# The Wayward Duke

Also by Katrina Kendrick

*A Bride by Morning*
*Tempting the Scoundrel*
*His Scandalous Lessons*
*A Touch Wicked*

# The Wayward Duke

KATRINA KENDRICK

*An Aria Book*

First published in the UK in 2024 by Head of Zeus,
part of Bloomsbury Publishing Plc



9 7 5 3 1 2 4 6 8

A catalogue record for this book is available from the British Library.

ISBN (PB): 9781837931538
ISBN (E): 9781837931507

Cover design: Meg Shepherd | Head of Zeus

Typeset by Siliconchips Services Ltd UK

Printed and bound in Great Britain by
CPI Group (UK) Ltd, Croydon CR0 4YY

Head of Zeus Ltd
First Floor East
5–8 Hardwick Street
London EC1R 4RG

WWW.HEADOFZEUS.COM

# I

## London, 1874

Caroline, Duchess of Hastings, eyed her canvas with murderous intent. She clenched the paintbrush, fighting the urge to plunge its tip through the layers of oil and pigment.

"Turn towards the light, *s'il vous plaît*," she said, struggling to keep the frustration from her tone.

Laurent shifted his bare body to catch the rays slanting through the window. He was an artist's dream given form, yet the painting continued to elude her. Colours crashed and careened, composition crumbling into chaos. The smudgy blobs seemed to mock her, tangling into an unrecognisable jumble of limbs.

With a defeated sigh, she dropped her brush into a jar of spirits to soak. "I'm afraid that will be all for today, Laurent."

The model began dressing without complaint, donning his clothes efficiently from years of serving as an artist's subject. Caroline tidied her supplies, removed her gloves and smock, and escorted Laurent downstairs.

"When should I come again?" he asked at the foot of the stairs, buttoning his coat.

"I'll send for you," Caroline promised, then kissed both his bearded cheeks in farewell. "Ask cook for some scones before you leave. She made a fresh batch this morning."

It was the least she could do after the poor man had endured her foul mood all afternoon. Laurent made for the servants' entrance – the one route guaranteed to avoid stray visitors. Caroline would never hear the end of it if someone spied him leaving her home in broad daylight.

A scuff of footsteps behind made her turn. "Percy," she began absently, still lost in thought, "please remind the maids not to enter the studio for cleaning. I have everything just where… I…"

Her voice faltered as she took in not the slim frame of the butler but the imposing presence of her estranged husband.

The Duke of Hastings was as gorgeous as ever, tall and broad-shouldered, with gleaming black hair that tumbled rakishly over his forehead despite his valet's best efforts. He had always had a commanding air to complement a ruthlessly handsome face.

Now those glacier-blue eyes fixed on her, pale and remote as the northern seas. Once, they had thawed for her alone. Before their affection soured. Before everything fell apart.

Now, their marriage was one of carefully arranged and maintained neglect.

"Hello, Julian," she said softly.

"Linnie." The old childhood nickname was more dagger than caress.

There were a hundred things she could say to this man who was her husband in name alone. Recriminations and regrets piled on top of one another from years of separation. Years of silence and distance yawning between them like a grave.

But all she could summon was, "You look well."

And he did – time had honed his beauty to a sharp edge. He still had the shoulders of a dockworker, strength evident in every inch of his tall, strapping frame. His face had the colour of time spent in warmth and sunshine far from London. From her.

All while her thoughts tangled in memories pressed between the pages of her many sketchbooks.

"As do you." His gaze flicked towards the servants' door

through which Laurent had departed moments before. "Busy too, it seems."

Annoyance flared, white hot. "Why are you here, Julian?" she asked, refusing to dignify his crass assumption with a response.

Julian removed his gloves before tossing them onto the hall table. Like a man readying for a duel.

"I'm between residences at the moment," he said. "The tenant in my apartments needs time to finish moving. Rather than take rooms at a hotel, I decided to make use of my perfectly serviceable townhouse."

His words were casual as he twisted the knife. Julian hadn't set foot in this house since they married.

Caroline stiffened in disbelief. "You plan to stay here?"

He lifted a shoulder in a careless half shrug. "I have a room, don't I? Or have you given it over to a frock museum in my absence?"

He didn't wait for her answer, brushing past her to ascend the stairs. To seek out the bedchamber that had once been his refuge. Theirs.

"*Julian*." Caroline hiked up her heavy skirts and hurried after him.

She wouldn't – *couldn't* – allow him to barge back into her carefully orchestrated existence. Not when she'd finally learned to breathe around the hole in her chest he'd carved open with his abandonment.

Her husband didn't so much as turn. "It's only a few weeks, Linnie."

"But I—"

He turned to face her, pinning her in place with those wintry eyes. "But what?"

Caroline flinched. "The ducal chamber is my studio."

For several heartbeats, Julian just looked at her – time and tragedy stretched taut between them. Then he climbed the last few steps up and tore open the door to what had once been his room.

Julian's gaze traced over it all with clinical precision, no doubt taking in every telling detail. Everything was exactly as she'd left it earlier. The space was filled with half-finished canvases propped at odd angles to catch the light, jars of linseed oil and bottles of pigment scattered on every flat surface, the crimson divan placed strategically beneath the wide studio windows.

Nothing of his old room. No evidence of their intimacy. Their marriage had been put on a pyre and set alight, and the only thing that remained of it was the ashes of their former life.

His focus snagged on the easel, where the nude painting of Laurent sat half finished, in all its garish and horrific glory. Caroline's cheeks reddened. Somehow, that portrait seemed like a mockery, a reminder of her ineptitude. No matter how many years she spent trying to forget Julian, no one else would compare.

Her husband, after all, had been her first model. Her first secret painting.

Her first everything.

"I saw work like this at Marlborough House." His voice was soft, and yet it shared nothing. "Your brushstrokes, your method, your lighting." He moved his fingertips over the canvas, not quite touching. "But it wasn't your signature in the corner."

It had not occurred to her that he would recognise all the intimate details of her work, but Julian had such a keen eye. An artist's heart, if not the talent at putting paint to canvas. And so he had once given her the artist's heart of him, and she – selfish creature in her youth that she was – had desired more.

Too much.

"Grace suggested Henry Morgan as my *nom de guerre* when I first started painting," she said quietly. "Remember?"

She shouldn't ask. Shouldn't care. But his memories of their oldest childhood friend – the third of their trio – were woven through hers, a thread binding their frayed edges.

Grief ghosted across his features. Then it was gone. "I do."

She cleared her throat. "I decided it was best to use it for my more… scandalous pieces. I wasn't aware you'd seen my work since…"

*Since you were the one who posed for me.*

Julian's hand dropped. "I admire exceptional art where I find it." He spoke softly, each word clipped. "And yours has always been my favourite."

Her traitorous heart gave a twist.

She studied the lines of his face, trying to remember the last time she'd kissed him. The last time she'd felt his touch. Every moment was documented and stored in her mind behind shards of jagged glass as reminders that their marriage began as a mistake.

When he'd left her, she'd done nothing to stop him. Just stood there, mute and stupid, while he walked away.

"I'll stay in one of the guest chambers until my departure," Julian said. "I leave for Italy at the end of the month."

She shook her head. "I'll have the servants remove my things from in here—"

"No." Julian's expression remained unreadable, as closed to her as a locked tower. "The afternoon light slants in here the way you like it, and a guest room would be more than suitable for me."

Of course it would. That would put him on the other side of the house, putting as much distance between them as their residence allowed.

When her thoughts turned poisonous, Caroline sometimes wondered if Julian had simply decided he loved Grace. If their friend's sudden loss had cracked him open in some fashion, made him realise the depth of his affection only after it was too late. Made him regret the impulsive circumstances binding him to Caroline now like shackles.

After all, he'd left Caroline behind the moment Grace drew her last agonised breath. And she went from being one-third of *Julian, Grace, and Caroline* to being utterly, wretchedly alone.

And now their peers whispered behind fluttering fans,

speculating endlessly on why the Duke and Duchess of Hastings avoided each other's presence.

Caroline's lips twisted. "I understand you care very little for our marriage, but I've tried to maintain a reputation that doesn't besmirch yours. I can hardly say the same about you."

Julian's eyebrow raised in surprise. "I've often complimented you in polite company. Certainly, no one can claim I've insulted you."

A lick of fire burned within her. Eight years of this. *Eight years*. "You compliment me," she repeated. "And yet you're never seen with me, never present in my home, and depart for the Continent the moment Parliament so much as recesses. Now you suggest withdrawing to a distant guest bedchamber while in the same house, as if our servants won't notice the slight."

"And do our servants not notice your… *slight*?" His eyes flickered to the painting of Laurent.

Caroline straightened. "If they notice anything," she said in French, "it's that my languages have improved through various tutors." She switched to German. "You speak this, don't you?" Then to Italian. "My husband is so well travelled, maybe I hope to find common ground if he should ever deign to put himself in my company." And then to Spanish. "Or perhaps you'd like to check my progress in mathematics, *o debería parar ahora*? I have a tutor for *that*, as well."

"Enough with the games." He lapsed back into German, the language of strategy and science. Of ruthless sensibility. "Just tell me plainly what you want."

She wanted impossible things. Things lost to the ash and rubble of their grief.

"Board your ship to Italy in four weeks," she said. "But until then, you'll play the role of my husband, and we'll show a united front to society and in our home. We'll share a bedchamber. You won't humiliate me in my own house. If all of this poses a problem, I suggest you lie convincingly. I'm sure you can manage."

His cold blue eyes drifted down her body. "And I suppose you'll want me to fuck you as well."

Crude words from an elegant mouth – designed to shock, to push her away.

Caroline stepped closer. "You don't have to play the dutiful husband behind closed doors," she snapped.

"One month of pretence then," Julian conceded, in a tone that promised retaliation. "For the sake of appearances. Does that satisfy you?"

As she scrambled for a response, his attention snagged on the painting of Laurent – and his mask of indifference slammed firmly in place.

This man was not her husband. Not anymore.

"I'll be out for the day," he said curtly. "Don't bother waiting up."

He strode from the room without a backwards glance.

As though he hadn't just ripped the foundations out from under her for the second time.

# 2

The afternoon sun spilled across the redbrick façade of Marlborough House, bathing the building in liquid gold as Julian ascended the front steps. Inside, the butler rushed to greet him and relieve him of his hat and gloves.

"The gallery today, Your Grace?"

"Yes. No need to accompany me. I know the way." Julian kept his tone clipped.

With purposeful strides, he made his way through the winding halls towards the gallery tucked away at the rear of the house. He knew the route well, had walked these corridors many times over the years, both as a casual visitor and a connoisseur of the fine arts. But today, he knew which paintings he wanted to see.

He prowled down the hall lined with paintings and sculptures, the artworks separated by narrow pillars. Searching.

Until…

A harsh breath escaped his lips unbidden. There. Just as he recalled them. Two canvases tucked against the eastern wall. The first captured Achilles in all his rage and glory, muscles coiled to strike as he stormed the walls of Troy. And the second, of Galatea and Pygmalion in an embrace, Galatea's marble body thawing to flesh beneath her lover's touch. Both neoclassical works stood resplendent, evoking an intensity of feeling that seemed to leap from the very artwork itself.

When he'd visited the gallery years ago, he'd been drawn to them. Many were, for the realistic and frank display of the nude human body. But, as always, it was the artistry itself that captivated him. The way shadow and light blended, the delicate precision of every brushstroke, the heady balance of shape and composition. The emotions displayed through the positions of the bodies, the tension in their musculature – elements that seized hold of his senses and refused to let go.

No. Not refuse. Beckon. These were brushstrokes and lighting and a harmony of colours he knew with bone-deep intimacy.

Of course it was her. He had watched her develop her budding skills during their youth, had sat there with her as she blossomed through her talents. And, once upon a time, he had provided the figure for her paintings. Lent her his body in the absence of his skill. He was not an artist – but he loved watching her paint.

*Don't come back. Stop visiting. Just get out and leave me alone.*

Julian closed his eyes against the memory. The sudden hollow ache in his chest, as if someone had taken a sharp blade and carved out some vital piece of him.

A polite cough pulled Julian back into the present. Habit had his expression smoothed to indifference before he turned. Mattias Wentworth, an operative Julian knew at the Home Office, observed the paintings with intensity, shoulders straining against his tailored jacket. The man was built for violence, though he hid it well under expensive trappings.

"A masterful work," he said, his voice almost reverent.

Julian tamped down the riot of emotions clamouring for release. "Indeed. Are you here for the gallery, or following me?"

Wentworth smiled slightly, though it didn't reach his eyes. "Both, actually," he said. "I have an appreciation for art, as well as for discretion. And you're the most discreet man I know." Wentworth sobered, tone sharpening. "I require your expertise."

"Mm." Julian looked back at the painting. "I've thought a lot about the last time you required my expertise and why you travelled all the way to Vienna for it."

Julian had often interacted with diplomats and ambassadors in his social circles, aware that many of their public-facing roles hid more unsavoury activities in spycraft. And among Her Majesty's operatives, he'd developed a reputation for his aptitude in languages and cryptography.

"I've always liked you, Julian," Wentworth said. "You're clever. And even better, you know how to keep your mouth shut. A rare characteristic among men."

Julian glared at him, then gestured with one hand. "Give it."

Mattias pulled out a folded sheet of paper from his coat. The paper was creased and the ink smeared, but the letters and symbols were still legible.

Julian rubbed it with his fingers. "How many people have tried to solve this?"

"Enough for me to resort to a duke in an art gallery," Mattias said, his words dry. "What do you see?"

"A letter written by a man of French extraction with sloppy penmanship and a fundamental lack of cryptographic skill. Amateur work, practically a child's practice cypher." Julian pursed his lips in annoyance as he handed the note back. "Give me the actual thing you want me to solve, or get out."

Mattias let out a low laugh as he withdrew another paper from his coat. "Will this do?"

This one was pristine, not a single crease, and the ink was fresher – written by a different hand. Gone were the uneven strokes of the first attempt. Julian studied the rows of figures and letters. He reached for the patterns lurking beneath, the hidden mathematical structure on which the code was built.

"Do you know who wrote this?"

"Not the specifics," Wentworth said. "But it's imperative that we develop a way to crack his messages."

"How imperative?"

Wentworth's jaw tightened. "The man who wrote it is dangerous and already responsible for two mass casualty events to assassinate his specific targets. I'm taking a risk trusting you with it."

Julian studied the cypher once more, the rows varied and different. This unknown man had a clever mind.

"I may be able to break this, but I'll need more of his writings to compare it against. As much as you can secure me."

Wentworth gave a nod. "I'll deliver them to your apartments."

Julian pressed his teeth together. "Stafford House. I'm in residence there for the rest of the month."

A knowing gleam entered the other man's eyes. "Reconciling with your wife, then?"

Caroline was right – everyone had noticed the diligence with which they maintained their separation. Eight years with no ducal heir had drawn attention.

"I've no interest in discussing my personal affairs." Julian folded the cypher and slid it into his pocket. "Excuse me."

Four more weeks. He need only endure four more weeks entangled in the thorny disaster of his marriage to Caroline.

In four weeks, he'd be able to breathe again.

# 3

## Ravenhill, 1865

*Nine years ago*

Caroline added another ruined sketch to the pile by her feet. Failure after failure after failure mocked her from the grass. At the rate she burned through paper, she'd soon be reduced to sketching in the dirt.

"Oh dear, not another for the bonfire," said a voice, soft with sympathy. Caroline glanced over at her oldest friend, Grace Harcourt, where she lounged on their picnic blanket. "What a pity. I was rather fond of that one."

Despite herself, Caroline let out a laugh. "You must be joking. I made you look like Medusa. Perseus should be swooping in to lop off your head as a trophy."

"Medusa was a great beauty before she was cursed." Grace straightened the brim of her hat, preening. "I'll take it as a compliment."

"Yesterday, I gave you three hands. Like some infernal chimera."

"Ah, but what exquisitely shaped additional hands they were," came the ironic drawl as Julian stepped from the forest path.

Caroline's pulse quickened at the sight of him stripping off his riding gloves. The afternoon sun gilded his black hair, setting it in stark contrast to his pale skin. There was an innate sensuality to his beauty, a leonine grace with which he moved and spoke and observed.

"I see I've arrived just in time to save Linnie from her artistic wallowing," Julian said, settling beside them on the blanket. "Please tell me there's wine left."

"Plenty of wine and an abundance of despair," Caroline said. She wrinkled her nose at the artistic proof of ineptitude scattered around her. "I'm getting worse with each effort."

Julian picked up one of the discarded pages, studying it critically. "The shading here is nicely done. You ought to revisit this technique." His gaze softened almost imperceptibly as it shifted to Grace. "And you've captured the fire in Gracie's eyes quite beautifully."

Caroline snorted. "I know you're lying. That horror resembles Grace as much as I resemble the Queen."

Grace nudged Caroline's shoulder. "The Queen should be so lucky. Why don't you try your hand at the lovely willows by the pond for a bit? Give yourself a rest from portraiture."

Caroline sighed, flipping back through her artistic endeavours. "Trees and flowers I can render passably. But people… I'm hopeless. Especially the hands. More claws than human appendages." She scowled down at her latest effort and fought the urge to ball it up. Such a waste of expensive paper. "At this rate, I'll be restricted to pets and flower arrangements. And that's assuming I can keep the pets from resembling some unholy mating of nature and nightmare."

She had to master her craft. It was the only way to save herself and her mother from destitution now that marriage seemed an unlikely prospect. As the sole daughter of the late Baron Winslow, their family name had once commanded respect, but scandal had forced them from London while Caroline was still a girl. Her father had then drunk and gambled away the remains of their modest fortune.

Now her dowry consisted of little more than her mother's genteel manners and Caroline's passable charms. Hardly enough to catch the eye of a peer with deep enough pockets to rescue them from penury. Which left her with only one choice: establish herself as a sought-after portrait artist. Painting was the sole talent she possessed in abundance.

"I'm certain you'll improve with time and practice," Julian said. "What do you think, petal? Think our Linnie might progress beyond shrubbery?"

Grace made a face at the dreadful nickname. "Must you call me that? Mother is now convinced we're all but betrothed after overhearing you last week."

"A dreadful prospect, I'm sure," he said dryly.

Grace laughed. "Hastings, I value you far too much to subject you to a lifetime of my company."

Something unreadable flickered in Julian's eyes before his polite mask slid into place. He plucked a lone daisy from the grass and held it out to her. "Let's try an experiment, shall we? Gracie, come here." He tucked the flower behind her ear, his fingertips skimming down the curve of her jaw. An intimacy that fractured something deep inside Caroline's chest. "There. Flawless as ever. Now, turn your profile to Linnie, petal. I suspect she'll fare better from this angle."

They were a study of contrasts – Julian carved from shadows and Grace spun from gold and porcelain. Little wonder the gossips predicted their betrothal with each passing day. Watching them together was like pressing on a wound, a sharp stab of pain that never quite faded.

Grace sighed. "As delightful as it would be to remain your subject, Mother is waiting for me at home. Another gown fitting." She pressed swift kisses on Caroline's and Julian's cheeks. "I'll see you at cards on Tuesday. Do try not to get into too much trouble without me."

Then she was hurrying off, disappearing down the path in a flutter of skirts.

Julian stared after Grace with an unreadable look. "Do you think she'll accept if I offer for her this Season?"

Caroline forced air into her lungs before trusting herself to answer. As gently as one might pull shards of glass from a wound, she said, "I suspect she'll refuse you. She's made her feelings quite clear."

His jaw tightened, but he nodded once. "That's rather my expectation as well. But if no one suitable proposes to her by summer's end, I intend to ask anyway."

Caroline worried her lower lip between her teeth before saying what was required of a friend. "If Grace asks my opinion, I'll give you both my blessing."

Julian's expression gentled at that. "And what about you? Any potential matches capture your fancy?"

"Respectable offers will be thin on the ground for the daughter of a baron who quit London under a cloud of scandal and treason," she said with a brittle smile.

Over a decade ago, her father's close associate had betrayed military secrets to the Russians during the Crimean War. Whispers speculating on her father's possible involvement had ravaged her family's reputation long before his gambling debts finished it off.

"That was years ago." Julian waved a dismissive hand. "No one even remembers."

"Perhaps."

"You're brooding again. Time for a much-needed distraction." Julian retrieved the abandoned wine and took a bracing drink from the bottle. "God knows I'll need the courage for what comes next."

Caroline shot him a puzzled look. "What now?"

"I intend to offer myself up as artistic sacrifice." His lip lifted in a small smile. "You've spent months attempting portraits of Grace. It's time you switched to another subject. One more accustomed to critique."

Caroline made a derisive noise. "You'll probably end up resembling a tree stump with warts."

"A harsh blow to my vanity, softened by the wine." He settled back on his elbows, every line of his body speaking of lazy elegance. "Unless you'd rather admit defeat?"

"Of course not." She flipped to a fresh page with renewed determination. "Fine, let's see if I can't make you moderately less hideous than my other efforts. But you may want to brace yourself."

"Do your worst, Miss Winslow."

Caroline focused on her sketchpad. She carefully outlined the angle of his jaw, the sharp slant of his cheekbones. As she worked, Julian's aquiline profile took shape on the page, patrician features emerging from shadow and light.

Few men could boast bone structure as exquisitely wrought as the young Duke of Hastings. Here, at last, was a subject who rewarded her – the clean lines and symmetry of his face, a pleasing interplay of light and dark. Julian's aristocratic features lent him a commanding air beyond his twenty-one years. She softened the sensual curve of his lower lip with delicate strokes of her charcoal.

After a few more minutes, she angled the sketchpad to let him view her progress. "Well? Do you need to fortify yourself?"

Julian studied the sketch. "Not hideous at all. I'm impressed."

"I suspect you're half drunk. At this point, a tree stump would merit praise."

"I know good art when I see it, whatever my state of inebriation," he countered. "Comes with my own pitiful inability to create it."

"You make wonderful music. I can hardly play a note."

Julian gave a careless shrug. "I play the piano proficiently. You make something meaningful. Compelling, even at your worst."

Warmth blossomed in her chest. "You're an exemplary subject. Your bone structure is exquisite." Realising how intimate that sounded, she hastily clarified, "From an artistic standpoint."

A wry smile crossed Julian's face. "My most valued quality, to be sure. Would you like to try another drawing?"

"Yes." She studied the portrait. "My struggles are largely with light and shading. Capturing the way shadows interact with the human form. They say nude studies are most helpful for learning those techniques. Unfortunately, they aren't available to aspiring female artists."

"Then use me."

Caroline's gaze snapped to his. "You would be willing?"

He gave an elegant shrug, setting the bottle of wine aside. "We're friends, aren't we?" His fingers went to the buttons of his shirt, slipping them free one by one. "Just keep that sketchbook private and never breathe a word of this to Gracie."

*Friends. Just friends.*

*Never anything more.*

Helplessly, Caroline watched as he peeled the fine linen from his shoulders, revealing smooth skin and lean musculature. He removed his boots and stripped away his stockings before rising to stand barefoot on the grass.

"Trousers off or on?"

Heat scalded Caroline's cheeks. "Off," she said before she could stop herself.

Those sharp eyes stayed locked on hers as his hands moved to the fastenings of his trousers. Inch by inch, he revealed himself – lean hips, muscular thighs, until he stood before her nude and utterly unabashed.

Swallowing hard, Caroline forced her attention up from the enticing trail of hair below his navel, the jut of his cock.

"See anything of interest?" he murmured in amusement.

The blood roared in Caroline's ears as she tried to gather the tattered scraps of her composure. "Determining the best angle for my sketch. Taking note of geography. The, er, angularity of your..." She coughed into her hand. "Hipbones. That sort of thing."

"Well then, please inform me how best to arrange my... angular hipbones. What do you require?"

*You. Beneath me, behind me, inside me.*

Good Lord, where had that thought come from?

Pasting a smile on her face, Caroline lifted her charcoal. "If you could just lie back and relax."

He shifted onto his back, thighs falling open in casual disregard for modesty.

Swallowing hard, Caroline ignored the temptation now on display. She flipped to a fresh page and began sketching the lines of his shoulders and arms, the lean muscles of Julian's abdomen, the enticing hollows of his hipbones. The sketch became a detailed study rather than a chaste outline. She took longer than necessary shaping his powerful legs, smudging the shadows to suggest coarse, dark hair.

As she worked, the lingering awkwardness dissipated. Julian made for a mesmerising subject. His body was all lean, honed muscle, strong yet elegant. She lost herself for a time in the sure strokes of her charcoal, sketching curves into angles into planes. The world narrowed down to breath and motion and vision until Julian's likeness emerged beneath her fingers in painstaking detail. Dappled light and smooth skin. The shape of temptation scrawled across the paper.

When she finally set down her charcoal, a pleasant glow of accomplishment replaced her earlier frustration. "There, I believe I've finished for today." Pulse skittering, she extended the sketch towards him. "What do you think?"

For long moments, Julian stared at the detailed study rendered on paper. At the intimacy there.

Several heartbeats passed in fraught silence before Caroline asked, "Is it dreadful, then?"

His gaze lifted, blue eyes dark with hunger. Ferocity barely leashed. Caroline's breath snagged as his focus moved along her flushed skin.

"No." His voice came rough-edged. "No, it's magnificent. Now, all that's left is to sign it."

Caroline heard nothing except the pounding of her own heart. This felt like more than just a playful artistic study between friends. Some silent threshold had been crossed as soon as she put charcoal to page. Or perhaps it had been crossed long before, in furtive moments of connection neither had dared acknowledge.

A thing between them too new to name.

“We shouldn’t immortalise the scandal in ink,” she said softly.

His burning stare stripped her down. “Then let it be our secret.”

# 4

## London, 1874

*Nine years later*

Silence permeated through the rooms of the sprawling townhouse after midnight, smothering even the soft ticking of the clock. Caroline paced the bedchamber, her thoughts crashing together – memories, conversations, a relationship tangled and tossed. She thought back to her and Julian's childhood, when friendship came easy. To the early days of their marriage, when passion still burned hot.

Before all the grief that came after.

Before the open grave of the last near-decade.

And then, music – the first strains of a familiar melody plucked from the keys of a piano. Caroline froze, listening, rediscovering the shape of a song she had not heard since girlhood.

Before she realised she was moving, her feet had carried her out into the corridor, the floorboards silent beneath her bare soles. Drawn towards the sitting room by some invisible tether woven of memories and might-have-beens.

At the door, she hesitated, peering through the crack at Julian, his shoulders hunched as his fingers danced across the ivory keys. His eyes were closed, lost in some private memory. The song had layered complexity beneath its simple structure, rich and textured, speaking of things lost and found again. Caroline shut her eyes too, swept back through the years to girlhood afternoons in the grounds of Ravenhill. Back when his music was a gift just for her.

And now she listened to his music as if for the first time. As if she knew him and yet knew nothing at all, this man she married but who had become a stranger to her.

The melody crested and faded, the final notes hanging tremulously in the air between them. An ache bloomed in her chest as she opened her eyes to find him watching her in the darkness, shadows carving hollows beneath his cheekbones. His gaze was remote, the silence heavy with years of distance.

Turning away, Caroline retreated to the bedchamber. She lay between cold sheets, her thoughts too loud in the hush. Who were they to each other now? Not friends. Not lovers. Not even husband and wife, except as lines on a contract.

Only two strangers drifting alone in the wreckage left by time.

Sometime later, the door opened and closed again, stirring eddies in the silence. She held her breath as soft sounds marked his preparation for bed – the rustle of clothing, the silhouette of his frame in the darkness. He stood over her, silent. She listened to his breathing and waited for him to speak, wondering what she would say in return. Their hearts pounded together. They breathed together.

But no words came.

After a moment, he turned away, the mattress dipping beneath his weight as he slid beneath the sheets. Not touching, the yawning chasm between them wider than any ocean. Too many years, too much left unsaid to bridge with one tentative hand.

So they lay side by side in silence, strangers bound by vows turned brittle with neglect.

Caroline woke slowly, blinking against the morning light. Without looking, she knew the other side of the massive four-poster would be empty. Cool and untouched. Julian had slipped into her bed and slithered out again before the sun could catch him there beside her.

Of course.

Downstairs, the sounds of the house stirring to life filtered through the floorboards – the muffled clink of china as the maids readied tea, the soft susurration of servants speaking. Caroline threw back the covers and rose. After washing and dressing for the day, she lingered over breakfast.

She wasn't avoiding anything, she told herself. Certainly not him. But the moments alone settled her nerves. Fortified her.

Eventually, her procrastinating ran its course. As she passed the open study door, the silhouette of Julian's dark head bent over his desk arrested her steps. Morning light slanted through the windows, limning him in gold. He looked like something from a portrait – shirt collar undone, black hair falling across his forehead.

"Admiring the view or contemplating murder?" He didn't bother lifting his gaze from his writing.

A flush scalded her cheeks at being caught staring. "I reserve my murderous impulses for mornings when I awake to cold tea and burnt toast. I was just beginning to doubt whether you still had a voice at all, as you couldn't be troubled to offer a greeting."

At that, Julian cut his pale eyes towards her, ice blue and assessing. "And here I thought you were the one making impressions, looming in doorways. Do come in if you mean to stare at me all morning."

Caroline felt a reluctant smile threaten. "There it is. That infamous Hastings arrogance."

"Just giving you ample opportunity to admire." Julian held out his hand. "Come here." His voice was like silk. Smooth. Lethal.

Caroline's breath snagged in her throat, nerves and anticipation tangling together. She approached cautiously, hesitant to get too close. To let her guard down. He'd already flayed her open with his music, and she'd just managed to don armour again.

He caught her fingers in his and drew her to his side. "There now. You keep looking at me as though you expect I might bite, and I regret my promise if it makes you so uneasy in your own home."

Promise. The word was a knife sliding bloodlessly between her ribs.

"Your promise to behave as a proper husband?"

"Yes," he said, very softly. "That promise."

Silence stretched between them – not the easy quiet of the past, but a tense, thorny thing. Just like his music, comprised of sharp edges that she suspected he wanted her to feel.

She cleared her throat. "Are you going out today?"

Julian's shoulders tensed beneath his shirt and then he withdrew his hand. "No. I've business to finish while I'm still in town."

Dismissal. It rankled even as unwanted heat curled low in her core at his nearness, the clean scent of soap and skin. Once, she might have perched on the edge of his desk, stealing kisses until he laughed and pulled her into his lap.

Now, an ocean of loss separated them.

"Of course." She struggled to keep her tone light. Her gaze drifted to the papers on his desk, desperate for neutral ground. "Cryptography? That's your business?"

"A private project for an acquaintance."

Another dismissal, sharper than the first. Caroline bit her lip, fighting the urge to goad him. To pierce his poise and provoke a response beyond indifference. Better fury than silence. Better broken glass than distance.

She couldn't bring herself to anger him. Not when the ghost of his touch still whispered along her skin.

She leaned in to study the topmost page. "The code is more complex as it goes on?"

The faint scent of his shaving soap teased her senses. Julian's focus caught on her hand, where she trailed a nail along the cypher's edge. His eyes went dark, throat working on a hard swallow that made triumph surge in her veins.

*Good. Do you remember how brightly we burned?*

"Yes, but I can't determine the inconsistencies at the beginning—" Julian's words ended on a sharp inhale as her hip accidentally brushed his arm. Electric awareness sizzled in the scant space left between them.

Caroline's face heated, but she kept her tone composed. "Have you studied International Morse?"

His eyes lifted to meet hers. "I beg your pardon?"

Her next words tumbled out in a nervous rush. "International Morse code. Have you studied it?"

"No," he said shortly, clearly not interested in a discussion. "Only American Morse."

"Well, the international code incorporated additions from Herr Gerke and Herr Steinheil, and German umlaut vowels are used to refine the alphabet, and someone has cleverly employed the international code within the enciphered message. So you might borrow one of the books from my library and inform yourself."

Julian stared at her for a long moment, his guarded expression cracking into surprise. "I wasn't aware you still practised code-breaking. I thought you might have stopped after…"

*After.*

*After us.*

She squared her shoulders, donning a mask of casual indifference. "When my duties permit. Of course, never anything as interesting or complex as your vulgar letters written in code."

His expression tightened, and his gaze dropped back to the codes. "I suppose I gave you plenty of practice."

"You did," she said tightly. But Julian's coded letters today were none of Caroline's concern. She had appearances of her own to maintain now, pretences that did not include a man who had shed her like a snake's old skin. "I've been invited to Thornfield House tonight for Lady Arundel's birthday."

Julian did not glance up from his work. "Would you like me to accompany you?"

Ever the proper gentleman. As if she couldn't hear the reluctance beneath his offer.

"No. The seats have been decided. If you've read the gossip sheets, you'll know my cousin, the Earl of Montgomery, married my friend Lydia Cecil recently, and I intend to congratulate them on their new marriage. I'm giving you fair warning that this will be my last social engagement attended alone until you quit this house, board your boat, and do whatever it is you intend to do to avoid me."

It was petty, but the words grounded her somehow – an anchor in choppy waters. For the span of a heartbeat, Julian's composure cracked, echoes of shared grief and loss flashing raw across his face. Caroline's breath caught at the glimpse of the man she once knew, the wound that had never healed.

But Julian looked away. "Then enjoy your evening," he said.

Dismissing her yet again.

Biting back angry words, Caroline turned on her heel. But before she could storm from the room, his voice stopped her.

"Caroline."

Something dark and fragile strained his tone. She waited, body coiled tight.

"Remove the tulips."

The words were a slap – a reminder of their final exchange eight years ago. Caroline turned her attention to the vase of flowers on the edge of the desk. One she kept there every day as a reminder.

"You used to bring me tulips every day," she said. "For months. Because you knew they were my favourite."

When the hurt had been so sharp, Caroline had wanted to tear him to shreds with her parting words.

*I don't want you bringing me flowers or telling me about the weather. I can't bear the sight of you.*

*Don't come back. Stop visiting. Just get out and leave me alone.*

A pause, weighted. His knuckles were white around his pen. "Please."

The single word severed the fragile threads of the moment. Her jaw clenched. Without another word, she grasped the vase and left, the door clicking shut behind her.

# 5

Julian drank at his usual spot at White's. The club's public rooms were subdued this afternoon, most members not yet recovered from last night's entertainments. Newspaper pages rustled. Teacups rattled. Julian savoured the respite from Stafford House.

When he boarded his ship to Italy, he was going to get raving drunk to forget Caroline again.

A movement in his periphery tore him from memories. He nodded in greeting as Mattias Wentworth made his way towards him.

"Duke," Wentworth said, taking the seat across from him. "You're looking rather worse for wear today. Trouble at home?"

Wentworth wore politeness with deceptive ease, like a bespoke jacket concealing weapons underneath.

"As I've made clear, I don't discuss personal business with the Home Office." Best to get this over promptly so he could return to brooding. Julian reached into his pocket and flicked the folded foolscap onto the table.

"I appreciate your speed," Wentworth said, pocketing the missive.

Julian leaned back and sipped his drink. "I doubt I would have been so quick if the duchess hadn't contributed her insight."

The other man gave him a stern look. "I believe I ordered discretion."

Julian stared at him. "I may not know the exact nature of your true profession, but I'm not an underling, nor someone to whom you can give orders. My wife is just as skilled at code-breaking as me. She has a better mind for certain patterns."

A muscle jerked in Wentworth's jaw as he handed Julian a new coded letter. "I need this one quicker than the last."

Julian let nothing show on his face as he studied the symbols. Snatches of conversation from nearby drifted over to him, fragments of gossip from men talking about their mistresses, political projects, and investments. Julian ignored them.

After a few minutes, he blinked. "A polyalphabetic Vigenère tableau, maybe," he murmured. "More complex than your last. Have you annoyed someone?"

Mattias's smile was wry. "I'm always annoying someone."

"Mm." Julian considered the code again. "I couldn't help but notice that your last was in Russian, but the boastful notes you gave me were in German and Italian. This individual has used such an interesting collection of languages to taunt you after taking responsibility for the steamboat sinking. The Earl of Stradbroke was on it, I recall. Didn't the thing disappear into the Atlantic? Three hundred souls lost, I believe."

The other man's expression became shuttered, dark eyes turning to ice. "If you're about to ask a question, I suggest you rethink it."

"I'm relieved to hear we have progressed from ordering to suggesting," Julian said. "But I'll ask it, anyway. Who are these letters from?"

The other man hesitated, reluctance weighing down his words. "We don't know his name. Six months ago, the letters started arriving, and our code-breakers could never solve them in time to prevent two tragedies – the steamboat, and a building collapse that killed fifty, including Lord Baresford. Whoever this man is, he enjoys being chased and outsmarting us. So I need you to work quickly. That letter was sent a fortnight ago, and if the pattern holds, we have a catastrophe about to happen. Yes?"

"I'll need to ask my wife to assist, then."

Mattias gave him a sharp look. "You'll both be discreet, or I'll ruin you."

Easy words to intimidate a lesser man.

"Don't make me regret helping you, Wentworth," Julian said, very softly.

A charged beat of silence followed between them. Wentworth broke it first, expression unreadable as he stood. "Don't make me regret asking."

Julian watched him go before letting out a long breath, his mind turning to the task at hand. Asking Caroline for help meant putting them in even closer proximity – forcing them together more than they already were.

He didn't know how long he remained at the club, deep in thought, but as he rose to depart, his attention fell on the group of young gentlemen clustered around the betting book. They looked his way and made some hushed comments, laughing.

Julian passed them by – but then he noticed the bet that had made the idiots go silent.

*Lord Rivers bets Lord Alington one thousand pounds that a duke and duchess understood between them shall divorce on or before this day six months.*

*Lord Rivers makes the same bet with Mr Payne.*

"A foolish wager to make," he said to Lord Rivers, very softly, "when a man doesn't have one thousand pounds to lose. Good day to you, gentlemen."

*

Julian had been hunched over the coded letter until his shoulders knotted and his neck ached. When the old grandfather clock tolled midnight, he finally admitted defeat. For now.

With a quiet groan, he tucked his work away and turned to the sideboard, pouring two fingers of amber liquid into a crystal tumbler. The whiskey burned going down.

He'd just poured another glass when the front door groaned open, followed by the tap of brisk footsteps – the familiar, no-nonsense cadence that could only belong to Caroline.

His sweet fucking torture was home.

Julian tracked her path as she strode down the hall and slowed outside the open study door. Silk skirts whispered, and then she stepped into the firelight.

He froze, the tumbler halfway to his lips. Good God. The thing she wore could barely be called a dress. It was an artful arrangement of pink silk doing its damnedest to preserve modesty and failing on every account.

It was suddenly vitally necessary that Julian finish his drink. Now.

"You're still awake," Caroline said, her voice curling through the room like smoke and sin.

A voice designed to bring men to their knees. Designed to drive him mad.

Julian lowered his glass slowly, as if disarming a weapon. "As are you. I expected you hours ago. Did you attend a birthday celebration" – his gaze dipped over her attire – "or a Roman bacchanalia? You look as though you're dressed for a night of debauchery. Not that I object."

That earned him a smile. "Are you ogling your wife, Hastings? I'm shocked."

"Perish the thought. I'm merely taking note of how you put that scandalous silk to shame."

"I suppose most gentlemen find bare shoulders absolutely riveting."

"Among other things, I'm sure." His gaze drifted over the tops of her breasts.

Her gaze turned mocking. "Do go on. I'm finding your ogling most educational."

Julian glanced away and reached for the bottle again because he was a gluttonous bastard when it came to her – always had been. Even when she sliced at his heart, he wanted to bare his throat for more.

"Does it count as ogling when a man stares at his own wife's dress?" he asked. "Most gentlemen present likely spent the evening contemplating what you're wearing beneath it."

*Or what he might do to divest you of it.*

Her smile sharpened. "Should they come knocking, I've no doubt you'll unleash that infamous glare and turn them to stone."

"Why turn them to stone when I can watch in amusement as they piss themselves in terror?"

"Careful," she said in amusement. "Your protective streak is showing."

"It's the whiskey. Lowers my defences. Did you enjoy yourself this evening?"

Julian watched as Caroline claimed a seat by the fire. Watched the way shadows danced over her bare skin. "Reasonably. Though my cousin remains an unmitigated idiot."

A wry huff escaped Julian. "Doesn't half of London compose sonnets to Montgomery's charm?"

"Oh, Monty plays the charming rake to perfection," she said. "But he's desperately in love with his new wife and is already finding creative ways to muck it all to hell and back. Truly, most gentlemen are tragically lacking in emotional intelligence."

"We do blunder about until fate deigns to boot us up the arse a time or two."

*Or three, or four, or…*

Her smile faded. "Speaking from personal experience?"

A harsh breath escaped him. She could always strip him raw. "With you?" He sighed. "Always, sweetheart."

Their gazes caught and held, a familiar tension charging the air.

Then she cleared her throat and subjected him to the same scrutiny she employed when attacking her canvases. "You look dreadful, by the way. Don't tell me you forgot to sleep again."

He schooled his features to impassivity. "I've been occupied."

"Mm-hmm. Let me guess – mysterious papers have been holding you hostage all day. More cryptography, or something equally dire?"

"You know I lead a thrilling life," he said dryly. "Cryptography and confidential diplomacy until dawn, policy reform over breakfast. By midday, I've sorted out a rebellion or two."

"And how many languages has your thrilling life equipped you with by now?"

His mouth quirked up. "Ten. Would you like a drink?"

Surprise flashed in her features, there and gone. "Yes. Thank you," she said.

Julian strode to the sidebar and poured two fingers of whiskey. When he turned back to offer her the glass, he was all too aware of their fingers brushing as she took it from him.

Caroline sipped her drink. "I'm swiftly reconsidering everything I know regarding your travels. Tell me, were the Alpine vistas more or less intriguing than the notorious Third Section? That coded letter I saw earlier looked quite official."

Damn. Too sharp by half. "Ridiculous notion. Dukes make poor spies." He lifted one shoulder in a shrug. "We simply allow our expertise to be discreetly used from time to time by Her Majesty's operatives."

"Ah. And how often does your sense of patriotic duty compel you into cryptographic service?"

He turned his glass between idle fingers. "Often enough to develop something of a reputation for code-breaking."

Now he had her undivided attention. "And what are you working on now? Still International Morse?"

For a moment, he saw a glimpse of the old Caroline. The woman who once looked at him with such affection and desire. Before grief carved out softer emotions, leaving them both hollowed out.

He didn't want to lose that fragile connection.

Standing, Julian went to his desk, unlocked the top drawer, and pulled out the encrypted letter he'd been labouring over for the past eight hours. He held it out to her like a white flag of surrender.

Or a plea for parley.

"This came to me just this afternoon."

Caroline set her glass aside and took the letter, scanning the sheet of unfamiliar symbols. "Not International Morse, then. What language do you suspect?"

"Possibly Russian." He paused. "Do you know Russian?"

"I took a tutor," she said quietly. "After I heard you'd been to Moscow. Brushed up on my Cyrillic and vocabulary."

Something possessive and heated unfurled in his chest. She'd kept track of his travels after he fucked everything all to hell.

"When you said you were learning languages to find common ground..." He rolled the whiskey between his hands, amber liquid catching the light. "I didn't think you meant it."

*I thought you'd said it to hurt me.*

She cleared her throat. "Well, I did." Caroline scrutinised the cypher now. "Polyalphabetic Vigenère tableau, possibly."

A smile touched Julian's lips. "There's that spark. The only time I've seen your eyes light up like that is with cryptography and—"

"Painting," she said. "I know."

A long breath left his lungs. "When I pleasured you," he corrected quietly.

Her tongue darted out to wet her bottom lip in a nervous

gesture he instantly recognised. "It might be double- or triple-encoded," she said.

"Or encoded backwards. With null cyphers embedded." He met her eyes. "Would you like to work on it with me?"

A beautiful smile played on her lips. "If you think I'd be of help. I'm afraid most of my prior expertise in cyphers remains your filthy notes."

Bright and painful memories flashed of all the notes he'd written her during their marriage. Daily letters of increasingly complex codes detailing every lurid fantasy in the most vulgar terms – papers he'd known she would solve in the middle of ballrooms, at dinner with guests. And then she would pull him to secret alcoves where he would shove up her skirts and fuck her against a wall.

He leaned back. "Well, I did show off by composing those notes with advanced cryptography. I had to impress you somehow."

Her teeth flashed in a grin. "Then I'll help. But I require at least a few hours first. I may present a pretty picture, but I'm about three cups deep in champagne on top of the whiskey." She hesitated, then seemed to firm her resolve. "Will you come to bed?"

In answer, Julian extended his hand. Caroline twined their fingers together and didn't let go, even as they crossed the threshold from formality into intimacy.

Once within their rooms, she presented the row of buttons down the back of her dress. "Well?" Caroline said, glancing at Julian over one shoulder. "Going to stand there or offer your assistance?"

Reverently, Julian stepped close and rested one palm between her shoulder blades as he began working the tiny buttons free, parting silk inch by devastating inch.

His breathing turned ragged, and arousal pounded a merciless beat in his blood. Still, he devoted himself to his delicate task, following each pearl button down... down... until he reached the dip of her waist and the top of her bustle. The material slithered down over her body to pool at their feet. Easing apart the laces of her corset revealed her thin chemise, and as he slid that last gossamer barrier off her shoulders, he traced the ridges of her spine with his thumb.

He wanted to press her down into the bed. To fill her with every dark, wordless thing inside him.

But he refused to be careless. Refused to be anything less than gentle. Caroline deserved better from the man who had failed her so catastrophically years before.

When she finally turned to face him, Julian's breath arrested in his lungs. She stood luminous in the soft firelight, all sculpted curves and smooth skin. Utterly, heart-stoppingly beautiful.

"Now *that's* ogling, Hastings," she murmured.

He gave a huff that was almost a laugh. "I do appreciate beauty where I find it."

She said nothing as she pulled a white nightdress on. He watched the play of firelight over her body's silhouette as she crossed the room and slid beneath the sheets.

Julian stripped out of his shirt and trousers and joined her, all too aware of her soft warmth. The floral scent of her skin teased his senses. He pressed the heels of his palms against his eyes, praying for strength or, failing that, cold indifference. No man, saint or sinner, could resist this temptation lying so close.

"Julian?" she whispered into the darkness.

"Hmm?"

"Will you attend Lady Fairfax's garden party with me in two days?"

He exhaled at the tentativeness there, as if she feared he'd refuse. "It would be my pleasure."

Then he felt her hand squeeze his. "Thank you. Goodnight."

"Goodnight, Linnie," he managed, past the ache in his throat.

When Julian finally slept, he dreamed of her.

# 6

## London, 1865

*Nine years ago*

Caroline fidgeted with her skirts. It was a finer gown than any she had worn before, pink sarcenet with tiny seed pearls sewn into the bodice, winking in the glow of the chandeliers. A stunning confection fit for any well-bred lady entering society.

But this was all a mistake; Caroline didn't belong here.

The stale, perfumed air was suffocating.

"Stop fussing," Grace hissed out of the corner of her mouth. "You look beautiful."

Caroline managed a wan smile for her friend's benefit. Grace's mother, Viscountess Harcourt, had used all her influence to secure the coveted Almack's vouchers. Caroline was grateful, but a soul-deep terror gnawed through her veins, whispering that she would fail.

Again.

And failure would mean utter ruin for her.

She forced herself to scan the opulent ballroom, but all she noticed were the shrewd eyes judging and finding her lacking. Cruel mouths curved in malice, waiting for her to stumble or misspeak so they could pounce.

And then she saw him.

Julian.

Even across the crowded floor, the Duke of Hastings' beauty

was almost violent in its intensity, aquiline profile and sharp cheekbones lending him an air of detached grandeur, as if he found polite society beneath his interest. Power and easy confidence clung to him, drawing eyes, though he remained largely indifferent to the speculative gazes following his every move.

Something hot and hungry curled low in Caroline's abdomen at the sight of him. She remembered too well all the times he'd posed for her in recent weeks – sprawled across the grass, lean muscle and warm skin painted gold by the sunlight.

But this reaction went beyond artistic appreciation or even friendship.

Julian glanced in her direction, and Caroline forced her gaze away. He was her friend. Nothing more. His heart was destined for Grace.

"Introduce me to someone amusing," she said to Grace under her breath. "Before I faint and make a fool of myself."

Grace threaded her arm through Caroline's. "If you do swoon, aim left. I've no doubt Lord Beaumont would be only too happy to catch you."

Caroline risked a subtle glance at the ruddy-faced viscount leering down the front of her gown. "I'd rather crack my head open on the marble floor."

A smile quirked Grace's lips. "There's that rapier wit I love so well. You'll have all the gentlemen eating from your palm."

If only Caroline shared her friend's confidence. She'd endured three disastrous balls so far, and not a single bouquet brought to the doorstep in the morning. Just crude ogling over weak lemonade. Each wasted evening was another nail in her family's financial coffin.

"I can hardly string two words together. I'm afraid I might resort to hiding behind the potted plants before the night ends." Caroline picked at her gloves, smoothing nonexistent wrinkles.

"Well, string three words together and aim for witty," Grace said. "Lady Asterley is waving us over. Time to work your charm."

She allowed Grace to tow her into the fray. For the next

torturous hour, Caroline echoed inanities about the weather and the latest *on-dits* swirling through the *ton*. All the while ignoring the way the gentlemen's gazes caressed her cleavage like groping hands. Bile scalded the back of her throat even as she maintained a pleasantly vacant smile.

Not a single gentleman asked her to dance. With each wasted moment, Caroline felt another unseen door closing in her face, locking her into penury.

Grace pressed close. "There are the first chords of a waltz. And don't be glum – at least a dozen gentlemen are ogling your bosom right now. We'll bring in reinforcements." She caught Julian's eye through the crowd and crooked a finger in summons.

"He ought to dance this set with you." Caroline kept her voice low, swallowing around the bitterness. Jealousy was unbecoming. "I suspect Hastings might be rather desperately in love with you."

Grace laughed, the sound soft and knowing. "I appreciate the confidence, but you think too little of yourself and too highly of me in this scenario."

Before Caroline could protest further, Julian arrived, inclining his head. "Miss Harcourt. You summoned me?"

"Hastings, time to do your duty by our friend," Grace said. "Linnie needs a handsome duke on her arm to strike envy into the heart of every gentleman present. You'll oblige us both, won't you?"

Amusement lurked at the corner of that stern mouth. "Hardly a trial, playing the besotted suitor to a beautiful woman. Consider me at your disposal." He swept Caroline an elegant bow. "Miss Winslow. Would you do me the honour?"

Caroline had little choice but to accept the proffered hand. His fingers engulfed hers, radiating warmth even through the fine kidskin. He ignored the curious glances as he led her onto the gleaming parquet.

When he pulled her close, Caroline inhaled his clean scent to steady her nerves – soap and spice.

"Just like when we practised in the meadow last summer," he murmured, evoking memories of their bare feet twirling in the grass. "You know this dance better than anyone."

The tender encouragement eased some of the tightness in her chest even as vicious whispers swirled around them now.

*"My, aren't they rather… intimate."*

*"Barely a step above a fortune hunter."*

*"I heard there was some scandal with her father…"*

Humiliation flooded Caroline's veins.

"Eyes on me." Julian's quiet command broke through her rising panic. His wintery gaze caught and held hers, an anchor in the fraying chaos. "Just keep looking at me."

He was so handsome, black hair gleaming under the chandelier light, a perfect mouth made for wicked smiles, though he rarely indulged in such shows of mirth.

But he smiled for her.

And in that moment, she was painfully aware of how much she loved him.

"That's it. Ignore them all," he instructed as they swept down the room's length. "Keep your gaze on mine and move as we've always done." The hand at her waist squeezed gently. "Just us two alone in that meadow."

She focused on him, allowing his steady presence to drown out the hostility pressing closer around them. The steps were etched into muscle memory until the outside world faded, her feet remembering this private language between them.

"That's my girl." His tender praise sank straight to her core as he spun her effortlessly through the next turns.

Around and around they whirled, lost in their own orbit. Until, too soon, the last notes dissolved into silence. They lingered a beat longer, neither willing to let go. But propriety reasserted its icy grip, forcing them apart once more.

Hastings bowed before turning to carve his way through the crowds. And the spell shattered. The vicious whispers and cruel laughter rushed back in like the tide.

*"Well, that's her moment over and done, I should think."*

*"She ought to show some gratitude for the opportunity he gave her."*

The weight of their derision an almost physical force. They looked at her as if she were something foul, scraped off a boot heel.

Grace appeared at her side, slipping a supportive hand beneath her elbow. "Wait a few minutes until their attention settles on something else, then get some air."

Chest heaving with barely contained sobs, she waited until Grace gestured to her, then slipped out the terrace doors into the darkened gardens beyond.

Out on the moonlit grounds, Caroline finally allowed the tears to fall. Furiously, she dashed them away, but more followed in an endless, bitter stream. She was the world's greatest fool, losing her heart to a man who would never think of her as more than a friend.

"Hiding again?"

Caroline whirled to find Julian emerging from the garden shadows.

"I just needed some air," Caroline lied, turning so he wouldn't see the slick tracks on her cheeks.

"This is the third ball where I've found you slipping away outside."

"I know," she admitted with a watery laugh. "I'm terrible at this."

Julian sighed. He drew a handkerchief from his pocket and gently dabbed her cheeks. The tender gesture threatened to undo her. "You were radiant."

She swallowed. "Careful, you might mar your reputation as the stoic Duke of Hastings."

"That's because I'm just Julian to you," he said softly, brushing his thumb over her skin. "Would you like me to get you something to drink?"

"I've drowned myself in enough lemonade tonight to float the navy. It didn't improve the night."

His expression softened. "Let them look and whisper behind their fans. But don't ever let them see you cry."

Caroline searched his eyes. "Why are you doing this?" she whispered.

Julian cupped her face with a tenderness that made her breath catch. Against all sense, she indulged a spark of wild hope he might lower his head and—

But then he withdrew. "Because we're friends," he said simply.

Nothing more.

Never anything more.

*We're friends.*

Friends. What a lie.

Friends did not look at each other the way they did. A friend did not ache to dominate her in every wicked way Julian's imagination provided. Ever since that first sketch, something fundamental had shifted between them. The space where friendship once dwelled had cracked open, hunger seeping through. Her gaze had ignited him, scorching away platonic bonds until all that remained was need.

*Not friends.*

He did not want her friendship. Not her kindness or compassion. Those things lived in the light, and what he wanted from her belonged to the shadows. He craved the slide of her body against his, her gasps as he pushed inside her. Wanted her *prima* untouched canvas marred by his hands, his mouth. No restraint. No going back.

"A few more minutes to restore your composure," he said, keeping his tone perfectly pleasant. Propriety in flesh and blood form. He wiped the last of her tears and tucked the handkerchief in his pocket. "Then back to battle. Plenty of dances left."

Her answering smile didn't reach her eyes. "Oh yes, I'm sure a queue of suitors is waiting to whisk me away. Maybe I'll just tell Gracie I want to go home."

"Don't flee just yet. I've seen a dozen idiots ogling your décolletage tonight."

And he'd wanted to throttle every last one of those leering dandies.

"Ogling is not the same as offering marriage."

"Then it's a good thing you've ample charms beyond your bosom, Miss Winslow."

Her answering laugh sounded brittle as glass. "And yet those manifold charms have not inspired a single suitable offer."

Julian winced. "Your prospects can't be that dreadful. Surely, some addled heir is ready to bumble his way into courting you. You might even inspire a baronet's third son with more hair than wit."

"Unlikely." Her mouth twisted bitterly. "My meagre dowry sends most gentlemen leaping for the balcony."

Julian knew he should jest, make light of it all. But an image flashed through his mind – her slim, talented hands motionless and idle, her paintbrushes abandoned. She'd progressed from artless childhood sketches to true mastery, bringing her visions to life in vivid oils. She'd painted him nude now countless times, and each day he could barely resist kissing her.

"Is your situation truly so dire?" The question tore itself free before he could stop it.

A muscle leaped in her delicate jaw. "With my father's debts, I'll be fortunate to catch a cit or a grocer this Season. Though I suppose there are worse fates than being a greengrocer's wife." She cast him a sidelong look through her lashes. "I could borrow one of your waistcoats and try my hand at chimney sweeping."

He could not share her weak attempt at humour. "I see."

Caroline swallowed and looked away. "It's fine, Julian. Being a grocer's wife is better than penury."

Her bleak acceptance echoed inside him. He had learned life's harsh lessons early. Life gave less than promised and took far more than its share. Sickness had stolen his family, leaving gaps nothing could mend. And now genteel poverty threatened to rob Caroline of the same – to deprive the world of her brilliance.

The notion was obscene. Intolerable.

"It won't come to that," he said. "I won't let it."

He could steal this small thing for himself. Gather this rare, bright creature close before she slipped through his fingers. He teetered on the edge of that precipice, poised to ruin them both.

But she was the one who moved first.

She rose on her toes and pressed her lips to his in a featherlight kiss. It lasted only the space of a heartbeat, but it jolted his world off its axis. When she started to pull away, some raw, primal need seized him. Julian clutched her waist and brought his mouth back to hers. Caroline made a faint, desperate sound low in her throat. She tasted of champagne and something sweeter, warmer – sunlight on bare skin.

Some distant shred of reason screamed this was madness. One stolen embrace would ruin them. But then her fingers twisted in his lapels as she pulled him closer, and Julian was lost. Beyond thought. Not when Caroline was soft and pliant in his arms, her lips parting so sweetly beneath his.

Not after every fantasy for months had been with this woman in his bed.

"We shouldn't be doing this," she murmured against his lips, even as her fingers speared through his hair.

"We absolutely should not. And yet here we stand, and I can't stop kissing you." He nipped down the slender column of her throat. She whimpered, nails biting into his shoulders. "Can't stop wanting you. Can't ever stop."

She was oxygen. He was suffocating. Nothing existed beyond the sweetness of her lips. Closer. He wanted her closer – always closer. Until need roared so loud it drowned out sanity.

Too late, Julian registered the approaching footsteps.

"Hastings?" A slurred, incredulous voice, then soft laughter. "Good God, man."

Caroline jerked as if scalded. Julian blinked away lust's haze to find two young lords gawping at them from the garden path, faces flushed with drink. Dorset and Hayes. Grasping gossipmongers.

They'd stumbled on prime fodder tonight.

With monumental effort, Julian wrenched himself under control. He gentled his voice, adopting his usual tone of bored condescension. "Dorset. Hayes. Do run along, please. The ballroom has shortage enough of wits without you adding to its deficit, and my fiancée and I would appreciate the moment of privacy."

Caroline sucked in a sharp breath at the significance of what he'd just done. With one impromptu declaration, he had bound them together.

Too late now.

"Fiancée, you say? Well, hang me, I hadn't heard. Our apologies. Congratulations to you both." Dorset grabbed his companion's arm. "Come along, Hayes. Back to the punch."

The drunken lords retreated down the garden path on unsteady feet.

Caroline stared at him wide-eyed, one hand pressed to her kiss-swollen mouth. "Oh God," she whispered. "You told them I'm your fiancée."

He offered a half smile. "A reasonable understanding, given recent activities. Unless you'd rather I withdraw my offer and deliver you to the first respectable cit who asks?"

"How can you possibly be so calm? You wanted to marry *Grace* just months ago. You were planning to propose to her at the end of the Season. Everyone will believe—"

"Who cares? Let them think what they want."

"I was going to say," she said very softly, "that everyone will believe I'm a calculating, destitute harlot who seduced a duke in a garden to get at his money."

She still didn't understand. Didn't understand that *she* was the only woman who had occupied his thoughts for months, and *they were not friends*.

"And when you're my duchess," he told her, "you have my enthusiastic permission to freeze them from across a ballroom with one chilly glance."

Emotion roughened her voice. "You're mad."

"No more mad than you marrying some cit to save yourself from poverty." He shifted closer, lips grazing her ear. "Tell me, Miss Winslow – how many times now have you watched me disrobe before your easel?" His hand at her waist tightened. "Studied every inch of my cock while you committed my form to memory?"

A shiver moved through her. But she didn't pull away.

"How often have you loosened your bodice when you returned home on those long, lonely nights?" he continued. "Parted your pretty thighs and imagined it was me stroking you there in the dark? Me fucking you until you screamed my name?"

Her lips parted. A visible tremble took hold of her.

"Well?" he prompted.

A soft sound. Then – "Too often for propriety."

Triumph roared through him. Yes. He was hers since she first put charcoal to paper and sketched the lines of yearning connecting them.

He pulled back. "Wouldn't you like to touch me in all the ways you've imagined? Be my wife, and I'm yours. Say yes."

*I'm already yours. I just want you to be mine.*

For several pounding heartbeats, he held still, waiting for her answer. Ruin and rapture balanced on the same razor edge.

Then she turned her eyes to his, soft and wondering, and she plummeted down the precipice with him. "Yes."

# 7

## London, 1874

*Nine years later*

The afternoon carriage ride to Lady Fairfax's estate felt endless. Caroline was too aware of Julian beside her – the solidity of his thigh pressed to hers, his clean scent teasing her senses.

When the charged silence grew too much, she asked, "How long has it been? Since…"

*Since you traced every inch of me with those elegant fingers until I was mindless with pleasure? Until I forgot everything but the taste of your skin beneath my lips?*

"Since we sat together in a carriage?" he supplied.

"Sat together anywhere. Attended an event. Had a conversation." She paused, then added in a softer voice, "Since I drew you?"

She heard the hitch in Julian's breath at the mention of her art, the intimate charcoal portraits she'd made of him so long ago. Theirs had always been a relationship defined by the spaces left unspoken.

"Eight years. Or seven years, ten months, four days, to be precise." Julian's voice was low, almost rough. "And you didn't draw me after our wedding."

The specific accounting was a blade slipped between her ribs, sharp and unexpected. He'd been counting the days apart as diligently as she had.

"I drew you from memory," Caroline confessed before she could think better of it. She gave a careless shrug, feigning nonchalance. "I can show you sometime if you'd care to see."

"I would enjoy seeing your work whenever you wish to share it," he said, his voice gentle.

"I'll look for them," she said, gathering herself. "They're probably buried under dust by now."

Where she'd once boarded up her tender feelings as one might shutter a crumbling ruin.

Sensing the need to redirect their discourse to less treacherous waters, Julian said, "We should prepare ourselves for scrutiny today. Have you heard the latest gossip about us?"

She gave him a wry glance. "You read the scandal sheets, Hastings? How shocking. What's next, playing whist and gossiping over cake with dowagers?"

"On occasion, one does overhear tidbits over cigars and port."

"I see." Caroline tilted her head, considering. "Go on, then. What did you learn about the estranged Duke and Duchess over cigars and port? Have we grown horns and tails in each other's absence?"

"They wonder if the duke keeps a mistress on the Continent to explain his long absences," Julian said bluntly.

There it was. Their fragile accord cracked beneath the sharp spike of jealousy that lanced through her at the thought of Julian in another woman's bed. She forced her tone to nonchalance. "And does he?"

"I thought I made it clear when we were young that I've no tolerance for infidelity or affairs outside of marriage. That hasn't changed."

The confession settled in her like a stone. Eight years apart, and he'd been faithful to her. The thought sunk deep, cracking open possibilities she'd long since boarded up.

"What about whispers regarding your duchess?" she asked, almost gently. "Has she taken someone to warm her bed while her husband was off on his adventures with the nonexistent Continental mistress?"

"No." Something dangerously close to possession simmered beneath that one clipped word. "As far as the *ton* knows, we're the picture of propriety and marital devotion. So very dull that we've lived apart nearly a decade with nary an unkind word between us."

"I'm rather disappointed we haven't been embroiled in any outrageous scandals during our separation. Maybe we ought to manufacture some for novelty's sake." Caroline gave him a playful smile. "Hurl insults in public. Overturn a tea table. Ravage each other on top of the *petit fours*."

The corner of Julian's stern mouth flickered. "Let's refrain from debauching on the baked goods, if you please. I do have some standards."

"Well, something salacious that won't get us banished from society for lewd acts. Anything else would be permissible."

Amusement warmed Julian's eyes. "I'll do my best to walk that fine line between scandalising dowagers and getting us exiled to one of my dusty estates."

"That's the spirit."

A crush of carriages and ladies arrayed in frothy muslin crowded the drive of Lady Fairfax's estate. Caroline gripped Julian's arm for balance. There were too many eyes on them. Too many whispers behind fluttering fans.

They strolled through the elaborate topiaries flanking the garden path, ignoring the stares following their progress. Julian's hand found the small of her back, spreading warmth even through layers of fabric as he guided her through the crush. The intimacy of his touch made Caroline's breath catch.

"Smile, my duchess. We're the very picture of connubial bliss." His breath stirred her hair, and desire curled hot and sweet inside her.

She threw Julian a dry look. "I'm contemplating how much laudanum in my tea might make this afternoon tolerable."

His thumb stroked a distracting pattern over her lower back. "Let's refrain from drug-induced stupors until after the dessert course. I know how you love your sweets."

"Oh, very well." She heaved a theatrical, long-suffering sigh. "I'll resist the siren song of drug-induced oblivion for the sake of the puddings. However—" A footman appeared bearing a salver with champagne. Caroline accepted one and gulped it down. "Champagne, I will have."

"Pace yourself," Julian said. "It's a bit early to be in your cups."

"It's either this or fashioning myself a noose from the table linens," she returned sweetly.

"Let's refrain from hangings, if at all possible." He plucked the empty champagne flute from her hand and passed it to a hovering servant. "It would put a damper on our performance of wedded felicity if you turn up dead in Lady Fairfax's garden. As would a drunken scene, no matter how entertaining."

"But aren't you curious how many glasses it would take before I'm compelled to fling myself into Lady Fairfax's garden fountain?"

"At this rate? I'd wager one more," Julian said dryly. "Behave, and I'll procure you a jam tart later."

She considered that. "Very well. But I insist on another glass of champagne as compensation for good behaviour. And a generous slice of cake to go with my jam tart."

"You drive a hard bargain."

"I always do."

Just then, Lady Fairfax bustled forth in a froth of violet silk. "Duchess! Here you are, and with your husband after all this time!" The countess's attention shifted between them. "We had quite despaired of your wanderings to the Continent, duke. I do hope you'll stay longer than the Parliamentary session. I confess I'm most eager to hear of your travels."

Julian's expression remained coolly polite. "I'll consider it. I'm finding much to enjoy in London after my travels."

"Wonderful." Lady Fairfax's calculating stare bounced between them. "You really must join Horace and I for dinner soon. I'd love to hear how you're both getting on." She lowered her voice conspiratorially. "And whether you have any happy news to share in the coming months."

*Happy news*. Caroline's emotions turned the simple statement into a blade that pierced deep. She blinked around the sudden tears, taken off guard.

But Julian didn't pretend to misunderstand. His hand came to rest again at the small of her back. "Should we be so blessed," he answered smoothly.

Oblivious to the turmoil roiling inside Caroline, Lady Fairfax beamed approval. "Lovely. Do come join us in a few minutes for a bit of sport. We're about to commence an archery competition."

And with that, she bustled off, leaving a heavy silence in her wake.

"Come with me." Julian tucked Caroline's hand into the crook of his elbow and drew her towards a secluded little alcove behind an artful screen of roses. Safe for the moment from prying eyes.

Caroline sucked in a lungful of air. Still, it couldn't fill the hollowed-out space left by Lady Fairfax's words. Children. A simple concept most husbands and wives didn't have to think twice about. But for her and Julian, it was a wound that would not stop bleeding.

"Are you all right?" Julian asked gently.

She focused on a point just beyond his shoulder, throat tight. "I should have expected that question eventually."

Julian shifted closer. "Expecting it and it not hurting are very different things."

Caroline gave a jerky nod of agreement.

"Would you like me to come up with an excuse? We could

slip away early." His knuckle skimmed her cheek in a caress that made her pulse stutter.

Stubborn pride had her shaking her head. "No. We still need to make a good showing. Give them something new to gossip over besides whispers of estrangement."

His expression shuttered. "Of course."

Damn it all, that had come out wrong. She grasped for the right words. "Just... just let me catch my breath."

Julian moved closer, rubbing his hands over her arms, the friction chasing away the chill.

"You were always good at knowing what I needed most," she admitted softly.

"I did once possess a singular talent for being your friend before I made a mess of being your husband." His tone took on a rueful note, though his gaze remained tender.

She turned her face up towards his. "You weren't terrible. We just... hurt."

Pain flashed in his eyes. "Yes. And I made terrible mistakes in how I handled that hurt." His knuckle grazed her cheek once more, touch achingly gentle. "Are you recovered now, do you think? We could stay behind the roses and drink champagne if you'd like."

Caroline straightened, shoring up the cracks in her armour. "I'm fine. Not blotchy, am I? Hideously splotchy and swollen?"

"Your face is lovely as ever." His lips curved as he held out his palm. "Was that in doubt?"

"A lady must always be assured of these things before presenting herself in public," she said, taking his hand.

Soon, a line of targets was erected along one edge of the garden for an archery competition. As Julian shed his coat and moved to take his turn, a ripple of appreciation went through the assembled ladies. The white linen of his shirt pulled taut, displaying the breadth of his shoulders. He took aim with flawless form and loosed the arrow. It struck the outermost ring with a solid *thunk*.

Ignoring the avid stares that clung to Julian, Caroline stepped up and selected her bow. She nocked an arrow with fingers that trembled. So many eyes on her. Too many whispers swirling.

She struggled to recall the cadence of air in her lungs, the proper stance. But her limbs had locked, every motion forgotten.

And then Julian was there, pressed against her back, his heat surrounding her. Strong hands framed her own, holding them in place. "Relax your shoulders," he murmured low in her ear. "You're fighting it too hard." His free hand traced down her arm in a whisper-soft caress that skimmed along every nerve ending, leaving gooseflesh in its wake. "Feel the tension here? Breathe through it."

Caroline shivered. "I don't think you're supposed to be helping. I'm your competition, remember?"

"They're all watching us." His breath stirred her hair, warm and intimate. "And we're meant to give them something scandalous that isn't debauching on a dessert table, remember?"

Heat scalded her cheeks at the words. "Oh, I think they'll be whispering about us over breakfast tomorrow."

"Good." Julian's voice dropped to a rough purr. "Now, just focus on my touch. Inhale..." His fingers flexed where they covered hers on the bow. "And loose the arrow as you exhale. There's my girl."

His husky praise sent heat curling through her veins. As she released her breath, the arrow sprang free in a silent blur.

Dead centre.

A smile curved her lips as applause and shouts erupted from the crowd. Lady Fairfax's voice rang out above the rest. "A perfect bullseye! Well done, duchess!"

Caroline barely heard it over the roar of her pounding pulse. For a suspended moment, Julian's gaze held a glimmer of unguarded warmth.

"Nicely done," he murmured.

"I'd nearly forgotten what an exceptional instructor you make."

Everything he had taught her – waltzing across meadows, nude portraiture, archery lessons stolen away from prying eyes… it all lingered still in muscle memory.

Something strained and raw flashed in Julian's eyes. But before Caroline could decipher it, he took the bow from her numb fingers and handed their equipment to a footman. Then he guided her back towards the gathering.

The afternoon wound down. As Julian handed her up into the waiting carriage, his fingertips seemed to linger at her waist.

"You were magnificent today," Julian said into the quiet space between them.

"So were you," Caroline returned softly.

*I don't want you to leave again.*

The words echoed unspoken inside her as the carriage rattled along the lamplit streets.

# 8

## London, 1865

*Nine years ago*

The room was dim, the heavy velvet curtains drawn against the morning light. Shadows cloaked the opulent furnishings, leaching all vibrancy from the space.

Caroline perched on a chair near the large canopied bed. Beside her sat Julian, elbows braced on his knees. Neither could tear their eyes from the still figure beneath the silken coverlet.

Grace.

Her charm and vitality had filled any room she occupied. Now, sickness had reduced their friend to a pale wraith, her lustrous curls damp with sweat. Grace's breath emerged in laboured rasps, a chilling percussion beneath the mournful tick of the bedside clock. Every exhale was wet with fluid and ended with a choked gurgle that made Caroline flinch.

Grace's eyes fluttered open, fogged with fever. They wandered listlessly before settling on Caroline and Julian. When recognition sparked, her cracked lips twisted into a ravaged imitation of her once radiant smile.

"You're both still here," Grace rasped. "Have you nothing better to do than watch me die?"

Despite everything, Caroline managed a wisp of laughter. "All society left after the Season," Caroline replied. "I'm afraid you're stuck with us."

Grace's mouth twitched again, wry and resigned. "Morbid creatures." Her gaze shifted to Julian, softening. "You've been so quiet, Hastings. Not a word of gloomy philosophy to share?"

He stared down at his clasped hands. "I find my well of wisdom has rather run dry just now," he admitted hoarsely.

A violent fit of coughing wracked Grace. She curled onto her side, her thin frame heaving beneath the bedclothes. When the spasms passed, her shift was dotted with vivid red. Blood speckled her wan lips.

"Here." Julian offered a handkerchief, averting his eyes from the grisly evidence. "Let us make you comfortable."

Between the two of them, they shifted Grace onto her back once more and wiped the blood from her mouth. Caroline's hands shook as she smoothed Grace's damp curls from her brow.

A gentle knock on the bedchamber door preceded Viscountess Harcourt's entrance, ragged grief etched in her features. She perched on the bed and took one of Grace's frail hands between her own.

"Mother," Grace breathed. "You're here."

Viscountess Harcourt blinked away her tears and brought Grace's fingers to her lips. "Of course, my darling. Where else would I be?"

The viscountess leaned forward and whispered something for her daughter's ears alone, pressing a kiss on her brow. When she straightened, resignation lined her ravaged features.

"It's time we let her rest." Viscountess Harcourt rose on unsteady legs and looked at Caroline and Julian. "Come with me to the hall?"

"Of course," Caroline said. "We'll return shortly, Grace."

In the sitting room across the hall, Viscountess Harcourt sank onto an embroidered settee. Her composure fractured at last, tears spilling down her cheeks. Caroline sat beside her and wrapped an arm around her shoulders. Her eyes burned, but she dared not loosen the ruthless hold over her emotions. Not yet.

After endless moments, the viscountess scrubbed at her face with a handkerchief. "I need to make the arrangements."

Caroline swallowed hard. "She might still pull through—"

"The doctor warned me she likely wouldn't last the night." Viscountess Harcourt twisted the handkerchief in her lap. "My husband is with Victoria in America, but I'm uncertain where," she said, referring to her eldest daughter. "New York, I think. But I can't let them find out about Grace by letter. That would be unthinkably cruel."

Julian took a slow breath. "I'll take a steamer and give them the news," he said after a long silence. "So you don't have to worry about anything but funeral arrangements. I'll leave tomorrow morning." He glanced at Caroline. "May I speak with you?"

Squeezing the viscountess's hand, Caroline hurried after her husband into the empty room down the hall. She found Julian leaning against the mantelpiece, staring at the cold grate. Before he could mask it, Caroline glimpsed the stark devastation hollowing his eyes. The raw agony he hid from all save her.

It cracked something wide open in her chest.

"Julian." He shuddered against her when she wrapped both arms tight around his waist. "I'll come with you."

"No." She heard him swallow. "We can't leave Gracie's mother alone right now. And I can't… I have to get away, duchess. Just for a little while."

A memory took root in her mind – Julian staring at Grace with open affection as he tucked daisies into her hair. If it wasn't for that night in the garden, he'd be proposing to Grace by now. Planning their wedding. Not waiting for her to die.

Caroline shook off the thought, leashing it ruthlessly and choking it into submission. That thought had no place in this room with them. "I'll write to you," she said.

"Tell me every detail," he said. "Promise to spare nothing."

"I promise," she said.

He turned, his gaze tracing over her. "Come here."

Caroline let him tug her down to the wing chair beside the hearth, settling her on his lap. The heat of him seeped into her skin through their layers of clothing. Julian's breath left him sharply as she shifted until her knees bracketed his thighs. The chair groaned faintly beneath their combined weight.

His hands came to rest on her waist – a silent query. In answer, Caroline draped both arms around his shoulders. Still, he withheld the embrace, studying her.

After a weighted moment, Julian spoke. "I want to hold you before I go."

Emotion clogged her throat. Caroline pressed closer, fingertips trailing through Julian's hair. "Hold me as often and as long as you like," she whispered.

At her words, the last of his restraint crumbled. He dragged her against his chest and buried his face in her neck, hugged her so tightly that her ribs creaked. Clutched her as if he was drowning.

Caroline clung back as fiercely. With Grace slipping away, it would be just the two of them. Childhood bonds fraying down to their final delicate threads.

They held each other as the candle flames died one by one. Until only the barest flicker remained, leaving them twined together in the looming dark. The entire world distilled to Julian's laboured breaths against her throat, his hands spread over every notch in her spine.

*If you loved her, I'm sorry for what happened in the garden. I'm so sorry you had to marry me to save me. I love you, and I'm sorry.*

"What are you thinking?" he asked.

Caroline closed her eyes tight. "That I'll miss you."

"I'll come home as soon as I can."

She let him hold her. Cradle her close. Lips brushed her brow and printed a benediction there.

The next day, she watched Julian leave. He slipped out the door, the latch clicking behind him with resounding finality.

# 9

## London, 1874

*Nine years later*

Caroline stared at the canvas on her easel, at the malformed creature taking shape there. She added another hopeless smudge of grey, as if she could capture life by slowly suffocating it.

"You're utterly hopeless," she muttered to the abomination.

A painting so abysmal it would bring the critics to her door like rabid dogs, ready to tear her apart with their teeth. No skill, they would sneer. No heart. A child could produce something better using their toes. Blindfolded.

"Talking to yourself?"

Caroline turned to find Julian leaning in the doorway, broad shoulders eclipsing the light from the hall. He looked as if he'd just rolled out of bed, hair mussed, shirtsleeves to the elbows.

"Scolding my painting." Caroline forced her lips into a brittle smile. "You look tired. That cryptogram still plaguing you?"

"Unfortunately. Though I confess it wounds my pride to be bested by random symbols on paper."

"I'd offer to help, but I'd likely only hinder you today." She waved a hand at the abomination on her easel. "As you can see, I'm busy attempting to insult this painting into submission."

He crossed the room on silent feet to stand beside her, and it took every ounce of her self-control not to reach out and trace the ink stains marring his elegant hands.

"And have your criticisms yielded any improvement?" His voice was cool, stripped of anything telling.

Caroline tossed her ruined gloves onto the nearby table. "God, no. It's an offence to painters everywhere." She pinched the bridge of her nose against the building pressure headache. "I ought to just quit now."

"You've always been unnecessarily harsh on yourself," he said.

"I'm serious. The proportions are atrocious. I've somehow made an attractive model look like some lumbering behemoth. With a face like a potato."

"But your technique is flawless. It's not without merit."

"You're being kind," she said. "Go on, give me your honesty. Tell me what you really think of this monstrosity." She crossed her arms, half hoping he'd tear the awful piece apart and give her an excuse to be rid of it. "You had no words for how I painted the subject."

But Julian only stepped nearer, so close she could feel the heat of him. "My preferences on subject matter may be somewhat biased where your art is concerned."

*Are you jealous?* she wanted to ask. *Or do you wish I'd paint you again?* Questions unspoken but pulsing against her skin like endless heartbeats – each one a plea, a prayer, a stinging accusation.

"Biased?" Her voice emerged thready.

"You mistake the root of the problem," Julian murmured. "It's not your technique. It's the emotion. What do you feel when you look at him?" His eyes raked over the painting of Laurent.

She swallowed, a strange tightness settling in her chest. "Nothing."

"And what do you feel when you look at me?"

*Everything. Alive.*

*Ruined. Like you're going to leave me shattered again once you board that damned ship to Italy.*

Another shuddering breath left Caroline, pain crackling

through her sternum. “I don’t know.” The lie scorched her throat.

“You don’t know.” His words were soft, but they fell between them like stones sinking to the bottom of a dark lake. Silent accusations.

Because they had softened towards one another in recent days but those were the words of two people irreparably altered. Two people forced to lie and evade, to shield themselves behind armour that had become second skin.

Before she could react, Julian grasped the hem of his shirt and peeled it off in one smooth motion. Revealed the expanse of smooth skin and lean muscle, the play of light across the hard planes of his abdomen. A body she knew intimately.

Her mouth went dry. “What are you doing?”

Julian lifted his shoulder in a careless shrug. Like this was nothing. “Taking off my clothes. What does it look like I’m doing? Or has it been so long that you’ve forgotten how this goes?”

*Forgotten?* She wanted to laugh. Or maybe scream. There wasn’t enough wine or laudanum in the world to erase him from her memory.

“Why, is what I meant.”

“That painting is a disaster, and I know from experience that we work well together. You’ve helped me with my cryptograms, so I’ll help with your art.” His stare turned mocking. “And since you can’t even put your feelings for me into words, it shouldn’t be a problem, should it?”

Julian’s eyes locked with hers, burning into her, as he flicked the buttons of his trousers open and let them fall to the floor.

His body was a work of art, and Caroline ached to reach out and touch him. The scar high on one shoulder from a childhood tumble. The thin silvery line across a hip where her nails had dug crescents into tender flesh. But she didn’t dare move.

Julian stepped closer. “Flushed skin. Racing pulse. Shallow breathing,” he murmured, bending to nip the tender spot where her neck met her shoulder. Caroline couldn’t stifle a gasp. “You don't know how you feel about me, my duchess? I think you're a liar." Julian reached for a piece of charcoal and pressed it into her trembling hand. "Now draw."

He sauntered to the chaise longue and sprawled across it. Head thrown back, every muscle on display.

"Well?" His voice was rough silk. "What are you waiting for?"

Somehow, she managed to face her canvas. With shaking hands, Caroline began to sketch. She started slowly, almost clinically, capturing lines and contours.

If he insisted on flaunting his body, then she'd feast. Gorge her starved senses on every angle until she'd had her fill. Until the pounding ache in her core no longer made her dizzy with lust.

Until she scrubbed her fevered dreams free of ink-stained hands and burning blue eyes.

Caroline drew across the page in bold slashes. Angled light played over the defined muscles of his torso and legs – muscle, sinew, poetry wrought in the flesh. A familiar heat bloomed inside her while she rendered each powerful contour. She smudged the shadows between his thighs before darting a shy glance upwards.

His stare held a knowing glint that made her skin flush hotter. Steeling herself, she continued her path downwards, letting her gaze linger on the thick length of his aroused cock.

"Stop drawing." Julian's voice came out rough. More command than request. "Take off your dress."

As if compelled by gravity, Caroline set aside her charcoal before crossing the room. She reached for the buttons lining the front of her day gown. One after another they slipped free, until she stood before him in only her thin chemise and stockings. When she shivered, it had nothing to do with the cold.

Julian's stare moved over her. "All of it."

The rest of her garments joined the pile. She tried not to fidget under that intense perusal. She saw herself reflected in his gaze – the rapid rise and fall of her breasts, the fine tremor in her hands.

Utterly exposed before him, flaws and all.

"Come here."

This time, it was less command, more the gentle beckoning of a lover. Caroline went willingly. Let him guide her down onto the divan so they lay pressed together, skin to skin. His fingers traced idle patterns over her hip.

Their lips met, and Julian kissed her until stars exploded behind her eyes. He relearned each sensitive spot that made her gasp and tremble. She drank him in – the taste of his skin beneath her lips, the devastating pleasure of his hands and mouth on her body. And when she finally pulled back, gasping for breath, he simply moved his attention lower, kissing down the column of her throat.

Caroline clutched at his shoulders, lost to sensation. She wanted this – wanted him with a desperation that went soul-deep.

Wanted to drown in him.

Julian stroked his fingers between her thighs. He kept her balanced on the precipice, denying her the penetration she craved.

"Now, I'll ask again, my duchess," he said. "What do you feel when you look at me?"

It took Caroline a moment to process his words. To understand the importance behind them.

But her heart was too bruised, too tender beneath its fortress of scars. Jagged at the edges, barely held together. He would leave her again, board his ship and pretend he didn't know her. She couldn't survive him carving her open a second time.

His gaze locked with hers, so intense it seared. "Answer me."

"I can't," she whispered.

Something dangerous sparked in Julian's eyes. He drove two fingers deep inside her, as if he could wring the truth from her trembling body. Caroline came apart on a sharp cry, shattering beneath his touch. Again and again, he brought her to the brink, stoking her pleasure until she was wrung out and gasping.

She expected him to find his own release then. Instead, he

gathered his discarded garments, donning each item with clinical precision. The distance between them gaped wider with each button refastened, each layer of clothing restored.

Until it was as if their interlude had never happened.

"Aren't you going to—" Caroline pressed her lips together, refusing to beg for it.

*You don't have to play the dutiful husband behind closed doors.*

Fully dressed once more, Julian leaned down to brush his mouth over hers in a kiss that somehow felt more intimate than all they'd just done. "When I fuck you," he whispered, "it won't be while you're lying to me." He walked to the door. "We're attending the theatre tonight. Don't keep our audience waiting."

Long after he had gone, she remained sprawled amid the wreckage of her studio. Still burning from the memory of his hands. Still devastated by the ruthless skill with which he'd shattered her defences, forced her to confront old agonies she'd never been able to cauterize closed.

# 10

The clock ticked out the minutes as Julian waited at the foot of the grand staircase. He adjusted and readjusted the silver cufflinks at his wrists, focusing on the repetitive motion to calm the sudden restlessness that had taken hold. It had been hours since he'd posed naked for Caroline, but his body still hummed with nervous energy.

He could not forget her fixed focus as she'd sketched him. The way her eyes had lingered on him with such intense concentration, as if he were the only other person in existence. She'd looked at him like that when they were young and still learning each other's bodies. When the press of skin on skin was art to them.

He shoved the memories away and focused on steadying his breaths. Listened for the telltale swish of silk that would herald Caroline's approach.

When she appeared, it stole the air from his lungs. The muted light gilded her pale hair and her ice-blue silk gown made her glow. No jewels adorned her save the simple gold band of her wedding ring.

*God, but you look breathtaking tonight. I can hardly breathe for wanting you.*

Even with her face schooled into politeness, he could read

the lingering tension in her slender frame. As she descended, her skirts sighed against the marble steps in a susurrus that scraped over Julian's senses and left them raw. He thought of fisting those silken skirts in his hands, dragging them up to bare her legs, revealing whether she still wore stockings and garters beneath. Pleasuring her again until she gave him answers.

He wanted to peel back her armour.

Julian dragged his gaze upwards. "The carriage is waiting."

Too brusque. Caroline's resulting flinch behind her polished smile cut straight through his ribs.

Outside, he handed her into the carriage and tried again while the footmen secured the door.

"You look beautiful." The words emerged rough around the edges.

Caroline blinked, her cheeks colouring. "As do you. The evening kit suits you."

Soft words rotting like carrion on the ground at their feet. He'd thought her softening – after Lady Fairfax's party, after their code-breaking – and he'd moved too fast.

And now he didn't know how to reach through the walls she'd erected around her heart.

So he held his silence during the ride as rain-slicked streets blurred past fogged windows. Tried not to notice how she shivered whenever their knees accidentally brushed in the confines of the carriage. How she worried her bottom lip between her teeth. Until he had to curl his hands into fists to resist the urge to kiss away the sting.

The discordant chatter hit his ears as soon as the carriage rolled to a halt outside the theatre. Julian stepped down into the glittering crush and turned to offer her his hand.

"I can practically hear your teeth chattering," he told Caroline in an undertone. "Relax, or they'll scent blood."

She slanted him a sly look, allowing him to help her down the steps. "What if I shatter a few champagne flutes out of spite?"

His mouth tilted up at one corner. "Be sure to let me know

so I can position myself out of glass range." As they crossed the threshold, Julian splayed his fingers at the small of her back, an unrepentantly possessive touch allowed by the performance she'd requested.

Only it wasn't a performance for him.

*"I'd heard they reconciled, but I didn't believe it..."*

*"... heard he left her after the wedding and stayed away..."*

Even here, he was attuned to her. To the stiffening of her spine as judgemental gazes crawled over them both, picking at old wounds. He longed to shelter her from their scrutiny, hide her away someplace only he could find her.

Instead, Julian nodded politely to acquaintances, ignoring their hushed speculation. He channelled arrogant disinterest as if he hadn't spent the last eight years longing for this woman now on his arm.

"I'd hoped Lady Fairfax's party would make this gossip stale." Caroline kept her voice low, but he heard the bitter edge sharpening each word. "Didn't their governesses teach them manners?"

His hand flexed against her back. "I think our appearance fuelled speculation on the precise nature of our estrangement." Julian guided her up the grand staircase towards the private boxes. "We're the most interesting gossip they've had in months, and it's killing them not to have answers. Does it help if I glower at them?"

"Immensely." A reluctant smile tugged at her lips. "Please scare Lord Ponsonby. I believe I heard him whisper earlier that you tried to ravish me during archery."

Julian narrowed his eyes at the young lord until the man blanched and scurried away.

"Much better," Caroline said in amusement. "Thank you."

As they walked, snippets of gossip reached his ears, each more outrageous than the last. But he forced himself to appear calm and unaffected.

*"... keeps a bevvy of exotic mistresses, I heard."*

*"... did you hear? At Lady Fairfax's party, he had his hands all over her in front of everyone."*

"How are you always so calm?" Caroline asked.

Julian let his gaze trace over her face, drinking her in. "Because the only person whose opinion matters to me is yours. I just ignore the rest." She froze, eyes widening. Before she could respond, he added, "Now show me that dazzling smile I love so much. Let them see it."

When she smiled at him through her lashes, playing along, it made his chest ache. He wanted to see her real smile. Wanted to coax laughter from her lips and kiss away the bitterness lingering there.

They were so close, her floral perfume teasing his senses. Unable to stop himself, Julian turned his head and brushed his mouth over her cheek in the barest caress.

She gasped, body jolting. The crowd released a collective breath around them.

"There," he murmured. "Let them talk about us over breakfast again."

Safely ensconced in their private box overlooking the stage, he finally trusted himself to meet her gaze.

"Was that necessary?" Caroline asked.

Julian lifted one shoulder in a casual shrug. "Perhaps not. But you asked for gossip fodder, and I aim to please. In a few weeks, their claws will retract, and they'll move on to newer scandals."

Behind the defiance burning in those blue eyes, he glimpsed the first faint cracks forming in her armour.

Her answering smile turned brittle and sharp. "Until you leave for Italy, of course."

That sentence shouldn't possess the power to flay skin from bone. And still, it shuddered through him, merciless as any lash.

His jaw tightened. "Yes. Until I leave for Italy."

The silence bloomed between them once more, full of hurts left to fester.

"I suppose I'll go to Ravenhill, then," Caroline said, turning back towards the stage.

He stared sightlessly at the performers, aware of her nearness.

The floral scent of her skin teased him with memories – the slide of her body against his, gasps muffled against his throat. He shifted in his seat.

Then her hand drifted to rest on her thigh, close enough to graze. Julian struggled against the madness whispering through his mind. Telling him to cover her fingers with his own. To tangle tight and never let go.

Before he could stop himself, Julian let his knuckles brush the back of her hand where it rested on her thigh. She jolted, sucking in a sharp breath. He froze, waiting to see if she'd pull away. When she remained motionless, he risked another tentative graze of fingertips over skin – an unspoken question.

Time slowed. Seconds stretched endlessly.

Then she turned her hand in invitation.

Julian's breath left him in a rush. He slid his palm against hers, threading their fingers together. Felt every desperate shred of self-control threaten to unravel at that small point of contact.

To sit beside her with her palm sliding against his was sheer madness. He told himself to release her. To rebuild the walls between them before they fractured beyond all hope of repair.

But he couldn't make himself let go.

Not when she shifted restlessly in her seat, soft thighs pressing together. Not when he felt the wild flutter of her pulse through their joined hands.

He stroked his thumb over her knuckles, unable to look away from their joined hands. She shifted beside him, the slide of silk over skin echoing in his ears. He imagined grasping her skirts, dragging them up to bare her legs, spreading her wide…

"This afternoon, I didn't want you to stop."

Her hushed confession froze the breath in his lungs. He turned towards her and saw the heated yearning in her eyes. His cock throbbed, pressure building.

"I would have told you," she whispered. "What you wanted to know."

Words that might've stopped his heart if he wasn't already

dying by slow degrees. If this was to be his last scrap of time with her, he would cling until his bones shattered.

"Can we go home?" Caroline asked.

"Yes. Let's go home." The words scraped his throat raw.

As he guided Caroline outside, his hand still tingled with the memory of her skin against his. With sense memories of her body in the studio.

This time, when she spoke, something fragile in her tone threatened to crack straight down the middle. "Thank you. For doing all this with me. I know you didn't want to."

Julian's breath tangled in his lungs. *Tell her everything*, the recklessness urged. *The sheer futility of trying to carve her out of your soul. Tell her so she understands a month more in her presence is the only thing tethering you to sanity.*

He opened his mouth to lay himself bare beneath the knife edge of her regard. To cut out his heart and offer it up.

*Ask me to stay, and I will.*

But before he found the words, the explosion tore the night in two.

# 11

Julian reacted on instinct, throwing himself over Caroline's slender frame. His shoulders curled protectively around her as they hit the cobblestones. Debris pelted his back, sharp and bruising even through the layers of his tailcoat. The wave of blistering heat seared across his back. His ears rang from the concussive force, deafening him until all other sounds faded to a dull roar.

And then, stillness – stripped clean in the wake of violence.

No. Not stillness. Slowly, sound filtered back in. A high-pitched whine where there should have been noise. The groan of twisted iron and splintered wood settling into unnatural shapes. Soft, ragged cries painted the silence in shades of pain.

Julian's focus narrowed on the woman beneath him. "Are you hurt?" His voice scraped raw and foreign to his own ears.

He scanned her for any sign of injury, every protective instinct roaring to life. She looked so small curled there on the ground, her coat spread around her like broken wings.

"I'm fine," Caroline managed, though her face had gone bone-white beneath the layer of grit.

Julian grasped her shoulders to help her stand, keeping hold of her when she swayed on her feet. Blood slicked his palms, rubbed open by their impact with the street. He hardly felt it.

All around them lay utter devastation. Plumes of acrid smoke clawed at the night sky, searing Julian's throat. Through the haze, he glimpsed the mangled wrecks of carriages and coaches strewn across the ravaged street. Wood splintered, ironwork twisted into jagged spikes, debris scattered into shrapnel.

Their footman came pelting up, his livery almost unrecognisable beneath the layer of soot. "Your Graces!" he gasped out. "Thank God you're alive. What should I do?"

Caroline straightened up, the picture of poise even when coated in dust and blood. "Go summon the constables," she said. "Fetch anyone available and tell them to bring doctors. Direct them here."

The footman nodded and raced off into the night.

Julian began stripping off his ruined tailcoat, the fine fabric shredded beyond saving now. "You won't go anywhere near that," he said, gesturing at the devastation. "I'll dig out the wounded. Stay back where it's safe. There might be another blast."

But Caroline had that stubborn set to her jaw, the one he knew all too well. "Don't be absurd. We'll work much faster together."

Before he could protest, she gathered her silken skirts and picked her way into the wreckage. Glass crunched beneath the thin soles of her slippers.

"Damn it," Julian growled. Cursing under his breath, he had no choice but to follow her.

The world was reduced to a blur of smoke and agony. Together with the gathering crowds, they shifted heavy planks by inches. Ragged edges scraped Julian's knees and palms raw. Grit coated his tongue, acrid and bitter.

He swallowed back bile as shattered bones and mangled limbs were jostled. Screams filled the night. As he moved debris and stones aside, Julian kept an eye on his wife. Caroline tore strips of fabric from her ruined gown, wrapping the silk around wrists, arms, legs – any injury she could bind up and staunch the bleeding. Her makeshift bandages shone like gossamer against torn flesh.

All the while, she kept up a constant soothing stream of encouragement. "There's a good lad. Just lie still, the pain will pass."

And to another, "It's not so very bad, miss. You'll have a dashing scar to impress the gentlemen."

If he hadn't already loved her desperately, Julian thought he might have fallen in love with her then and there. The sight of her easing people's agony with her gentle words and makeshift bandages brought an odd lump to his throat.

As they laboured on, more bystanders trickled in to assist. Men and women of all classes grasped the broken planks and moved rubble at Caroline's crisp commands. She was in her element here – organising rescue with brisk efficiency even as her pristine silks became filthy rags.

Julian redoubled his own efforts, pulling apart the wreckage with single-minded focus. When he lifted a cracked wooden panel to reveal a bloodied elderly man pinned beneath, he called over his shoulder, "Caroline, I need you."

In an instant, she was beside him. "Let's get him out quickly. I'll brace his head."

Together, they shifted just enough rubble aside to pull the elderly gentleman free. Caroline cradled the man's head in her lap, heedless of the blood streaking her gown.

"Is he—?"

"Alive," she confirmed. Caroline's voice was steady, betraying none of the bone-deep weariness Julian knew they both felt. "But concussed and in need of a surgeon."

Another low moan drew their attention. Peering beneath the ruins of a splintered carriage, Julian spotted a young woman pinned under a heavy oak beam.

"Damn it all," he growled, wrapping both hands around the jagged edge of the wood.

He tensed and heaved upward. But the beam barely budged, weighed down by bricks and debris. The woman's whimpers faded to silence.

Julian braced his feet and gripped the wood once more. "Take her hands the instant the beam lifts," he said to Caroline. "Pull her free quickly and get clear yourself. Understand?"

Caroline gripped the woman's arms. She cast Julian a resolute look, ready for his signal. "One..." Julian tensed. "Two..." He drew breath scorched by smoke and gritted his teeth. "Three!"

Digging his heels in, Julian heaved upwards with every shred of strength left in his ravaged body. The beam shifted just enough for Caroline to act, and she dragged the woman's battered form free. Then Julian's strength gave out, and the beam crashed down once more in a plume of dust.

They collapsed together onto the blood-slick ground, chests heaving between wracking coughs. After a moment, Caroline crawled to the survivor's side and pressed an ear to her heart.

Relief broke across her dirt-streaked features. "Her pulse is weak, but it's there."

Julian clasped her shoulder with a filthy, bloodied hand. "Well done."

Caroline's eyes warmed at the praise.

In the distance, the clatter of approaching horses and carriage wheels swelled through the smoky air. The authorities were finally arriving. Julian rose unsteadily and pulled Caroline up beside him, keeping an arm wrapped around her shoulders.

Together, they watched as constables and medical personnel swarmed the devastated street. Blanket-draped bodies were loaded onto stretchers while bobbies struggled to hold back crowds of shocked onlookers. Mattias Wentworth stood in the road, his face etched into harsh lines as he surveyed the destruction. Catching sight of Julian, Wentworth picked his way over through the rubble.

"Good God," he said. "Are you both all right?"

"Nearly weren't," Julian replied.

Wentworth nodded once. "Meet me at White's tomorrow at midday. We need to talk." His eyes flicked to Caroline in polite acknowledgement.

Questions scorched Julian's tongue, but this was not the time or place. "Tomorrow then," was all he said.

Carefully steering Caroline through the chaos to their untouched carriage, Julian handed her inside. As soon as they were alone, he took Caroline's hands and carefully turned them over. Her palms were scored with angry scratches and scrapes, her knuckles raw and bleeding.

They regarded each other for a long moment – the weight of everything unsaid pressed between them until Julian broke the silence.

"You took ten years from my life out there," he said. "It was reckless of you to run into that catastrophe."

"Only ten? I'll have to try harder the next time I rush towards the danger." She studied him as the horses lurched into motion. "You know who was behind that explosion. Don't you?"

Julian's jaw tightened. "Not yet."

Her gaze dropped to her hands, studying the angry scrapes marring her skin. Evidence of how close she'd come to harm. After a moment, she asked quietly, "But this has to do with your code-breaking?"

Julian hesitated, then gave a terse nod. "I believe so, yes."

Caroline exhaled. "I thought as much. For Mr Wentworth?"

He didn't reply, focusing on her torn dress. "Any other injuries? The absolute truth."

"Bruises and scratches. Though I may need to burn this gown now." She attempted a wan smile, but it faltered at his stony expression.

What had once been an exquisite, gauzy confection was a tattered, filthy rag. Julian's throat tightened at the visible evidence of what she had faced tonight. He could have lost her.

Wordlessly, he brought her abraded hand to his lips, breathing in the scent of her skin beneath the smoke and dust. Then he threaded his fingers through hers as the carriage rolled on through the streets.

# 12

Caroline stared out the carriage window as London sped past, buildings reduced to shadows and fragmented light. Julian's thumb swept her knuckles in steady rhythm, anchoring her amid visceral memories churning through her thoughts. The bone-jarring explosion. Debris searing her skin. The hellish landscape of torn bodies and crumbling ruins, rubble shifting beneath her boots. She could still taste the acrid tang of smoke coating her throat.

The carriage rolled to a stop, wheels a distant crunch over the gravel drive.

"Let's get you inside," Julian said gently.

He alighted first, then turned and lifted her down. He steered her straight upstairs to the washroom and eased her onto a stool beside the copper tub. "Wait here while I fetch supplies and draw you a bath," he instructed.

When he returned, his arms were laden with linen, scissors, brandy, and a steaming basin. He set them on the tiles before her and knelt, taking her bloodied hands between his own.

"This will hurt," he warned. "But I need to clean them properly. I'll be quick."

She sucked in a breath, bracing. "I know. Just do it."

Even with warning, she still flinched at the first touch. Julian kept his grip gentle as he swabbed every cut, clearing away blood and grit. Caroline focused on him – shirtsleeves rolled to the elbows, exposed forearms corded with muscle. Here knelt the elusive Duke of Hastings, scion of one of the noblest families in the kingdom, a powerful man humbled before her. Not a hint of impatience marked that austere face, only calm competence.

Unexpected tenderness pierced her, stealing her breath. This man had shielded her body with his own – and now he scrubbed the blood and grime from her torn flesh as if she were infinitely precious.

"I'm sorry," Julian said when she gasped. His touch remained gentle. "I know it hurts like the devil."

"A small price to pay for having all my limbs still attached."

"You were brave," he said, continuing his ministrations. "Quite commanding."

"Well, there are some benefits to this duchess business. At least people snap to attention when I start bellowing orders."

Amusement softened his tone. "Like a general marshalling troops into battle."

She gave a laugh. "Yes, I'm sure that's precisely how I looked. Covered in blood and soot, gown ripped to tatters. People will probably describe me as a deranged harpy."

His hands stilled on hers. "I think what people will tell me is that my wife was ferocious tonight."

*Wife.*

The word resonated through her chest. Spoken in that smoke-rough voice, as if he were relearning her measure.

"They might," she conceded. Casting about for safer conversational ground, Caroline ventured, "You needn't wait on me, you know. I'm perfectly capable of bathing alone."

"Have you seen the state of these hands?" he asked. "I doubt you could even unbutton your gown."

*Stubborn man.* "You underestimate my determination regarding personal hygiene."

"And you underestimate my determination regarding you. Now stand so I can undress you."

Too weary to argue further, Caroline rose to her feet. Julian's hands went to her waist, steadying her. She shivered as his warm breath tickled her ear.

"There's my good girl," he all but purred.

Liquid heat pooled between her thighs. God, she wanted those elegant hands on her body again. Stroking her. Taking her hard against the tiles as her world fractured apart. This man's calm, stoic demeanour had always aroused her so effortlessly – that unwavering focus on her alone.

Before she could think better of it, Caroline let her eyes slip shut and surrendered to the sensation of Julian's fingers moving down the line of tiny buttons on the back of her tattered gown. She focused on the delicate rasp of fastenings slipping free, each baring another sliver of her bruised skin. The tender drag of his knuckles down her neck, her spine.

To be undressed this way after so many years apart felt too intimate. Exposing. As if he slowly peeled back the layers of pretence and performance that comprised her armour, stripping her down to the most vulnerable parts of herself. When he eased the ruined gown from her frame, she heard his sharp inhale ghosting against her bared nape.

Julian efficiently divested Caroline of her chemise, leaving her clad only in tattered stockings gartered high on her thighs. She watched in the mirror as he sank to his knees. His fingers scorched trails of fire along her legs as he removed those last wisps of fabric. She saw it in his eyes – the hunger. Felt it simmer in the heavy air between them. For a suspended heartbeat, she thought he might grip her hips and drag his mouth up her inner thighs, licking over sensitive flesh until she shattered with his name on her lips.

*Put your lips on me*, she wanted to say.

But Julian only rose and pulled her back against him. "Get in the bath before I forget to be a gentleman."

Caroline angled a look at him over her shoulder. "And if I don't want you to be one?"

He froze. Hunger blazed in his eyes, silver-bright. But then Julian took a slow, deliberate step back from her. Cold air raised the fine hairs on her bare arms.

"Forgive me," she said. "That was too forward."

"Don't ever apologise for telling me what you want."

*Want.* That word ricocheted between them. What did she want? Not just tonight, but for the endless nights and days after?

Julian looked away when she said nothing. "In you go, Linnie."

Caroline sank into the tub, limbs heavy. She let her eyes drift shut as warmth seeped into her muscles, loosening knots. The hot water lapped at tender places and turned her skin pink. Steam curled around her, blurring the sharp edges of recent memory into something softer.

Silence enveloped her, broken only by the soft sound of Julian's clothes hitting the floor, followed by the gentle displacement of water as he joined her. When she forced her eyes open, it was to find her husband sitting across from her, close but not touching. Julian's stern features appeared softer through the film of steam wreathing his face, blurred at the edges. Younger somehow, like a half-remembered dream.

"You're injured," she realised, jolted back by visible proof marring smooth skin. She reached out, unthinking, to skim her fingers over the angry welts slashing his face. "You're bleeding."

Julian caught her hand. "Just scratches. Nothing to fuss over."

*Lie.*

She read it in every bruised line of him, tension wound tight beneath the skin. Julian was very much not fine. Then again, neither was she.

"Tonight is for you," he insisted when she opened her mouth to argue.

She traced her fingertips over the fresh cuts marring his knuckles. "Says who? I don't recall signing that decree."

The barest ghost of a smile touched Julian's mouth. "Always so stubborn."

"Resolute is the word, I think. And you're clearly not fine, so stop pretending."

"Determined," he allowed. "But I want to take care of you right now." His voice gentled, turned reverent. "All right, Linnie?"

The old nickname speared her heart. Swallowing around the ache, she nodded. Let him shift closer until his thigh pressed to hers beneath the water. Let him ease her back until she floated, supported and safe.

Julian took up a sea sponge and began to wash her. As he worked, Caroline studied his face, taking in the faint lines etched at the corners of those pale eyes – lines that had not existed before. She had loved learning the landscape of him once. Had traced every part of him with curious fingertips, greedy lips – memorising the geography of this man who was hers. Now he seemed some half-remembered country glimpsed through morning mist. So achingly familiar, yet unknown.

She wondered if her own face betrayed similar stories, mapped by the trauma and loneliness he had not been there to witness.

"You do that well," she murmured.

"You used to tell me I was good with my hands," he said, brushing the sponge over her shoulders.

"You still are. I love your hands. I used to watch them for hours – while you wrote, while I drew you. While you played the piano. Especially then."

Julian went very still. "Did you?"

Heat crept up her throat, but Caroline made herself continue. "Of course. You don't really think I didn't treasure those moments when you made music?" She touched the back of his hand with her fingertips. "I was quite taken with your hands."

*With you. I was so in love with you, I could hardly breathe.*

Julian's eyes fell shut. He turned his palm upwards in silent invitation.

Caroline traced the hills and valleys of his knuckles, the delicate tracery of veins inside his wrist. The years peeled back like old wallpaper. She was an infatuated girl again, and Julian the charming boy who featured in all her youthful daydreams. It was a language written into her very bones, into the deepest parts of her soul.

Something she had thought turned to ash long ago.

"And the rest of me?" Julian whispered into the swirling steam between them. So softly, she almost missed it.

As if her answer meant the difference between forever and nothing at all.

"As I recall, the rest of you was my undoing," she said wryly. "I remember meeting a brooding boy in your father's gardens and thinking him the most interesting creature I'd ever encountered. All sharp cheekbones and brooding countenance. Utterly magnetic. Until you opened that mouth of yours and told me people bored you."

The barest smile touched his solemn mouth. "And you proceeded to declare plants better company and lectured me at length on the superiority of most flora over humans for the remainder of that afternoon."

"Naturally. You needed schooling."

"I stand by my original assessment that most people are terrible company. With two notable exceptions."

Caroline's breath snagged.

Grace had been his other exception.

"Do you think Grace would be happy to see us together?" she whispered.

Old grief flickered over his features. "She would scold us both about the last eight years, I think."

Steeling herself, Caroline whispered the long-held fear that had corroded her from the inside out. "Did you love her very much?"

There. The poison was out. Now, she could only wait for the blade to fall.

Julian searched her face. "You believed I was in love with Gracie."

Caroline forced herself to hold his gaze. To speak the thoughts locked away in the deepest vaults of her heart. "You intended to propose to Grace at the end of that summer, and you only married me because my reputation was compromised. And when you left after we lost her, I thought maybe you—"

"No." A sharp inhale, then softer, "No, sweetheart. I did care for Grace once, but I lost my heart to you that summer."

Hope and uncertainty warred inside her. Who knew if this fragile *détente* would last beyond the confines of this room? One truth didn't undo the shared grief and distance between them.

"I lost my heart to you, too," Caroline replied.

Dropping a kiss on her hand, Julian took up the sponge and resumed washing away the last traces of blood and soot. She remained pliant, craving the solidity of his hands on her skin.

When he had finished, Caroline drew a steadying breath. "Let me return the favour."

They did not speak as she swept the sponge across the sleek muscles of his shoulders, his broad chest – along the cuts and bruises that were evidence of the protective way he'd curled himself around her during the explosion. With reverence, she traced old scars, though she did not ask about them. Those stories belonged to another Caroline, one who had shared this man's past as well as his bed. One who had lost the right to such intimacy and hadn't yet earned it back.

When she gestured for Julian to turn, he complied without argument. The rigid line of his spine was an accusation, his body coiled tight as if bracing for something. As if he, too, expected this moment between them to snag on all the jagged glass of their history. Caroline set her teeth against the threatening sting behind her eyes and resumed washing him with meticulous care.

By unspoken accord, they left anything below the cloudy bathwater untouched.

Without a word, Julian rose from the bath in a cascade of water. The lean muscles of his back and thighs flexed as he wrapped himself in a length of linen.

"Let's get you to bed. You need rest."

Caroline dutifully donned the nightclothes Julian held for her. Allowed him to tuck the sheets around her as she sank onto the mattress.

Yet when Julian made to pull away, some starved, wild thing inside Caroline stirred. Her hand darted out to capture his wrist in silent entreaty. "Come here. Next to me."

A rough breath tore from his throat. For an endless moment, she thought Julian might refuse. Might turn his back on this fledgling tenderness. But then the mattress dipped beneath his weight as he slid beneath the sheets.

The empty gulf between their bodies echoed the years, yawning wide and fathomless. Caroline's chest constricted with uncertainty. Then she could bear it no more – she turned onto her side to face Julian's remote profile. His eyes remained fixed on the ceiling, body held apart from hers.

She dared to trail her fingers down the rigid line of Julian's forearm, touch whisper-soft in silent entreaty. In unspoken apology for everything left unsaid between them.

Then she found the courage to whisper, "Will you hold me?"

With a low groan, he turned and hauled her into his arms. Caroline pressed her face to the warm skin of his throat, inhaling cedar and soap.

"Julian?" she whispered into the intimate darkness.

He tensed. "Hmm?"

"The answer to your question… When I look at you, I feel *everything*," she whispered. "And I'm so sorry for pushing you away. I didn't know how to fix us."

For an endless moment, Julian simply held her in punishing silence. Then, "Never apologise for me leaving you to bear losing Grace and our son alone. I didn't know how to fix us either. After that."

Their shared grief lodged like a spike in her throat. She stroked Julian's back in silent apology, wishing she could erase the damage done.

Then she closed her eyes and let the rest of the world fall away.

# 13

## London, 1866

*Eight years ago*

The rain drummed against the carriage's roof as it rumbled down the muddy road. Julian stared out of the fogged window, though there was nothing to see but grey. Just endless, featureless grey.

The dismal weather matched his bleak mood. He had thought returning to London might lift his spirits after so many dreary months abroad, but the city's familiar streets only echoed with absence. With loss.

Five months had passed since he'd last left England. It felt like a lifetime. An interminable torrent of storms had battered his journey to America, delaying his search for Viscount Harcourt and Grace's sister Victoria. Not in New York or Boston. Not in Philadelphia nor any of the eastern cities. He had pressed onwards, chasing elusive whispers and rumours west across a vast continent. Enduring icy rains and towering snowdrifts as winter sank its teeth deep, until he reached San Francisco, where Harcourt had gone with his new son-in-law to establish business contacts in the maritime trade with China.

Precious time lost. Time stolen he could never regain.

Julian swallowed against the hollow ache building behind his ribs. He had missed Grace's funeral. Missed holding Caroline in those first raw days of grief.

His hands curled into fists against his thighs. Grace's death had splintered something vital inside him. Unleashed a feral, wounded thing driving him halfway across the world just to outrun the pain nipping at his heels. Finding what remained of Grace's family had seemed noble, a way to wrest meaning from senseless tragedy.

But distance had made things worse. He wanted his wife.

Stafford House's glowing windows beckoned through the gloom. As soon as the carriage halted beneath the portico, Julian pushed open the door, heedless of the rain gusting in freezing sheets. His boots sank into the mud, his greatcoat sodden by the time he mounted the steps.

The blessed warmth of the hall enveloped him, chasing away the pervasive chill. His butler approached, unruffled as ever. "Welcome home, Your Grace. Shall I have a bath drawn?"

Julian handed the man his gloves, hat, and cane. "In a moment. Is Her Grace in residence?"

The butler hesitated. "She's been at Ravenhill for some months now, Your Grace."

Julian dragged a hand over his rain-slicked face, regret and self-loathing threatening to choke him. Exhaustion pulled at his limbs, but he needed to see her. "Tell the staff not to unpack my things. I'll travel on shortly." As an afterthought, he added, "Any letters arrive in my absence?"

"Allow me to fetch them for you."

The storm redoubled its efforts, lashing the tall windows in wild fury, as Julian waited beneath the crystal chandelier. He thought of Caroline alone in England while he roamed a distant continent on a fool's errand. God, how she must hate him.

At last, the butler returned with an armful of correspondence. "Your letters, Your Grace."

"Thank you." Julian took the stack and turned for the door, eager to be off.

Once ensconced in the carriage, he rifled through the pile of envelopes. Estate business. Parliamentary matters. Tenant messages. Halfway through the stack, his frenzied shuffling slowed. Then stilled altogether.

A letter penned in Caroline's graceful hand stared up at him. Addressed to the hotel in New York where he'd stayed on arrival in America all those endless months ago.

*Returned undelivered.*

Julian was scalded by dawning horror. With a curse, he sifted through the remaining letters. All bore that damning mark. *Returned undelivered. Returned undelivered. Returned undelivered.*

Dozens of letters she had dispatched to bridge the ocean between them. None had found their way into his hands. And the letter he had sent informing her of his passage to San Francisco must never have reached English shores. Their correspondence had been two ships passing in the night.

"Damn it all to hell," Julian rasped.

Hands trembling, he unfolded the delicate, creased parchment of Caroline's first letter. Just the sight of that beloved script raised a lump in his throat.

> *Dear Julian,*
>
> *Grace's funeral was beautiful. I held Lady Harcourt's hand as the choirboys sang a dirge. Lady Harcourt kept her composure through the ceremony and the wake, but it was difficult, I think, without her husband here with her. I hope you find him quickly. I miss you.*
>
> *Ever yours,*
>
> *Caroline*

Swallowing hard, Julian moved on to the next letter. This one later, the cheer more forced. As he progressed through the stack, she wrote chatty accounts of her days, sparing no detail. Determined to hold them together somehow.

And loneliness bled from every line. It was scrawled between each word in the spaces where affection once resided. He could read the silence stretching taut and thin between his departure and her waiting.

Shame scalded his throat. Then he reached a letter that made his hands tremble so violently he nearly dropped it. The strokes seemed firmer, the prose suffused with joy. He glanced at the date – three months ago. Written while he was on that damned fool quest across a continent.

*Dear Julian,*

*Some happy news that I hope you take with you on your travels. We made a child. It's difficult to tell how far along after our vigorous first few months of marriage. Let us vow never to tell this child the particulars of its conception, shall we?*

*Ever yours,*

*Caroline*

Julian froze.

A child. Their child. They had made a baby.

Her subsequent letters detailed the quiet joy of watching herself swell with pregnancy, the change of the seasons as summer's long days faded to autumn's vibrant hues. A happiness polluted with loneliness and worry. He had missed so much – all those milestones vanishing like smoke.

*Dear Julian,*

*I can't sleep well in winter, even under the best circumstances, but your child seems to enjoy kicking me awake each night. I am also growing quite large and ill-tempered, so perhaps it is fortunate you have been away. I've written so many lists of names that I've murdered all the inkwells in the house, but I settled on Tristan for your heir or Violet for a girl. I can't wait to meet our Tristan/Violet and see which one of us our baby resembles most. Between us, I hope it's you. The men in your family have superior bone structure.*

*Ever yours,*

*Caroline*

He shuffled to the final letter – dated three weeks prior. Ink blots marred the heavy parchment, the strokes jagged and sparse – a brutal blow straight to the heart.

*Duke,*

*Our child was lost this morning.*

*He was to be named Tristan.*

*Caroline Hastings*

Gone. Their baby was gone before he could even meet it. Before he could cradle the small body in his palms and marvel at tiny fingers and toes. Only a handful of letters shaped a name for a life extinguished too soon.

Tristan.

His name was Tristan.

Hot moisture burned Julian's eyes, obscuring the page. He pressed a fist against his mouth to hold back the howl clawing up from his throat. *Duke*, she'd called him. *Caroline Hastings*, a cold, impersonal signature – a damning verdict of his failure.

Christ, what had he done?

He could scarcely draw breath for the rest of the bleak journey. Wind and rain lashed the carriage as it rolled up the winding drive. At last, Ravenhill loomed ahead, pale and imposing. Julian burst from the coach before it stopped, taking the front steps two at a time.

"Your Grace," the butler said when he stormed into the house. "We weren't expecting you—"

Julian barrelled past. Up the grand staircase, down the shadowed corridor to the duchess's chambers. Towards her. He had to see her, had to beg her forgiveness—

Julian paused outside the carved oak door, breath sawing in his lungs. Then he turned the knob and stepped inside. The heavy velvet curtains blocked most of the watery daylight. Shadows cloaked the bed at the far end of the room, where a figure lay motionless beneath the coverlet.

*Caroline.*

His heart clenched. Julian moved slowly nearer, afraid to startle her. She showed no sign of noticing his presence until he stood over her.

"Linnie." The name dragged like broken glass from his throat.

Caroline's eyes found his. Then, her face crumpled as a fresh wave of tears streamed down her hollow cheeks. A low, keening cry tore from her.

"Shhh. It's all right," Julian murmured, reaching for her. But Caroline shoved him back with shocking force for one so frail. She recoiled against the headboard, body wracked by heaving sobs.

"Don't touch me," she choked out.

Shame and regret crushed the air from his lungs. "I never received your letters until today. I sent a letter when I reached New York that Viscount Harcourt had gone. The correspondence must have been lost."

Another wrenching sob escaped her. She wept with the devastation of one whose heart had been shattered beyond repair.

He had done this. Made her grieve Grace. Grieve Tristan.

Grieve *him*.

"Linnie, if I had any idea—"

"Get out." Her entire body shook with the force of her voice. "*Get out!*"

Each wretched shout felt like a physical blow. Julian retreated across the carpet on wooden legs. At the door, he paused, casting one last anguished look at his wife's crumpled form swallowed by the shadows.

He had broken her. Abandoned her when she needed him most. An unforgivable transgression. So he slipped out, drawing the door closed behind him. As he strode down the corridor, his wife's ragged sobs echoed through the darkened manor.

Julian returned again. Day after day. Week after week.

Each time, the mansion was silent. This house did not welcome him. It loomed like a mausoleum, all dark wood and velvet drapes blotting out the sun. Shadows clung to the corners.

Julian paused outside the bedchamber door and held his breath. She'd stopped rejecting him weeks ago. Now, she wouldn't speak. But he kept coming. Held her cold body in his. Waiting. Hoping.

Praying that one day, she'd turn in his arms and hold him back.

The hinges uttered no protest as he swung the door open. Weak light cast the room in shades of gloom. The air hung stale and untouched, a sickroom sealed shut from the world. Julian's heart clenched at the sight of the figure curled on the expansive mattress. The same place she'd been since he'd returned to England two months ago.

"Good morning, sweetheart," he said softly. Julian approached the bed with care. "Would you like me to open the curtains for you?"

She said nothing. She lay on the silken coverlet, still dressed in a creased nightgown. Her lovely blonde hair spilled across the pillow in limp disarray. Dark hollows haunted the delicate skin under her eyes.

Perching on the bed's edge, Julian noted how sharply Caroline's collarbone protruded above the sagging neckline of her gown. How wan her skin had become, pulled taut over the elegant scaffolding of bones beneath – wasting away despite everything he did to get her to eat.

"I've brought you more flowers," he murmured, replacing the wilting blooms on her nightstand with the fresh bouquet. The vivid new blossoms seemed garish – an offence to the atmosphere of decay. Tulips were her favourites. So he'd brought her red for love and purple hyacinths to beg her forgiveness. "These are from the garden. The magnolias are in bloom now. Will you come outside and see?"

Caroline's vacant stare drifted over the colourful bouquet. Then away. She had not spoken a word to Julian since the day he returned. She simply existed here in this elegiac tomb, staring into some middle distance only she could see. The entrance sealed shut behind her.

His chest constricted. He kept bringing flowers anyway, stubbornly strewing beauty among the ruin. As if their ephemeral loveliness could pierce the armour of Caroline's grief. As if anything could.

Gently, Julian lifted one chilled hand in his, chafing warmth back into her icy fingers. "Won't you eat something today, Linnie?" he murmured. "I'll have Cook prepare anything you desire. Chocolate. Pastries with clotted cream and jam on top. Cake. Just say the word, and you can indulge in the most hedonistic diet imaginable."

Nothing. Caroline stared through him, lungs rising and falling in a listless rhythm beneath her nightgown. Barely breathing. Barely alive.

Julian stretched out alongside her on the mattress. With

utmost care, he gathered her into the circle of his arms. She remained limp and unresisting in his tentative embrace. Julian rested his cheek against her hair and exhaled unsteadily.

Too thin. She had lost so much of herself, wasting away before his eyes. He wouldn't tell her that, though. Wouldn't add fuel to the fire laying waste to the woman he loved.

"It's warm outside today," Julian whispered, brushing a kiss across her cheek. "Would you join me for a walk?"

For the span of a heartbeat, Julian thought he glimpsed awareness stir behind Caroline's hollow stare. The barest flicker of life in the ashes. But it guttered out, and she turned her face in wordless rejection. Shutting him out – a door slamming closed.

Frustration roiled in Julian's chest, but he leashed it ruthlessly. None of this was her fault. The blame rested on his shoulders. He'd abandoned her when she needed him most. Now, he could only weather her bitterness and try to reach past the armour she had locked around her heart.

So Julian held her too-slight frame, stroking her limp hair. "Then we'll stay in today," he conceded softly. "Lounge around in bed."

He pressed another tender kiss on her temple, willing his touch to penetrate her shell of grief. But Caroline remained removed. Her rejection pierced Julian's heart like a blade. Twisting with every breath.

At last, she parted her colourless lips. "I don't want you in this bed with me," Caroline rasped. Her voice was cracked and ravaged from disuse. "I don't want you bringing me flowers or telling me about the weather. I can't bear the sight of you."

Each ragged word lanced through Julian's heart, but he drank them in desperately. Proof that she lived. Still felt *something*.

Even if it was hate.

A broken sound tore from Caroline's throat. Her fingers knotted in Julian's shirt, twisting it as she collapsed against him. Her body shook with the force of her sobs, guttural and cracked.

"I hate you," she wept. "I hate you so much."

Agony splintered through Julian. He cradled her closer, wishing he could absorb her anguish. He stroked her hair and pressed kisses on her brow, offering comfort as she shattered in his arms. As the tide of her agony finally crested and broke.

When her sobs dwindled at last to hiccupping breaths, Julian shifted back. He smoothed her tangled hair from her wet cheeks with tenderness. Cupped that ruined face between his palms and met her wild gaze.

"I know," Julian whispered. And then, giving voice to his gnawing guilt, "God above, I know. I hate myself, too."

Hated himself for leaving her. For not being there as she grieved for Grace, endured her pregnancy and childbirth alone. For not being there during the death of their son. For sailing halfway around the world on a fool's errand while she weathered the unimaginable back home.

Yes, Julian hated himself.

Caroline looked as frail as cracked porcelain in his arms, her skin nearly translucent with a faint tracery of blue veins. Dark hollows clung beneath her eyes. She had slipped back into silence once more. Lost again to a fathomless grief beyond his power to penetrate.

"I'll come back tomorrow," Julian said, brushing a thumb across her ashen cheek.

"No." Her voice was iron this time. "Don't come back. Stop visiting. Just get out and leave me alone."

Those words sank their claws deep as Caroline released him and turned away.

Everything in Julian railed against leaving. If he walked away now, she might seal herself off from him entirely. Yet he'd never denied Caroline anything she asked – even this ruinous request.

So Julian rose to his feet. Paused with his hand on the door, composure fracturing. "I love you," he whispered. "I just want you to know."

And then he left her there in the decaying opulence of their home. Left her to fade day by day among the ghosts.

In the following weeks, Julian forced himself to go through the motions of living. He remained in London but kept vigil over Caroline from afar. Ensured the staff attended to the house and grounds despite the absence of its master and mistress.

Eventually, a letter arrived, penned in the housekeeper's graceful script:

*Her Grace has departed for Brighton to continue her convalescence by the sea.*

Relief crashed through Julian. Caroline was up, dressed, and well enough to travel. The breath Julian released shook his entire frame.

*I suggest you let her recover without looming*, Mrs Gibbons added.

Delicate words meant to hurt. She had been with Caroline through the childbirth and the aftermath – his wife's loyal ally in his absence.

Hands trembling, Julian folded the note and placed it on top of the stack of business letters requiring his attention. He would pen a response later with instructions for the staff to provide anything his wife desired. For now, work beckoned. There was always work to lose himself in.

He would wait until she asked to see him again.

The weeks turned to months. The months became years. When Julian learned Caroline had returned to London, he waited for a letter that never came. Her voice echoed through his mind, a toxin spreading.

*I can't bear the sight of you.*

Three years after she had banished him from her life, Julian stood in the portrait gallery at Marlborough House. He stared up at a large canvas that had stirred excited whispers and scandalised gasps: a lush, radiant painting of a muscular Achilles before the gates of Troy. The rendering was so lifelike – every detail of the model's physique was captured with devoted precision. From the sculpted muscles, down to the fine tracery of veins in the arms.

Julian recognised the elegant brushstrokes instantly. The subtle interplay of light and shadow. The tender devotion in each motion of the brush. After years apart, he still knew Caroline's artistic talents intimately.

In the corner, a bold signature: *Henry Morgan.*

A false name. But the artistry was undeniably hers. Julian stared up at the riveting portrait, chest hollowed by loss. She had found a way to channel her gifts, at least. Had begun to paint again. To live again, somewhere beyond his reach. Without him.

"He's extraordinarily talented, isn't he?" a voice spoke at his shoulder. A gentleman was also studying the painting, keen interest etched on sharp features. "One can almost feel the warmth of the skin."

"Remarkable," Julian agreed, keeping his tone neutral. "The name is unfamiliar to me."

"Newly ascendant talent. Morgan's work is coveted for all the finest aristocratic collections." The gentleman shot Julian a knowing look. "Rumour has it he once served in the military. Perhaps was even the captain of a ship. Accounts differ."

"How mysterious," Julian said. His eyes lingered on the play of light over the muscular curves so lovingly rendered.

Grace had suggested a *nom de guerre*, he remembered suddenly. *You should use a man's name to sell them to the unsuspecting masses. Something dashing and mysterious.*

They had laughed together once, the three of them. Two lives lost, now. His family whittled down to ghosts and painful memories.

Before grief could choke him, he said brusquely, "If you'll pardon me."

He walked away, putting distance between himself and the pain of seeing how far she had moved on without him. How separate their lives had become. In the three years since she banished him, Caroline had learned to subsist without his presence. Even thrive in her own way.

Julian still woke reaching across the empty sheets for her. Still wandered his palatial home, half convinced he could hear her soft laughter around the next corner.

Still longed for her.

But she despised him now. Could not bear the sight of him. She had made that plain.

So he boarded a boat bound for the Continent and put miles between them. As more years passed, Julian learned to slowly and painfully live without her.

It was nothing less than he deserved.

# 14

## London, 1874

*Eight years later*

The afternoon sun slanted over the streets, gilding the city in shades of gold. But its radiance did nothing to pierce the restless fog that shrouded Julian's mind as he strode along the cobblestones, his boot heels clicking out a crisp rhythm.

He fixed his gaze straight ahead, cutting a direct path through the bustling crowds that parted before his imposing form like minnows scattering from a shark. No one dared meet the eye of the Duke of Hastings this morning. Julian barely saw the people scrambling out of his way.

Caroline consumed his thoughts – the feeling of her body, soft and warm against him the night before. *You're hurt*, she'd whispered. *Will you hold me?* He could still hear her. Still see the honeyed strands of her hair spilling over his chest as she slept. Her breath whispering against his throat.

The overwhelming rightness of having her in his arms again.

*The answer to your question... When I look at you, I feel everything.*

A confession between them in the dark – like a tentative hand across the continents that had separated them.

So he'd set a note on the bed beside her. An olive branch she could ignore or accept. One last lifeline cast into the fathomless rift torn between them.

Then he'd left Caroline sleeping, achingly lovely amid the tangled sheets. Departed the house without a word, to the safety of formality and distance, just in case she refused him. God, how he wished he could snatch it back now, destroy the evidence of his weakness. His mind still keenly recalled her rejections eight years earlier. The memories were blade-shards under his skin, making him bleed with every step.

As White's gentleman's club came into view, he paused to compose himself. He drew a deep breath, clearing his thoughts of everything but the task ahead. There would be time to obsess over tangled sheets and silken skin later. Now duty called.

Once he had donned his customary ducal mask of haughty composure, Julian proceeded inside. He moved through the interior, ignoring the gleam of polished wood and rich furnishings. His stride was that of a man with an urgent purpose. In the back corner sat Mattias Wentworth behind a spread of pastries and the day's paper.

He glanced up as Julian approached. "Afternoon. Fancy a scone?" he asked, raising a half-eaten one in salute.

Julian remained standing, eyeing the tea and pastries on the table. "You said it was urgent we meet."

Wentworth took another hearty bite, unperturbed. "Digestives fuel the mind. Have a seat." He gestured at the empty chair. "You're looming."

With a sigh, Julian settled into the wingback chair across from him.

Wentworth tossed over a folded broadsheet. "Seen this morning's edition?"

"'The Duke of Hastings Shields His Duchess from Fearsome Blast,'" Julian read aloud. He looked up, unimpressed. "How gallant of me, apparently."

"The story's got tongues wagging," Wentworth said, eyeing the groups whispering nearby. "The most powerful duke in England reunites with his estranged wife, scandalises all and sundry with public affection, and then rescues her from a dastardly villain's evil plot. My God, you've just inspired legions of debutante fantasies."

Julian thought once more of slowly undressing Caroline. The way she'd looked at him in the bath. She'd wanted him – that much was clear. But he wanted more than a brisk coupling wrought from heightened emotion.

He wanted something he wasn't sure either of them could have again.

"If you believe everything you read, perhaps," Julian said dryly. "The reality was rather less glamorous."

"I'm sure you were every inch the gallant rescuer. Scooping your duchess into your manly arms to protect her from the blast."

Julian's mouth twitched. "She was commanding the rescue efforts, covered in blood and soot, while I lifted beams and rubble out of her way. But that doesn't sell papers."

Wentworth let out an amused snort. "Well, you must admit, it makes for a fine story. Shall I order you a drink to celebrate your newfound fame as London's most heroic husband?"

"I'd rather you tell me why you wanted to meet, not waste time mocking newspaper drivel." Impatience edged Julian's tone.

"Very well. To business." Wentworth withdrew two folded papers from his coat and passed them across the table. "New acquisitions for you."

Grateful for the change of topic, Julian picked up the first cryptogram and unfolded it. The rows of symbols leaped out at him, their sequencing less intricate than the last coded missive – one already solved by someone in Wentworth's employ. "He left it simple intentionally?"

"Just so. A direct claim of responsibility for last night's bombing. I'm sure the cryptogram you hadn't solved before the attack would have been the warning."

Guilt twisted in Julian's chest. If he'd deciphered the warning faster, lives could have been saved. He thought again of Caroline bandaging bleeding strangers heedless of her own torn flesh. Ice slithered down his spine.

The penned words swam before his eyes, full of vindictive satisfaction at the destruction caused, the gloating pleasure in outsmarting them once more. Julian's fingers curled, crinkling the paper.

"I see," he said. "So his letters are pure malice now."

"Without a doubt. Which is why I summoned you." He tapped the still-unread second cryptogram between them. "Another encoded threat, no question. Solve it quickly, duke. Time is imperative."

Julian lifted his gaze from the letter, anger and frustration simmering beneath his skin. "Just speak plainly."

Wentworth drew a breath. "Very well. That explosion was intended to detonate when the streets were choked with carriages leaving the theatre." His eyes glinted like steel. "Had it gone off as planned, we'd have been scraping half the *ton*'s corpses off the cobblestones."

Julian's gut churned. "Your flair for vivid description is unmatched."

"Not a pretty picture, no. But an accurate one." Wentworth's fingers tapped out an agitated rhythm on his armrest. "The bomb was placed beneath Worthington's carriage. The earl died in the blast, but the timing suggests the goal was to inflict as much carnage as possible in the aftermath."

"You've looked into Worthington?" Julian asked. "Asked if he had enemies?"

"His wife couldn't point to a single person who would want him dead, and there's nothing connecting him with the tragedies involving Stradbroke and Lord Baresford. They moved in different circles. You said your wife has an eye for patterns and helped you before. Use her again if you must, but solve it swiftly."

Julian glanced up. "Last night changed things. I won't put Caroline in danger."

Wentworth's expression went cold. "I'm not asking. And I suspect if I approached her directly, she wouldn't appreciate you making that choice for her." He arched a brow. "From what

I saw, your duchess barks orders like a general. Doubt she'd welcome being wrapped in cotton wool now."

Julian considered that for a moment before conceding reluctantly, "No, she wouldn't." Caroline would be furious if she learned he'd denied her the chance to stop a killer. He picked up the intricate new code, turning it over in his hands. "I'll tell her she has the option to help," he said, scanning both letters.

"The sooner, the better, if you please." Wentworth made to stand.

"Wait." Julian's eyes narrowed as he scrutinised the cryptogram more closely. A niggling sense of familiarity teased him, though the specifics hovered just out of reach.

Wentworth paused. "Do you recognise something?"

Julian's gaze remained fixed on the letter as he mentally sifted through everything in the mocking phrases. The subtle revelation continued to elude him, as slippery as smoke. "I need to study it further before I can pin down precisely why. But this brand of smugness rings familiar."

"Keep studying it until you can grasp the elusive memory. Let me know what you find. And give my message to your duchess."

Then Wentworth turned on his heel and strode for the exit. The cryptogram seemed to scorch Julian's fingers.

He could almost see the blood that would spill if he failed.

# 15

Caroline awoke to the lingering scent of cedar and soap that clung to the sheets.

Julian's scent.

A breeze sighed against the window, and she shivered, burrowing back into the safety of the blankets. As sleep's grip receded, her mind pieced together fractured memories of the previous night. Strong arms around her. Gentle hands tending to her wounds. The glide of the sponge down her spine.

She reached across the mattress, seeking the solid warmth of his body. But her fingers met only cool sheets. Caroline's eyes dragged open. His side of the bed was empty, with only the indent of his head left on the pillow.

He was gone.

Again.

Sitting up sent a bolt of pain down her side where she'd struck the hard cobblestones. Her ribs throbbed in time with her heart as she took stock of her aching muscles. But Julian's diligent care had left the scrapes on her hands and knees cleaned as well as any doctor.

She flexed her fingers gingerly, remembering the tender meticulousness with which he'd bathed each small abrasion. The way those hands had cradled hers.

She could almost feel the heat of his palms sweeping down her skin.

Had she dreamed it all?

No – there, on the pillow, lay a folded piece of foolscap. Caroline's heart missed a beat as she reached for it with trembling fingers. She traced the sharp slashes of ink, the shape of each letter in Julian's decisive hand.

A coded note.

Like the lurid ones he used to slip her across crowded ballrooms during the early days of their marriage – which seemed like a lifetime ago. The ones that always left her flushed and dizzy with wanting, hands shaking as his scandalous propositions took shape – all the wicked things he wished to do to her. Things they would later act out in the dark intimacy of their bed.

Caroline's face heated at the memories. Of sneaking away to decode them in some shadowed alcove, always biting her lip to contain her reactions. The way he would catch her eye over the dinner table, so proper to all outside observers.

Their secret game.

*When I fuck you, it won't be while you're lying to me.*

*The answer to your question... When I look at you, I feel everything.*

She understood now. Here was a bridge built of paper and ink – a reward for her confession.

With the reverence of a penitent at prayer, Caroline pushed aside the blankets and moved to the escritoire to withdraw her pen. She memorised each symbol before decoding his note one letter at a time, savouring the ritual. Her cheeks flamed as vivid fantasies unfurled across the page in his bold script. Clearly, Julian had been in rare form when he composed this coded missive.

*Linnie,*

*You used to love it when I wrote these, so I hope you don't mind if I renew our correspondence.*

*I wanted to perform every depraved act I could think of last night in the dark theatre box. But let me give you one fantasy now. You sitting primly beside me in that gorgeous blue gown, hands folded in your lap. I would sink to my knees before you in the concealing darkness. In my fantasies, your breath catches on a question –*

*What are you doing?*

*What if we're seen?*

*But you keep silent, transfixed, as my hands slide your skirts up slowly. My palms glide over silk stockings until I reach those pretty garters snapped into place. Until I reach the silk barrier of your undergarments.*

*I imagine that catch in your breath as I slide your drawers down and put my hands on you at last, finding you wet with wanting. My fingers sink into you, and you have to bite your knuckles to keep quiet. As I lower my head between your thighs and press my mouth there, your hips shift eagerly. You make the smallest noise of shocked pleasure, but I squeeze your thigh in reminder –*

*We could be caught.*

*We could be seen.*

*Don't you want me to keep going?*

The lurid details seared her mind as clearly as if he whispered them aloud in her ear, his voice a devastating caress. Caroline clutched the letter as Julian's fantasy ignited a liquid heat low in her core.

*I'm ravenous, watching you writhe as I pleasure you with my fingers. Until I wonder whether you can remain quiet, or if you'll break and give us away to any who might be listening. I pleasure you again and again – until you have to bite down on my fist to keep from crying out in ecstasy.*

*That pain-pleasure hardens my cock until I ache with wanting. Until I long to cast propriety and manners aside and pull you into my lap to see how quiet we can be when I fuck you.*

*But I'll save that fantasy for another letter.*

*Yours always,*
*Julian*

Caroline came back to herself slowly. Her skin still thrummed where phantom touches had ignited trails of fire. Nerves singing with remembered pleasure.

She stared at the letter, its ink smudged now from her too-tight grip. This coded olive branch couldn't erase the yawning gulf of almost a decade between them – the wounds they'd inflicted on each other.

Caroline vividly recalled the bleak years of silence and separation after their marriage had fractured. The grief of his absence after Grace died. The anguish of losing their son and enduring the pain alone. And then, later, his return.

And she had pushed him away. Again and again. He'd kept coming back with flowers. His hand massaging her back as she lay in bed, unable to move in her anguish. And she had whispered poisonous words intended to shatter him.

*Don't come back.*

*Stop visiting.*

*Just get out and leave me alone.*

The thorns of that memory pierced deep. After months and

months of those barbs, he'd stopped coming to her door. He'd retreated behind the infamous Hastings reserve, becoming more of a stranger with each passing year. Never seeing her again, just as she'd asked. They'd spun in remote orbits around each other since, neither daring to draw too close.

It was easier to pretend the other didn't exist.

But his note was an offer of temporary amnesty. Trace the faintest line back to the man and woman they had once been before tragedy carved them hollow. Back when hope wasn't a blade poised over an exposed heart.

She thought of Julian's hands bathing her wounds. The solid anchor of his body curled around hers through the night.

And Caroline realised with dizzying clarity that she desperately wanted to meet him halfway.

# 16

London was wreathed in grey as Julian arrived home. The silhouette of Stafford House blurred at the edges, softened by the mist. Inside, all was still and quiet. Too quiet for his liking after the chaos of last night.

He took the stairs two at a time, boots thudding against the carpet runner. As he neared the upper landing, the muffled rustle of movement met his ears. Julian paused, angling his head to listen. Caroline's studio. She was safe, occupied. The knot of dread that had coiled in his chest loosened. Julian moved towards the studio, floorboards groaning faintly beneath his steps despite his care.

He nudged the studio door open. Caroline sat perched on her stool, limned in honeyed lamplight. The glow gilded her unbound hair and glinted off the elegant column of her throat. She looked like something he might conjure from a dream, lovely and untouchable – too perfect to be real. Julian drank in the sight.

Because she wasn't painting one of her other models.

She was painting *him*.

"I hope you don't mind being an absent subject," Caroline said, eyes never leaving her work. "Though you're rather difficult to capture from memory."

In truth, he had feared her recollections would be tattered and moth-eaten by years of separation. That he would be reduced to a blurry afterimage in her mind's eye, the pigments faded by grief and regret. This vibrant testament to the contrary stole his breath.

"Not at all," he managed, once he trusted his voice not to betray him. "You know I've no objection to serving as your model, whether or not I'm in the room."

A smile played about her lips. "Even without the benefit of clothing?"

"Especially without it." The words tumbled free before he could bite them back.

He drank her in, soft and unguarded, in this space that was hers. Here, the ugliness from the bombed theatre seemed a distant nightmare.

"I thought you would still be abed at this hour," he said.

Caroline's gaze lifted, eyes sharp as cut glass. "I woke to cold sheets beside me, wondering where my errant husband was. For such a diligent, disciplined man in society, you don't seem interested in keeping a schedule with me."

Julian curled his fingers into his palm. "You needed rest. I didn't want to disturb you."

"How considerate." Dry amusement laced Caroline's words. Whether she believed his paper-thin veneer of manners or simply ignored the blatant untruth, she let the matter lie unchallenged. "You look ready to crawl out of your skin. I take it your meeting with Mr Wentworth didn't go well?"

In answer, Julian withdrew the new cryptogram and held it between his fingers.

Caroline set aside her tools and crossed the studio, skirts whispering over floorboards. She plucked the paper from his grasp. "Another message from that terrorist?" At Julian's grim nod, she turned the page this way and that as if it were a puzzle box she could unlock by sheer force of will. "This one looks more complex than your last."

"I'll need your help if you'll give it."

Determination settled on Caroline's features. "On the divan, if you please. And remove your clothes. I need to paint first if I'm to think clearly."

Julian shed his garments piece by piece. Coat, waistcoat, shirt – all discarded onto the floorboards until he stood bare before her bold gaze. Her eyes swept over him, missing nothing. That shameless perusal left him restless, pulse stuttering as she handed him pen, ink, and paper.

"For your analyses," Caroline said.

He took the items and sprawled on the divan, angling his body towards the light. The universe narrowed to this room, its familiar smells and gentle susurrus of Caroline's movements. Julian felt some of the coiled tension leach from his frame.

"Just relax and work out your code while I get the texture correct," Caroline said. She retrieved her palette and selected a fresh brush. "You know I prefer you unstudied. Natural."

"What man could possibly relax with you looking at him like that?"

She saw too much, stripped him down to sinew and bone. Julian had forgotten how vulnerable she could make him feel with only a look.

How she could flay him wide open and expose the most hidden parts of himself, as dangerous as any blade.

"Like what?"

*As if I'm the only solace in a world determined to grind us into dust. As if I'm the only source of air in a room starved of oxygen.*

Julian bit the inside of his cheek until he tasted blood. "As if you're deciding precisely how you'd like to debauch me."

Safer to jest than speak truths that could cut to the quick. He had learned that lesson long ago where she was concerned. Levity was armour. The right words from her lips could slice him wide open, expose all the naked wanting beneath.

"Stop trying to distract me, duke."

"Far be it from me to interfere in the creation of great art," Julian replied.

The gentle sound of brushes sweeping over canvas filled the space again – an oddly soothing rhythm, one familiar from their youth. A familiarity he had thought lost forever amid the ruins of their marriage. Yet now here they were, tentative travellers picking their way across the rubble towards each other once more.

Julian hardly dared breathe for fear of destroying this fragile truce. But Caroline, bold and skirmishing as ever, seemed determined to provoke him.

"You're thinking very loudly," she chided.

With effort, Julian schooled his features to impassivity. "Apologies."

"You've always been so skilled at cryptography. What has you so distracted?"

"You." The admittance fell softly into the quiet between them. "I should think it obvious that I find it arousing when you make art."

Caroline paused, attention flickering over his blatant arousal. "Would you prefer I avert my eyes?"

Julian smiled slightly. "When have I ever given you the impression I want you to stop looking?"

The weighted silence returned as Julian forced his focus to the cryptogram's strange lettering. The temptation to provoke her further pulled at him, restless and insistent. Let her feel his nearness as acutely as he felt hers.

With care, Julian shifted on the cushions again, stretching his arms high overhead before settling back against the velvet. The move coaxed his muscles into longer lines, an enticement designed to draw her eye. As intended, Caroline's gaze dipped along the nude length of his body before skittering away. That subtle surrender unfurled vicious satisfaction through his veins.

He couldn't help but want to remind her. Eight years, and he'd been with no other woman. Julian only wanted this one.

"You know I would pose more intimately if you asked." He wrapped a hand around his cock. "For the sake of artistic accuracy."

Caroline's hand stilled, breath audibly snagging in her throat. "Mr Henry Morgan will already have to keep this particular painting for himself even without you doing that," she said. "I can't bring myself to share your beautiful physique with anyone but myself."

Only iron control kept Julian's lips from curving. "Do enlighten me on the precise attributes that make my physique ideal."

"You're quite tall. Long of limb. Your musculature is well defined but not overly bulky." She bit her lip. "The candlelight loves you."

"Go on," he encouraged. "I'm finding this assessment most educational."

"The angles of your facial structure are exquisite." She paused. "Also, you have a finely shaped backside."

"And my cock, duchess?" Julian gave himself a slow stroke. He wanted her hungry for him. "You've examined every inch of my anatomy. I'm certain you have notes."

"Many." Caroline's voice was a ragged whisper. "But as much as I enjoy your devotion to sensual art, that cryptogram requires your focus." She returned her attention to the painting.

Resigned, Julian released himself and studied the cryptogram with renewed focus. But the nonsensical symbols blurred before him, their meaning sliding out of reach. Out of the corner of his eye, he noted how Caroline worried her lush lower lip between her teeth when lost in thought, or how the tip of her tongue darted out to wet her lips when she changed brushstrokes.

He noticed.

He noticed it all.

Control. It was all Julian had left. He clung to the fraying edges of restraint even as he wanted to pin Caroline down and kiss her. This woman had a way of fracturing the barriers he'd constructed between *want* and *take* and *mine*.

After a while, she glanced over. "How goes decoding the message?" Her voice was like a fingertip brushing his shoulder blades, smooth and lovely.

"Not well," he admitted.

"Perhaps your coded Cyrillic needs practice," she said.

*Or perhaps I find myself too distracted by fantasies of my wife spread out before me, begging to be fucked.*

Julian wanted to ruin her composure, leave her breathless. Wanted to watch those sharp eyes glaze with lust as he drove into her again and again.

He made another note on his page. *Control.* "If you'd like to come over here and show me how it's done, I'd be more than happy to oblige you."

Colour bloomed in her cheeks, but she cleared her throat. "Very well. I suppose I've had enough painting for today."

He shifted to make room, and she sank on the divan. Lush curves pressed to his side, searing him even through the layers of her clothing.

"Rub my lower back," Caroline said, presenting the rigid line of her spine to him.

"So demanding," Julian murmured, even as his hands moved to obey. Kneading the tense muscles elicited a soft noise. "You carry too much tension here. It's no wonder your back pains you."

"Mm. That's why I keep you around. To rub all my sore spots," she said, bending over the cryptogram. All business. He wanted to shatter her.

*Control. Get yourself under control.*

"A modified Vigenère tableau to start, I think." Caroline traced the intricate rows of symbols. "But there seem to be varying patterns layered throughout. Have you done a frequency analysis?"

In answer, Julian retrieved the tidy columns of numbers from beneath the rumpled sheets of foolscap scattered on the divan. Caroline studied them, frowning in concentration as she tallied letter frequencies in her agile mind.

"The frequency for this symbol" – she indicated the triangle – "changes here, do you see? It disappears. This is a distinct code after line twenty, with another shift after line thirty. This pattern strikes me as different from a Russian distribution."

"Some others were in German and Italian," he said, continuing to massage her back.

Caroline's gaze cut sideways to meet his. "So a scholarly terrorist. But how many of those with vendettas against the *ton* would have fluency across multiple languages?" She shook her head, not waiting for his answer. "I'll determine the length of the keyword used to encode this and then break the message into a single alphabet."

Julian watched his wife work, her movements deft and precise as she devised a mathematical formula to calculate letter repetitions in the coded text. That brilliant intellect spinning out statistics and permutations, seeking a pattern in randomness. She was mercury, quicksilver. Never still, never idle. Always in motion.

Quick slashes of ink filled page after page with translations and frequency analysis. He soaked up her small noises of excitement, the way she gnawed her lower lip in concentration. Desire kindled, gathering intensity.

He marvelled that of everyone in London, only he got to see this side of her. The cool aristocrat. The barefoot woman with ink-smudged fingers. Both were seated here now, balancing on his bare thighs.

And both were his. Still.

*Always.*

When she had finished dividing and re-dividing the encrypted text, Caroline blew out a frustrated breath. "No wonder you were struggling. This isn't Russian, German, or Italian. The frequencies don't match." A delicate furrow formed between her brows. "Perhaps French?"

He wanted his teeth on that graceful neck. Wanted to mark the flawless canvas of her skin until she wore proof of his claim for all the world to see. Until no other man dared look too long, much less touch what was his.

*Mine.*

He fought against a low groan.

After double-checking her calculations, Caroline gave a decisive nod. "Definitely French for the latter portion. Eight single alphabets total, by my estimation." She straightened, rolling her shoulders again beneath Julian's idle palms. "Would you like to help me determine the Vigenère alphabet for… each…"

Her words trailed off as she glanced up, finally noting the naked want burning in Julian's stare. He surged forward to capture her mouth with his. Nipped at her lower lip, coaxing until she opened with a shuddered gasp. He swept his tongue alongside hers, and she arched into him, nails biting into his bare skin. He swallowed her moans, tracing fingertips down her throat.

A memory, that kiss. Their bodies were a language they shared, unchanged even after all this time.

Julian drew back to press his forehead to hers. "You solving cryptograms is the most erotic thing I've witnessed in my lifetime."

A flush darkened her cheeks. "It's just statistical analysis," she demurred.

"Mm." He leaned in to brush his lips along the shell of her ear, eliciting a visible shiver. "Employing Kasiski examination and identifying isomorphic alphabets. Talking maths and logic and order while perched on my thighs."

Before she could respond, he twisted his fingers through her elegant chignon. Julian's teeth grazed the skin over her frantic pulse, mapping the graceful arch of her throat with lips and teeth. "I love watching you work," he said. "What would you do next?"

Caroline's response came on a panting exhale as his hands

rucked up her skirts. "Write out possible permutations for each column until the letters are revealed."

Julian's lips curved against her fevered skin. Even now, poised on the crux between logic and desire, that formidable intellect would not yield.

She was a challenge, his wife.

Sliding his palm down to her breast, he murmured into her ear, "Quantify the letter values, and I'll slip my hand beneath your skirts and make you come."

"I want more than that," she said. "You left me unsatisfied last time."

*Unsatisfied?* He'd have to remedy that. "Me inside you? Is that what you want, my duchess? Very well, then. Quantify the letter values, and I'll fuck you on this divan."

An answering wickedness sparked behind her eyes. "*You* quantify them." Caroline extricated herself from his embrace and stood up. "For every five letters you can decipher based on my frequency analysis, I'll undo a button. Solve the entire cryptogram, and these undergarments come off."

There stood his wife, debauched and daring, using her prodigious intellect in service to desire. She wore a deep blue dress, her luscious curves visible beneath the fabric. She hadn't bothered with a corset or petticoats this morning – fewer garments to remove.

This game was in his favour.

"And then?" he asked.

She gave him a wicked smile. "I'll let you do whatever you want to me."

Caroline Hastings completely at his mercy. He almost groaned.

*Control. Just a bit longer.*

Julian snatched up the cryptogram and set pen to foolscap, attacking it with single-minded focus. Logarithms and letter frequencies soon filled the page in bold slashes of ink. The orderly rows and columns made sense, each one bringing him nearer to the prize of Caroline stripped bare before him.

Letters correlated to numerical values, frequencies converted to probable words. Julian's pen scratched over the paper as his mind formed connections – code and pattern and mathematics coalescing into meaning. His reward came button by button. Pale skin unveiled inch by devastating inch. The slope of her collarbone. The swells of her breasts. The indentation of her waist.

The dress hit the floor.

Julian's breath fractured at the sight of her flawless skin, clad now in only a thin chemise and drawers. Christ, she was exquisite.

Caroline raised one challenging eyebrow as if to say: *Is that the best you can do?*

Common letters formed common words. *Je. De. Un. Est.* Index of coincidence correlated probable phrases as the remaining letters took shape. Julian scribbled faster.

At this point, he would write out the entirety of Dante's *Inferno* if that's what it took to get her naked.

As the last word fell into place, Julian tossed the papers and pen aside. He grabbed her, tearing the gossamer fabric of her chemise in a violent motion that bared her naked body to his starving gaze. All patience shattered. Hauling her down onto the divan, Julian claimed her lips in a fierce kiss, a conqueror revelling in his spoils.

He rocked against her, his cock nudging between her thighs. They had drifted far too long, twin planets sprung from alignment. But gravity was reasserting its claim. He needed her too much for tenderness.

Fortunately, Caroline did nothing by halves – she responded to his claim with equal fervour. "Tell me precisely how you want me to reward you for solving that code."

He kissed her again, rough and deep. Pinned her wrists overhead, stretching her body taut beneath his.

"What I want..." His heated stare raked over her. "I described it explicitly in yesterday's letter. How I want to spread your thighs so I can pleasure you with my mouth. Until you're dripping wet and begging for my cock. How many times do you think I can make you climax tonight?"

A breathless laugh escaped her. "Why don't you find out?"

The wicked challenge sank into his bones, molten and merciless. Ruthless satisfaction ignited within him – here was his Caroline, bold and defiant.

Just as it should be between them.

"Don't hold back your cries for me." His voice was rough. "Let the entire house hear how thoroughly I satisfy my wife."

Then he blazed a path down her body, branding her skin with nips of his teeth. Her throat, the swells of her breasts, the taut plane of her stomach – all bore the marks of his claiming. When his fingers drifted between her thighs, he found her so ready. Wet and wanting. Perfect.

And absolutely his.

The first lick of his tongue stole Caroline's breath. Julian added two fingers, thrusting into her as he pleasured her. Vicious satisfaction clawed through him at her bitten-off sounds of pleasure.

"Inside me." Caroline's nails raked his nape. "Now."

But he'd made a demand, and he intended to see it through.

"My name, duchess," he said. He thrust his fingers hard. "I want to hear you scream it first."

He pressed his mouth to her, used his tongue until she was squirming beneath him. Her nails scored through his hair. Then his name – *thank God* – his name tore from her in a gasping shout that seemed to echo through the room as she climaxed.

Julian smiled as he rose over her. "That's it. Good girl."

His teeth scraped her jaw as he lined himself up and pushed into her. He had to pause, jaw clenched against the searing pressure threatening to end him right then. Christ, she was exquisite. Sublime. The vision of her wanton and pleading had shaped his every fantasy these past endless years. Having her again was raw and visceral. Primal as a heartbeat.

"Make me feel it tomorrow," Caroline said.

A savage thrill went through Julian at her breathless demand. Holding her stare, he withdrew halfway before slamming into her again. Hard. Deep. Taking her with powerful strokes designed to brand her. Julian shifted his angle until Caroline bucked and twisted, hitting that spot guaranteed to ruin her.

He wanted her senseless before chasing his climax. Wanted to drag out every dark, depraved desire.

Their eyes locked, and he saw the instant ecstasy crash through her. He gentled his grip but kept thrusting through the aftershocks, determined to make her come again. She was magnificent when pushed past sane limits – and he would push her as far as she could take tonight.

"There's my gorgeous girl," he murmured. He didn't slow his punishing tempo. "Let go for me again."

"Kiss me," she managed.

Julian obeyed, sealing his mouth over hers even as he pounded into her slick heat. When she tensed again, he wedged a hand between them to circle her with his fingers. Ruthless precision guided each stroke over the sensitive bud until she gripped his back. Only when she climaxed again did Julian let his control shred. Animal need obliterated conscious thought, narrowing his world down to friction and the harsh bite of her nails into his skin.

His release slammed through him. Their ragged breaths filled the art studio as he collapsed on top of her, their bodies still joined. Skin slid against skin, damp and fevered. Julian curled around her, one hand tangling in her mussed curls.

"Three," she said faintly.

Julian gently bit her neck. "Who says I'm finished?"

She shifted against him. "I'll need a moment to recover the feeling in all my limbs before you try again."

Julian brushed his knuckles along her cheekbone. "Very well. Pass me the code? In my haste to get you naked, I didn't see what it said."

Caroline's answering laugh came out husky and sated. She leaned down to retrieve the discarded cryptogram, scanning the rows of translated text. "Here – a place, date, and time. 'Two o'clock, fifth of July. Charing Cross.'" She shot him a meaningful look. "Do you think he'll target a train?"

Julian accepted the letter, ice creeping into his veins as he took in the chilling words now laid bare. Casual, smug – the tone set his teeth on edge. He rifled through the pile of foolscap until he located the other cryptogram Wentworth had given him. "Read this one. Tell me if the voice strikes you as familiar."

There was no other sight more beautiful in the world than Caroline Hastings, thoroughly debauched, using her clever mind. "'No one attacks me with impunity,'" she said. "*Nemo me impune lacessit*. From an obscure poem – very obscure, I'd almost forgotten it existed."

Julian froze, and a memory clicked into place. "I recall it once said by Edgar Kellerman," he murmured. "He quoted it in an argument. And the smug note reminds me of him."

Caroline's brow squeezed. "The financier? Isn't he quite beloved by the aristocracy?"

Julian brushed his lips below her ear, unable to keep from tasting her. "Not by me. I've had words with the man regarding his shady business practices and some venture involving Brazilian exports." He pressed a kiss on the smooth slope of her shoulder. "I'll tell Wentworth about the threat. Kellerman stays between us. I want to watch him first. Can't accuse a man based on a poem and a hunch."

"Very well." She took his jaw in her hand. "But only if you let me join in your clandestine stalking."

"Linnie..."

"Shh." And then she kissed him, and he forgot all of his protests.

# 17

Caroline studied her husband's profile as the carriage rumbled through the lamp-lit streets. Julian was the very picture of elegance – all sharp lines and brooding intensity. Even in partial silhouette, he was striking.

Just looking at that stern mouth made Caroline's toes curl. He was not so proper when he put that mouth on her.

"You're staring, my duchess," Julian murmured, attention still fixed out of the window. Amusement lurked beneath the velvet timbre of his voice.

Emboldened by the dark intimacy of the conveyance, Caroline allowed her gaze to trace the angles of his face, the broad expanse of his shoulders. She felt no shame in looking.

He was all hers.

"And if I am?" she challenged. "Shouldn't a wife look her fill of her husband?"

One dark brow was arched, though Julian kept his face averted. "My physique is yours to admire as you please."

"Oh, I fully intend to take advantage of that privilege. Perhaps I'll sketch you just like this later. Strong jaw clenched in concentration, eyes fixed on the streets ahead. A brooding Byronic hero."

"Byronic heroes meet rather tragic ends, if I recall their adventures correctly."

"True, but they enjoy scintillating escapades along the way."

All too soon, the carriage rolled to a halt at their destination on Threadneedle Street. Caroline straightened, smoothing her expression back to impassivity. Time to don her mask – the polished veneer of the Duchess of Hastings. Charming. Poised. Utterly unruffled.

Julian's hand engulfed hers, radiating warmth even through two layers of fine kidskin. "Ready?"

At her nod, Julian helped her down to the pavement. Together, they climbed the stone steps of the looming edifice that housed Edgar Kellerman's offices. Golden light blazed from the windows, almost garish in its opulence.

Inside, the heavy oak door admitted them into a richly appointed antechamber. Crimson walls and dark wainscoting lent the cavernous space an imposing weight. The whole design intended to intimidate.

At their entrance, the clerk behind the mahogany desk in the foyer snapped to attention. "Do you have an appointment?"

With an air of bored impatience, Julian withdrew a calling card from his waistcoat. "Please inform Mr Kellerman the Duke and Duchess of Hastings are here. I believe he'll make time to receive us."

The clerk's Adam's apple bobbed. "Right away, Your Grace."

He scurried through a rear door, leaving them alone in the oppressive room. Caroline glanced sidelong at her husband. "You nearly scared that poor man witless with one look."

"I'm the stoic duke, remember?" Julian murmured.

"Oh, I remember." She leaned up on her toes, lips grazing his ear. "But not in bed."

Heat sparked in Julian's gaze, though his expression remained like granite. "Careful. We've business to conclude here, and I've yet to have my fill of you this morning." His voice was silk and smoke, designed to make her squirm.

Caroline forced herself to look away from Julian's distracting nearness to scan the cavernous antechamber – anything to anchor her thoughts. Vast windows overlooked the bustling London streets, yet no shout or rattle of carriage wheels penetrated the thick glass. Velvet drapes muffled all sounds from outside.

At last, the clerk returned. "Mr Kellerman will see you in his office. If you'll just come this way."

They followed him through a maze of wood-panelled corridors adorned with imposing ancestral portraits and Greek statuary – more displays of wealth.

The clerk rapped on the double doors before pushing them open. "The Duke and Duchess of Hastings, sir."

Behind a polished mahogany desk sat Edgar Kellerman. At their entrance, he rose from his leather chair. "Duke and Duchess, welcome. What an unexpected pleasure."

Something about his demeanour set Caroline's teeth on edge. Kellerman's features seemed a mask, readily donned or discarded.

A snake shedding skin.

"Mr Kellerman," Julian said in greeting.

"To what do I owe the honour?" Kellerman asked, gesturing them towards the chairs opposite his desk.

Julian's hand pressed against Caroline's lower back. To an observer, his expression remained remote. But Caroline sensed his tension.

"I've heard some gossip about your Brazilian venture," Julian remarked as they settled into the plush leather seats. He crossed one leg over the other – the picture of leisurely disinterest. "I'd like to apologise for my previous harsh words when we first spoke about it some months ago. It's an ingenious scheme, from all accounts."

Kellerman tilted his head. "I appreciate your interest, duke. But my ventures are often speculative in the early stages. I try not to speak of them prematurely and risk disappointment." His attention shifted to Caroline. "I also know wives find these conversations tedious."

Caroline forced a smile. "Don't hold back on my account, sir. I never interfere with my husband's business."

Julian patted her hand. "Do allow my wife the pleasure of feeling involved, Kellerman," he said. "I've come to discuss investments."

"I'm delighted. But I understood you to be rather discriminating."

"I am. And I'm told you're worth my time."

Reaching inside his coat, Julian produced a silver cigar case and extended it to Kellerman. After a brief hesitation, the financier accepted the gift with a deferential tilt of his head.

Julian placed his own cigar to his lips and lit it. He inhaled deeply, letting the fragrant smoke wreathe his patrician features before he continued speaking. "As it happens, I've recently found myself free of certain properties in the West Indies. A surplus of capital could be redirected towards your scheme if I'm persuaded of its merits."

Caroline watched the entire performance in admiration. Her husband spun flawless lies with virtuoso skill.

Kellerman's hooded stare turned calculating – scenting opportunity. "Of course," he demurred. "Forgive my surprise, duke. It's only that you seemed rather… firm in your reluctance towards investments of this nature before."

"My inclinations are often complex, and my reasons are my own." Julian reclined in his chair, one hand draped negligently over the carved arm. He tapped cigar ash into the finial dish, every movement screaming bored wealth and refinement. "I understand from my peers that you mean to corner the South American shipping market. All that lush, untapped land newly opened to commerce." He paused, holding Kellerman's gaze. "I'm interested."

A definite gleam entered the hooded eyes. Even a whiff of ducal interest would grant Kellerman's scheme legitimacy and influence.

"Well." His thin lips stretched into a smile. "I admit, having a man of your eminence involved would be… advantageous."

"The risks sound thrilling," Caroline said. She filled her voice with honeyed sweetness befitting the useless aristocratic wife Kellerman took her to be. "I should adore an adventure."

Kellerman's expression turned indulgent as his stare settled on her. "Do you? I'd thought you a more retiring creature."

Caroline resisted the urge to grind her teeth. Instead, she let girlish excitement spread over her face. "In my youth, certainly. But recently, I've been reminded how much I've allowed myself to settle." She fluttered her lashes at him. "Haven't you heard? I was nearly blown to bits attending the theatre with my husband. All of London is abuzz."

"Yes, I had caught some idle chatter about an incident." His assessing stare moved to Julian. "And yet you emerged unscathed. Impressive."

Something close to possessiveness ignited in Julian's pale gaze. "I protect what's mine."

The blunt words raised the fine hairs on the nape of Caroline's neck. Spoken as both a warning and a dark promise.

"Some concern for your lovely wife's safety might be wise in the future, duke," Kellerman said. "Danger lurks in unlikely places these days."

"Oh, I'm not worried about my safety. My husband is quite devoted in that regard." She cast Julian a glance that she hoped read as besotted infatuation.

"Back to business, darling," Julian said gently, redirecting the conversation. To Kellerman: "How much capital have you amassed?"

"Your peers have committed enough privately to finance a ship or two." His fingers drummed an agitated staccato on the desktop. "However, these funds will be but a fraction required to launch commercial trade on a global scale."

"Naturally." Julian waved his cigar once more. "One must think bigger than two paltry ships to dominate South American markets. My man of business estimated I could divert thirty thousand pounds to you if sufficiently motivated."

Enough to purchase a small fleet. Caroline watched, fascinated, as Kellerman visibly struggled with his composure.

"That is… most generous, duke," he said.

Julian shrugged. "I reward those who prove themselves deserving."

After a moment, Kellerman mastered himself once more. His gaunt features resumed their mask of oily charm. "Yes, well, you'll find me most deserving indeed. In fact, one of my partners is hosting a party in three days." He glanced at Caroline. "Various investors will be there – and their lovely wives. It's certain to be quite a crush."

"Excellent. We look forward to it." Julian ground out his cigar in the finial dish and rose to his feet.

"Allow me to walk you out." Kellerman escorted them back through the foyer to the front steps, a model of deference. "I'm eager to get to know you both better at the party." Kellerman bowed as he handed Caroline into the waiting carriage. "Until then, duke, duchess."

Julian rapped with a walking stick on the roof to signal to the driver.

Caroline sagged against the seat. "Ugh. I feel unclean."

"You were flawless in there," Julian murmured.

"As were you. I'd nearly forgotten how imposing the Duke of Hastings can be when he's determined to be ruthless." She braced her hand against the armrest as the carriage lurched. "Do you think his venture is legitimate?"

"No." He removed his gloves, finger by finger. "If he's the man who wrote those letters and his targets are aristocrats, I believe he's using this scheme to lure them within reach."

Caroline's stomach twisted. "Get their fortunes first before killing them, you mean?"

"It's possible." He set his gloves aside. "But these assassination attempts are personal. He's set this up to gain confidence for a very specific reason. We just need to find out why. We'll attend

Kellerman's party. Watch how he interacts with the investors he's reeled in. The wives often know more gossip than the husbands."

"Be careful," she said. "He thinks I'm a useless society matron, but you promised him thirty thousand pounds."

"I'm nothing if not careful." He gestured with his fingers. "Now come here, my duchess. I solved your note this morning, and I believe it mentioned I had yet to pleasure you in a moving carriage. I wouldn't want to disappoint."

# 18

Julian surveyed the glittering ballroom. Around him, the cream of London society mingled and laughed, resplendent in their silks and feathers. Liveried footmen wove through the crowds, bearing trays laden with fluted champagne glasses. An orchestra occupied the minstrel gallery above, sawing away at their strings to provide a sonorous backdrop to the mingling aristocrats below.

But Julian only watched one man.

Edgar Kellerman.

Even in this crush, the financier stood out with a calculating gleam in his eyes as he scanned the room. Cloying charm oozed from every word as he bent his listeners to his will.

Julian recognised more than a few eager faces in the crowd surrounding him – second sons and ambitious heirs greedy for easy fortune.

He could not confront Kellerman directly, not yet. Despite his suspicions, Julian lacked definitive proof. He needed Kellerman to lower his guard first. To believe Julian an easy mark ripe for manipulation.

An unpleasant role but a necessary one.

Julian took a glass of champagne from a passing footman and leaned with bored indolence against a nearby pillar.

"If you were going to brood alone, you ought to have told me," came an amused voice at his shoulder.

Julian glanced over to see Caroline approaching. He let his gaze trace over her, drinking in the sight. She had swept her blonde hair up in an elegant coiffure, with a few artful curls left loose to caress her neck and shoulders. Her ivory silk gown was overlaid with intricate black Chantilly lace, the scalloped neckline accentuating the graceful arch of her throat. She'd chosen a dress to bring men to their knees while still appearing a proper duchess.

*His* duchess.

"Just observing," he said.

"You do realise you're glowering at our gracious host as though you'd like to skewer him with an olive fork?"

"Can you blame me?"

"No, but we need him to believe he's lured you in. Which will prove difficult if you insist on mentally eviscerating him all night." She took another sip of champagne. "Now stop looking so murderous before someone thinks to call you out."

"You know I only save my best behaviour for you. But I promise to glower more politely moving forward," he said. "How are you getting on with the wives?"

"I could fill a hundred scandal sheets with the idle chatter I've endured tonight over lukewarm lemonade, but none relating to Kellerman. I spied you over here, brooding in the corner, and thought I'd offer my sympathies. How fares our host this evening? Still reeling in his besotted fortune-hunting lambs?"

"One by one. With promises of fifty per cent returns within months. Probably streets paved with silver and diamonds growing on trees to be hand-delivered by next Tuesday or some nonsense."

Her laugh was more like a snort. "Ah, practically reckless fraud. He's desperate, then."

"Desperate men are dangerous men. I have a friend who's traded as far as Argentina, and he told me the ports are undeveloped and the terrain is inhospitable. Any investments would be sunk."

The Portuguese had held those colonies for centuries – if profitable ventures existed, they would have been seized long ago. It was easy to swindle aristocrats with little knowledge of the world outside London's parks and glittering ballrooms.

"I'm sure if you tried telling any of them that, they'd promptly declare themselves experts in South American shipping because they'd eaten a pineapple once," Caroline said. "Alas, when it comes to sense and sensibility…"

"… idiots prevail," Julian supplied.

His wife grinned. "I was attempting 'more money than sense', but yes, a parliament of raving idiots hits the mark."

Julian made a noncommittal noise, though inwardly, he agreed.

"Well," Caroline sighed, "I suppose I'll venture back to the crush of wives. You know where to find me if you need me."

After a few more minutes of covert observation, during which he learned nothing of value, Julian judged it time to engage his quarry more directly. He sauntered over to meet the cluster of gentlemen hanging on Kellerman's every word.

"Duke, how good of you to join us," Kellerman greeted him smoothly, shifting to make room for Julian. Behind his deferential smile, sharp eyes tracked Julian's every movement. No detail escaped Kellerman's notice.

He performed introductions, and Julian offered Kellerman's admirers a cool nod. "A pleasure, gentlemen."

"I was just describing my plans for Brazil. Sugar, coffee, cotton – plenty of sources for revenue. Such fertile acres."

Julian hummed in response. He knew the realities. The few small ports in Brazil were accessible only by hacking through dense rainforest. Heat and torrential rains would destroy cargo and breed fever before it ever reached the coast. Brazil was still decades away from the development required for massive foreign trade. But he needed to lure Kellerman into complacency, not arouse his suspicions.

"You paint quite a grand vision," Julian said, as though discussing the weather. "Tell me, what arrangements have you made with local authorities? Securing favourable trade relationships can be quite complex."

Kellerman flashed his teeth, shark-like. "Already in progress, duke. I have a man of business securing everything as we speak."

"Impressive. I've heard you boast rather incredible profits as well. Fifty per cent returns within mere months, wasn't it?"

"Indeed." Kellerman's smile turned sly. "Imagine profits to dwarf the East India Company in her heyday. Wouldn't the duchess enjoy dripping with Brazilian gems?"

A few chuckles from the other gentlemen. "Reunited, aren't you?" One of them said. "Planning an heir now, Hastings?"

Julian tensed, a memory flickering through his mind.

*Tristan. His name was Tristan.*

Kellerman watched him, doubtlessly looking for any potential vulnerabilities.

Mindful of his audience, Julian arranged his features in a mask of affability. "Should the duchess bless me with a son or daughter, I would be deeply honoured." He redirected the conversation to safer waters with practised ease. "But I understand Lord Delancey's lovely wife has recently delivered their first child. A little girl, was it not?"

Delancey blinked, clearly caught off guard by the abrupt change in topic. "Er, yes. Both are quite healthy, thank you for asking."

"Splendid news," Julian replied with sincere warmth. "Please give Lady Delancey my regards and congratulations when you see her."

Delancey drew himself up with pleasure at the acknowledgement. "Most kind of you, duke."

As the orchestra swelled into a lively waltz, Julian noticed Caroline across the room. Even at a distance, her radiance stole his breath. The glittering chandelier light caressed each elegant coil of her hair, bringing out glinting highlights of gold.

Despite the urgency of their purpose here tonight, Julian's gaze traced those seductive lines, his imagination filling in details of the body he knew so intimately beneath the fine silk and lace. The visceral need to keep her close clawed at his throat.

With effort, Julian wrenched his attention back to his task at hand. "My apologies, you were saying?" he asked Kellerman.

"We need an entire fleet of ships ready by year's end," Kellerman replied.

"Of course. Speed and decisiveness will be critical," Julian agreed. He turned the conversation to practical matters, probing for details. "What arrangements have you made? Commissioned shipbuilders, secured crews? Or would you purchase the fleet?"

He wanted to see how far Kellerman would spin this fiction to hook his victims. How intricate and layered the lies designed to reel them in.

As Kellerman expounded on timetables, shipyards, and a hundred other minor logistics, Julian catalogued details for later evidence. He needed to prove Kellerman was the man who had spilled blood in pursuit of some twisted vendetta. He needed to figure out who his specific targets were.

To avoid rousing Kellerman's suspicions, Julian said, "Send me the particulars in the morning, and I'll discuss them with my man of business."

Kellerman's thin lips curved. "Excellent. You won't regret this, Hastings." His signet ring flashed as he clapped Julian on the back.

That ring. Something about the large, vulgar piece sparked familiarity once more. But before Julian could grasp the elusive connection, it slipped away.

"In the meantime, enjoy the fete," Kellerman said. "I confess, such garish affairs are not usually to my taste. But one must keep up appearances."

"Of course." Julian nodded. "Appearances are everything in business."

# 19

The ballroom was full to bursting with London's elite.

Caroline nodded along as the ladies prattled on about fashion and gossip. Vultures dressed in silk and feathers. But behind her practised smile, Caroline focused on more valuable conversations. She had positioned herself near the wives of investors in Kellerman's dubious trade venture, listening closely.

The women tittered about the weather and speculated about the season's most extravagant upcoming ball, but nothing of consequence reached Caroline's ears. At least not until the hungry lions turned towards more tantalising fare.

"It's so lovely to see you here, duchess," Lady Kenilworth said, a sly smile curling her lips. "And your handsome husband, too, of course."

Ah, there it was. Caroline swallowed down a grimace. "Thank you. I'll be certain to tell Hastings."

"I heard he saved you from that dreadful bombing," Mrs Trumbull said, breathless. "That he held you in his arms after a dead faint. Did he truly carry you over the rubble to safety?"

Caroline resisted the urge to roll her eyes. Oh, for heaven's sake. She supposed the story of the formidable Duke of Hastings cradling his wife's limp form sold more papers than the truth – that she'd barked orders, covered in dust and blood.

"It was an alarming experience," she said. "Fortunately, Hastings proved himself quite gallant in the aftermath."

"I do hope they find the vile culprit," another woman fretted. "I almost didn't attend tonight, but I couldn't possibly miss it. Mr Kellerman's so charming, isn't he?"

Caroline tried not to glance at the man in question lest her distaste show. "I couldn't say. I don't believe I've made Mr Kellerman's acquaintance before this week." Time to redirect their hunger. "Tell me, how long has he been a fixture in London society?"

"Only since last year. He was abroad for ages before that." Lady Kenilworth lowered her voice. "But there are hints of rather low beginnings despite his obvious education and polish. I heard he began life in Cheapside. Or was it Spitalfields?"

"Surely not," another woman said.

"No one seems to know his family or origins," mused another gossip. Her predatory gaze tracked Kellerman through the crowd. "I've heard whispers he might be a tanner's son."

More dramatic gasping.

Caroline arched a brow, layering her tone with mild surprise. "How extraordinary. Though clearly, he has adapted himself well to high society." She filed away the gossip for later scrutiny.

Across the sea of feathers and finery, Julian stood scanning the crowd. When their gazes caught, he lifted two fingers in a subtle summons before turning to slip through the gilded doors.

With a final serene smile, Caroline made her excuses. "I'm feeling a bit hot. Do enjoy the rest of the evening, ladies." She abandoned her half-full champagne flute and departed the stuffy ballroom, ignoring the raised eyebrows.

In the muted hall, away from the revelry, she found Julian waiting around the corner. Before she could react, he grasped her wrist and tugged her into a darkened study. Caroline's startled gasp was muffled against his shirtfront as Julian kicked the door shut and backed her against it.

Warmth flushed through her. His clean scent surrounded her,

soap and starch and skin. She had forgotten how he could gentle her and inflame her in the same breath.

"Really, Julian. Must you accost me like a barbarian?"

Despite her chiding tone, she always loved seeing this side of him. The aristocratic polish stripped away to reveal the focused man beneath. The man only she was allowed to know.

Julian's mouth twitched. "My apologies. I needed to speak with you urgently, and discretion seemed warranted." Then he leaned in and nipped at her earlobe. "And I thought you enjoyed it when I let slip the civilised veneer."

Heat swept her cheeks, confirmation enough.

"This is hardly private," Caroline said, acutely aware of the ballroom's proximity, the faint strains of music penetrating the study walls. She resisted the urge to lean into his warmth. "What was so urgent it couldn't wait until we got home?"

"I need you to scrutinise something."

Frowning, Caroline accepted the page and angled it towards the meagre light. The outline of a heraldic crest was just visible, the ink still fresh. He must have scribbled it quickly.

"A family seal?" she murmured.

"On a signet ring Kellerman wore," Julian confirmed. "Have you seen it anywhere?"

"No. But the style does strike me as familiar. I can't say precisely why. With better light, perhaps—"

A scuffling outside the study door cut her off abruptly. In one smooth motion, Julian grasped her wrist and pulled Caroline through an inset door she hadn't even noticed, concealed in the ornate wood panelling. Pitch black inside, some kind of small storage closet or antechamber.

Caroline drew a steadying breath, intensely aware of Julian's nearness. She could just make out the angular lines of his face mere inches from her own in the gloom, feel the warmth of his lean body bracketing hers. His breaths whispered across her eyelashes. She should step back, move away. But the cramped space tethered them close, chests brushing.

In the next room, furniture creaked. The hiss and flare of a lucifer striking was as loud as a gunshot in the ensuing silence. Together, they waited, attuned to every sound filtering through the thin dividing wall. But whoever had entered the study showed no signs of leaving anytime soon.

When a thud sounded right outside the concealed door, Caroline muffled her gasp against Julian's shirtfront on instinct. His breaths came more rapidly now, grazing her cheek.

Julian turned his face into her hair and put his lips against her ear. "Don't move," he breathed. Gooseflesh swept down her neck and along her spine at the sensation. His voice dropped impossibly lower. "God, duchess, can't you feel what you do to me?"

He grasped her hips, pressing her against his cock. Caroline released a breath, eyes slipping shut. Then her lips parted on a silent gasp as his hand rose to her breast, his thumb teasing her nipple through the silk.

The door clicked shut in the outer room. Still, neither of them moved.

The air in the small chamber felt electric and alive. His grip tightened on her waist, a wordless warning.

Caroline was seized by a recklessness she hadn't experienced in years. When her mouth found his in the dark, the space between them fractured. Julian backed her against the wall. He kissed her with none of his usual careful restraint – all tongue and teeth and desperation. Caroline's fingers sank into his hair, opening for him eagerly.

He groaned against her lips. His hands slid down to grip her backside and tug her more firmly against him. He rocked his hips, teasing friction that was at once too much and not enough.

"Do you want me to fuck you?" His voice was sin in the dark. "Bend you over and take you hard the way we used to? Remind you who you belong to?"

Caroline shuddered, dizzy with need. Anyone could walk in

and catch them at any moment. But propriety and caution had melted beneath relentless desire.

"Yes," she whispered. "Here. Now."

Julian released a shattered breath. "Then turn around." The command was raw with wanting. "Fingers first. I want you writhing and desperate to stay quiet."

Then he slid his hand beneath her skirts to find the slit in her drawers.

"So wet for me already," Julian said, pushing two fingers inside her.

Caroline's head fell back against his shoulder, eyes fluttering shut.

Julian's teeth grazed the tender skin of her neck. "You've been imagining this all night, haven't you? Pretending to be proper while picturing my cock inside you, pleasuring you where anyone might find us?"

*Oh, God.* "Yes," she gasped.

The admission drew a rough, desperate sound from his throat. Caroline heard the rustle of fabric behind her as Julian freed himself one-handed. And then he thrust into her in a ruthless stroke that stole the breath from her lungs.

His hand clamped over her mouth at her sharp cry. "Hush now. Wouldn't want anyone hearing you beg for this, would we?"

The vulgar words sent heat spiking through her. All thought scattered, her world reduced to white-hot ecstasy. The obscene slap of skin, his breath rough in her ear, restraints of propriety stripped away until only raw need remained.

Caroline let him manoeuvre her wrists behind her back, pinned tight in his bruising grip – the restraint only heightening her arousal. Each powerful stroke built the pressure higher. Rational thought fractured to pure sensation.

When he laughed, it was a low, dark sound. "I love seeing you like this. This is what you wanted from me, isn't it?"

Caroline bit down on his palm. He played the perfect

aristocrat, but this was the truth between them. Here, away from prying eyes, there were no rules. No restraints to bind them.

"Julian—" She broke off on a shattered gasp as he quickened his pace again.

Nothing existed but Julian surrounding her. Possessing her. As her climax crashed through her, she muffled her noises against his hand. He followed seconds later, cursing rough and low against her throat, his fingers digging bruises into her hips.

Caroline felt untethered. Remade. As though he had reached beneath her ribs to touch some secret, vulnerable part of her.

Julian gently turned her in his arms, then opened the door a crack to allow in the light. His burning gaze took in her dishevelled appearance, something close to awe in his eyes.

"Here. Let me help set you to rights." He smoothed his hands over her tousled hair and rumpled skirts. When she was passably tidy, that devastating little smile curled his lips again. "One might accuse you of making me behave like a barbarian."

"One might accuse you of enjoying it." Caroline smoothed her gown, ensuring she looked presentable once more. Then she leaned to whisper, "I certainly do."

# 20

The humid summer air pressed down on Julian as he prowled the train platform, cataloguing each face, only to dismiss them just as quickly. Families bid farewell to loved ones, gentlemen hurried to board with tickets clutched in gloved hands, and ladies fluttered lace fans to combat the sweltering heat. None posed an overt threat. But Julian knew better than to take comfort in the mundane normality surrounding him.

Wentworth checked his watch for the third time. “Boarding should commence shortly.”

“You’ll snap your timepiece in half if you keep clutching it so tightly,” Julian murmured dryly, despite the apprehension singing through his veins. “Those things are delicate.”

Wentworth shot him an impatient look. “I wasn’t aware you’d developed a passion for horology.”

Julian’s lips twitched. “I wouldn’t want you to lose it during a time-sensitive operation. Though at the rate your jaw is clenched, you may crack a molar soon,” he replied, forcing calm into his voice even as his eyes tracked each passerby. Hunting anomalies. Seeking irregularities amid the mundane.

Wentworth did the same, assessing the steady trickle of travellers heading for the platform and mentally cataloguing potential suspects. But Julian's focus bent towards a different quarry.

Edgar Kellerman.

Wentworth remained ignorant of Julian's suspicions, and it was safer to keep it so until irrefutable proof came to light. But the pieces fitted too neatly for coincidence. Kellerman's dubious investment scheme gave him access to the aristocracy and their travel habits. And complex linguistic puzzles like the coded threats would be easy for an educated man like him to create.

Now Julian need only supply the evidence to hang the bastard.

He took stock of the train. Seven passenger cars, one luggage, three cargo. Numerous sinister possibilities for stowing an explosive device, poison, anything.

Wentworth's features turned grim, as if he read Julian's thoughts. "Any theories on the target, or shall we begin investigating every nook and cranny?"

"No theories yet. Your men are stationed nearby? I assume they're checking any aristocrats who board?"

A brusque nod. "Plainclothes. They boarded with the other passengers to keep watch."

Julian's gaze tracked a mother shepherding three children towards the platform. The young ones skipped and laughed, unaware of the danger.

"And the conductor has been advised to delay departure?"

"Yes. But the train must depart by half-past ten regardless, or the entire timetable descends into chaos." Wentworth's mouth flattened into a grim line. "We have two hours at most."

Two hours. Julian's pulse spiked. Two hours to identify Kellerman's mark and his weapon.

"This train alone stretches over a tenth of a mile. Ample territory."

Wentworth turned towards the platform gates. "Best we begin, then."

The next quarter hour passed swiftly as they conducted brisk searches of luggage, cargo, and passenger compartments, the plainclothes constables scrutinising all those boarding. But nothing sinister revealed itself – no wires or explosive mechanisms. No stashed weapons or vials of poison. Only innocuous items: books, travelling cases, parasols, and picnic baskets.

Unease skated down Julian's spine. Little time remained before the scheduled departure. He forced his breathing to steady.

*Think, damn you. Somewhere beyond the authorities' notice—*

"The coal," Julian said, already striding towards the back of the locomotive. "Get a combustible device in the firebox, and you've got a derailment."

Behind him came the smack of boots breaking into a run across the platform. "Check the tenders!" Wentworth barked. "Question the firemen!"

Julian vaulted up into the nearest tender car. When they entered, the fireman blinked at them in confusion. His youthful face was smudged with soot, cap askew.

"Sirs, if you're looking for the passenger compartments—"

Wentworth cut him off, tone brusque as he flashed his credentials. "Has anyone besides you accessed this car today?"

The young man paled beneath the grime coating his skin. "An inspector not fifteen minutes ago while I stepped out for a smoke."

"Get out," Wentworth ordered. "I need to take a look in here."

The fireman scrambled from the tender without argument.

As soon as they were alone, Wentworth stripped off his coat and took up a shovel. "The device won't be on top of the pile," he muttered, sifting through the gleaming coal with smooth strokes. "It'll be buried below the surface, ready to be shovelled into the firebox once the train is on its way."

Julian watched him work, swift and methodical. The shovel scraped over the coal, the only sound beyond their laboured breaths in the cramped tender car. Wentworth handled the tool with an ease that spoke of long practice. Of having performed such tasks countless times before in his shadowy profession.

Julian fought the urge to hurry. Forced his muscles to uncoil, adopting a casual slouch against the tender wall despite his thrumming pulse.

"How do you know what to look for?" Julian asked, breaking the tense silence.

Wentworth gave a dry laugh, not pausing in his efforts. "Captain Courtenay tried selling his design for the coal torpedo to Her Majesty's government."

"Courtenay of the Confederate Secret Service?"

"The very same." Wentworth kept shovelling, movements sharp with urgency. His shirt clung to his back beneath his discarded jacket. "He developed it to sink Union steamships and derail locomotives during the war."

Julian frowned at the mention of America's civil war, still so fresh in memory. "Tell me you didn't give that wretch a shilling."

The thought of the Crown funding such carnage turned his stomach. He'd seen the callous aftermath. The scorched earth and mass graves in America. All so the South could keep humans as property.

"God no," Wentworth said. "And from what I hear, neither did any other government. The man slunk back to America with his tail between his legs, where I hope he dies a miserable death." He hefted a lump of coal, scrutinising it before discarding it again. "Look for extra weight, distinct shape. Something that doesn't belong." The shovel scraped faster now, movements edged with urgency. "Looks like our culprit," he said, carefully lifting out the coal. He turned it over in his hands. "See the plug?"

It looked innocuous enough – Julian wouldn't have been able to differentiate it from any other piece of coal in that pile were it not for the visible metal casing hidden beneath a layer of soot filled with explosives ready to detonate. Capable of rupturing even a locomotive's robust boiler.

Wentworth's face was grim as he and Julian stepped out of the compartment. "Lads, we've got a live one!" he shouted.

A young officer approached from the platform. "Boss?"

"Take this," Wentworth said, passing it off gingerly. "Probably not a threat without a spark, but treat it like an active bomb, or I'll draw and quarter you myself."

As the man hurried away, Wentworth turned to Julian. "The bastard who planted it may still be here to finish the job."

Julian tensed, scanning the milling crowds with renewed scrutiny. He searched for any familiar face, any detail out of place. A stray breeze gusted, delivering the stench of smoke, sweat, and cheap tobacco. His senses strained, attuned to the most minute details.

There.

Near a pillar, a nondescript man in rough labourer garb stood smoking. To the casual observer, he looked like a worker enjoying a brief respite. But Julian noted how his posture radiated tension, shoulders too rigid beneath the shabby coat.

Unease skittered down Julian's spine. Every instinct screamed the man was no aimless loiterer. And he seemed to be watching someone. Following a well-dressed gentleman through the crowd with his gaze. Lord Amesbury, Julian realised with a jolt. He remembered the investor from Kellerman's party.

His instincts blared a warning.

With subtle signs, Julian directed Wentworth's attention towards the mysterious figure without being obvious. But their surveillance had not gone unnoticed. The man's head turned, eyes landing on Julian as he and Wentworth approached.

He bolted.

Julian and Wentworth broke into a flat-out run across the platform. Dodging around startled passengers, they closed the distance as the fleeing man knocked over baggage and barrels to slow their pursuit. But Julian would not be deterred. He poured on greater speed, lungs burning and boots slamming the pavement. The summer breeze plastered his sweat-soaked shirt to his back. He could hear Wentworth's laboured breaths several strides behind now. This prey was his alone to catch.

Just as Julian was poised to tackle the man, his quarry spun and produced a pistol from inside his coat and took hasty aim.

Only instinct saved him. Julian hurled himself into a diving roll just as the shot cracked as loud as thunder. A woman's scream rent the air as he came up in a crouch, heart hammering against his ribs. The bullet had narrowly missed him, biting into the platform boards instead. Julian surged back to his feet and ploughed into the man's midsection, driving them both to the hard pavement in a tangle of limbs.

They grappled together, landing vicious blows, fingers gouging for any weakness. The man fought like a feral animal. He clawed at Julian's face, his pistol swinging towards Julian's temple again.

Julian dodged the blow and seized the man's wrist, twisting viciously until he felt the delicate bones snap. A howl tore from the man's throat, but still, he thrashed like a rabid beast. Julian had to end this decisively before his opponent got off another shot at point-blank range.

He slammed the man's broken wrist against the pavement once, twice, until the pistol slipped free. Quick as a striking snake, Julian snatched up the gun and reversed their positions, pinning the man face-first into the rough boards. He jammed the pistol barrel into the vulnerable flesh beneath his opponent's jaw.

"Move again, and I'll splatter your brains across this platform," Julian snapped, panting hard.

The thunder of boots announced Wentworth's belated arrival with a clutch of bobbies. They hauled the cursing assailant to his feet. Julian relinquished his hold reluctantly, tension still thrumming through every fibre. His earlier calm had deserted him. That had been too damned close.

"Take him," Wentworth ordered his men crisply. "I'll be along to question him shortly."

After they'd marched the man away, he turned to Julian with a scowl. "Reckless stunt. He could've blown your fool head off, Hastings."

Julian slowly flexed his aching shoulder where he'd impacted brutally with the pavement. "Learn how to run, then, Wentworth."

A bone-deep exhaustion swept through Julian, leaving him

hollowed out and spent. He braced his hands on his knees, sucking in lungfuls of humid air.

Wentworth's heavy hand clasped Julian's shoulder, steadying. "You all right, Hastings?"

Julian straightened. "Fine. That man isn't the one who wrote the letters."

Wentworth's expression was unreadable. "I'd guess not. He didn't give the impression of a man fluent in multiple languages." He shook his head. "Just a hired thug."

"When you question him, ask if the man who hired him is tall, with dark hair and a moustache," Julian said, unable to resist one last attempt at driving the investigation towards his actual suspect.

Wentworth gave him a sharp look, gauging. "You know something."

"Nothing concrete." Not yet. But he would find it. "I'll bring you hard evidence when I have it. For now, watch him."

The other man nodded. "As you say." He clapped Julian on the shoulder again. "Go home, Hastings. Get some rest. You look like hell."

## 21

Caroline sat motionless in the sitting room. She watched dust motes dance through the bands of sunlight and tried not to think about Julian.

She'd been fretting since he'd raced off with Mr Wentworth that morning. When she'd objected to being left behind, Julian had pinned her with that intense, protective stare. The imprint of his blistering kiss still lingered, fogging her mind as effectively as any drug. She could summon the sensation too easily – the possessive sweep of his tongue, the bite of his teeth. A kiss designed to weaken knees and steal breath. Oh yes, it had done its work flawlessly.

And now there was nothing she could do but sit there, a dutiful wife biding her time.

Percy's arrival jolted Caroline from her dark musings. "A Mr Grey here to see you, Your Grace."

"Send him in, Percy." She cast her gaze over the picked-over sandwiches and pot of tepid tea. "And bring fresh tea, if you please. The good Darjeeling." She forced brightness into her tone that felt brittle even to her own ears. "Oh, and sandwiches. A lot of them."

Percy's eyebrows lifted a fraction. "A lot, Your Grace?"

"Oh yes. A frankly ludicrous amount. Enough to feed a regiment."

A familiar chuckle emanated from the doorway. "A regiment? My dear duchess, what sort of appetite do you think I have?"

Her closest friend, Richard Grey, sauntered into the room, looking too pleased with himself for the early hour. He moved with effortless grace, projecting the confidence of a man who knew his place in the world. Settling into the chair opposite her, he helped himself to a sandwich from the platter – one she'd been picking at earlier. Richard took an obnoxiously large bite and flashed her a shameless grin.

"Can you blame me for thinking you half starved?" Caroline said. "Every time I see you, my larders are mysteriously depleted. You descend like a scavenging fox set loose among helpless hens."

Clutching his chest as if affronted, Richard adopted a wounded expression. "Here I am, barely hours after kissing my darling wife and babe goodbye, rushing to attend to you in your time of need – ready to provide comfort and solace. And this is the thanks I get?" He took another defiant bite of the sandwich. "Have a care, Caro. I could waste away to a husk on such meagre rations."

"Oh yes, utterly selfless. Practically a saint." She reached over and patted his hand with fond exasperation. "I'm quite certain Anne knows precisely where you dashed off to this morning. Let me guess… was it a spot of light blackmail? Beating someone to a pulp in a back alley?"

Richard grinned, sharp and wolfish. "I'll have you know I'm an upstanding gentleman and devoted family man now." The twitch of his lips turned wicked. "I've already begun compiling prime blackmail material to share with Lillian when she comes of age."

"You'll do no such thing. Anne will string you up by your cravat if you corrupt the child too early. Can't you at least wait until she starts walking?"

"And deny my daughter her proper education? Anne's probably whispering seditious ideas to her. Mark my words, Lillian will have the pair of us wrapped around her little finger before long."

"And how is Anne adapting to motherhood?"

His smile softened around the edges. "It's been... an adjustment. Anne prefers to take on the role of the nursemaid, and it turns out an infant doesn't adhere to one's schedule or respect closed doors. All babies appear as angry, squalling potatoes fresh from the womb, but she's developed a distinct personality." He gave her a wink. "But Anne and I are managing well enough."

"Oh yes, I'm sure you are," Caroline said dryly.

Percy arrived with the tea tray. While the butler set the service between them, Caroline studied Richard, catalogued the new contentment. This man who had helped hold her fragile pieces together after she'd shattered. She was happy for him, truly. But the sentiment came with an edge of wistfulness.

An old grief that never faded.

She waited until they were alone again to ask, "Tell me more about how you and Anne are getting on. I want to hear everything about dear Lillian."

Richard helped himself to far more sugar than any grown man should reasonably consume. "Anne and I are deliriously happy but as exhausted as one might expect. Worth it, though." He took a slow sip, his keen gaze never leaving her face. "It takes some time, learning to put another tiny human's needs before one's own convenience. Much less sleep to be had. But I wouldn't trade it for anything." His smile turned self-deprecating. "Never pictured myself as the doting papa, yet here I am reading poetry to an infant more interested in gnawing the pages. Do remind me how you take your tea, darling. One lump or two?"

"Just one, please." She watched him plop a cube in her cup, followed by a careless splash of milk.

"I hear our wayward duke has finally deigned to grace your doorstep again after all this time." Richard's tone remained mild, but she detected the edge beneath the silk. Her friend had never cared for Julian, and clearly, that hadn't changed. "Shall I pry for details, or must I resort to bribing your staff?"

The question she'd been dreading. Caroline tensed, dropping

her gaze to the swirling eddies in her tea as she tried to corral her fraying thoughts. Their reconciliation was still so fresh, the old wounds barely beginning to knit. She hardly knew how to explain the jagged pieces of their history in a way that made any sense.

"His apartment in town was let, so he's staying here for now," she said. "And I'd like to ask him to remain indefinitely."

"Would you now?" Richard took a slow sip of tea, but his nonchalance didn't fool her. "I confess, it's difficult to be overjoyed at his return after so many years of indifference towards you. I'm half tempted to string him up in the courtyard, but Anne forbade it. Told me not to meddle."

Despite everything, Caroline let out a quiet laugh. "Anne is very wise. And I'm sure she'd be cross if you started brawling with a duke on a London street."

Richard's smile held an edge. "As if I'd be so gauche. There are subtler ways to make displeasure known." He set down his teacup with a soft clink. "But don't change the subject. You never told me what happened between you and Hastings."

Caroline stared down into her cup. "It's complicated."

Richard's voice remained patient. "I've put men in the ground for far less cause than having hurt you. Hastings will be no exception if that's what you want. Complicated intrigues me."

"It's difficult to explain," she began. "We were so young when we wed, and he'd originally planned to marry our friend Grace that year. But we both made a hasty decision in a moment of... well, you know how these things happen."

All humour fled Richard's expression. He reached over and covered her hand with his own, giving a gentle squeeze. "I believe I understand well enough."

The quiet empathy in his voice loosened some of the tightness in Caroline's chest. "And then we lost Grace shortly after the wedding. He left to give the news to her father and sister." She cleared the emotion clogging her throat. "And while he was gone, I lost our baby."

"Oh, Caro. I'm so sorry." Agony rippled across Richard's face. This new father would clearly burn the world down for his wife and child. "I didn't know."

Caroline managed a tremulous almost-smile, emotions scraped raw and bleeding. "It was a long time ago."

He shook his head, refusing to allow her to minimise the depth of those wounds. "May I hug you? You look as though you need one."

At her slight nod, he came around the table and sat beside her, wrapping her in a fierce embrace.

"I'm sorry," he murmured into her hair. "I didn't mean to cause you distress with my prying. Simply say the word, and I'll go outside and punch myself for my spectacular idiocy just now. I'd consider it a privilege."

A faint laugh escaped her this time. She gave him a final squeeze before relaxing back. "No fisticuffs required, but I appreciate the offer."

"Very well. But let it be known the offer remains open if you need it."

Footsteps echoed down the corridor before Caroline could respond. She glanced up as Julian appeared in the doorway.

Caroline watched his expression shutter as he took in the cosy tableau; Richard's arm was draped around her shoulders. For a heartbeat, his stride faltered. Caroline fancied she could hear the neat click of locks sliding into place. In the span of a blink, the remote and untouchable Duke of Hastings stood before them once more.

Without a word, Julian removed his gloves and overcoat, laying them neatly across a side table. He moved with calm, economical motions, giving no hint of his inner turbulence. When he turned back to them, his expression remained fixed in icy politeness. Only the arctic chill of his gaze gave any indication of his mood.

"Forgive the interruption, duchess. I wasn't aware you had a guest." He inclined his head in greeting. "Grey."

"Hastings," Richard returned coolly, still lounging on the

divan beside Caroline. He made no move to stand or withdraw his arm from around her shoulders.

Julian's gaze tracked the casual contact, pale eyes shuttering further. "To what do we owe the unexpected pleasure?"

Smooth as cream, that question. But the words dripped disdain.

Before Richard could come back with an equally biting riposte, Caroline interjected, "Richard stopped by to check on me. He wanted to ensure I was all right after the bombing."

"How thoughtful. As you can see, my wife remains quite healthy and intact. So your concern, while admirable, was unnecessary."

"One can never be too careful." Richard's own smile was tight. "I'll always be here when Caro needs me. Whether it's for cheering up or mending a broken heart. Wouldn't be the first time."

The temperature in the elegant little sitting room plunged. Caroline watched darkness sweep across Julian's expression, there and gone between one heartbeat and the next. His sculpted features might as well have been carved from marble. Beautiful. Remote. Untouchable.

Sensing the mounting tension, Caroline extricated herself from Richard's embrace and rose to her feet. She conjured up a smile that felt thin and brittle on her lips. "Thank you for coming, Richard. Do give your family my love."

Richard rose as well, blue eyes intent on her face. "Of course. Visit us soon, won't you? I'm sure Anne and Lillian would love to see you." Then he leaned forward and whispered in her ear, "Best brace yourself when I leave. But a little jealousy is good for the soul."

Before she could respond, Richard quickly kissed her hand and departed with a wink.

The silence left in his wake felt oppressive. Julian stood still in the centre of the room, muscles coiled tight beneath his expensive tailored jacket. A predator leashed by the barest of threads.

The stoic duke peeling away.

And then, gone.

Julian crossed the room in three swift strides and crushed his mouth to hers. No warning, no questions, just pure heat and blatant possession. His tongue swept past her lips to stroke along hers, staking his claim in no uncertain terms. Caroline melted into the contact, the heady taste and feel of him sweeping all coherent thought away in a hot rush.

Before she could catch her breath, Julian was lifting her into his arms. Caroline clung to him as he mounted the stairs, heedless of servants.

Once the bedroom door was shut and locked behind them, Julian set her back on her feet. His gaze scorched over her with its intensity.

"What happened at Charing Cross?" Caroline demanded breathlessly, still reeling.

"Crisis averted," he said, ruthlessly unbuttoning her dress. "I need you naked."

Desire speared through her, sharp and hot. "Are you jealous?" she whispered, arching her neck as his teeth grazed her throat.

A harsh exhale that might've been a laugh ghosted across her skin. "Furious with myself. Seeing him..." Julian's voice dropped, words scraping raw against her ear. "You called for Grey that night in Edinburgh last year when I pulled you from the flames. Do you remember? I was holding you in my arms, and he was the one you trusted. He was a comfort you needed, and I failed to provide."

Shame lanced through her. She had few memories of Edinburgh. Richard and Anne's hasty wedding, the sudden heat that filled her bedchamber – then hazy fragments glimpsed through smoke and fire-lit darkness.

*Take me home, Richard. Take me to Ravenhill. I want to go home.*

She remembered wanting to be buried beside her son. But the

admission lodged like broken glass in her throat, too jagged to voice aloud.

She hadn't realised how much that moment had hurt Julian. Taken all their damaged edges and fractured them further. Introduced more doubt to an already shattered foundation.

Before she could speak, Julian cut off her words with his mouth, fierce and uncompromising. She lost herself in the kiss, the possessive sweep of his hands over her bare skin. He touched her as if he were imprinting himself on her very bones, searing away any lingering ghosts.

There was only this – him and her.

And all the half-healed wounds between them.

# 22

Caroline awoke to the haunting strains of piano music drifting down the hallway. The melody washed over her, melancholy and aching, speaking of old griefs and memories worn thin by time.

Julian's music.

Caroline slipped from the bed and donned her silk wrapper. She made her way through the shadowed corridors, following the music towards its source. The notes hung suspended around her, strands of gossamer that clung and pulled.

What memories haunted him tonight? The same ones that haunted her days, she suspected. Whispers and echoes that never entirely faded.

Grace.

Tristan.

The wounds they had carved into each other with their silence.

At last, she came to the music room. Julian sat with his back to the door, shoulders hunched over the piano keys. Moonlight filtering through the tall windows glinted off the black waves of his hair. He seemed cast in shades of silver and grey, softened at the edges. The austere duke stripped away to reveal the man beneath.

Here was the brooding boy who had first caught her attention so many years ago in his father's gardens. Before he had slipped from her grasp like smoke, a half-remembered dream.

He did not turn or otherwise acknowledge her presence. The song flowed on, and Caroline closed her eyes against the hollow ache of it. She thought perhaps she would be content to stand there and let the notes crash and break over her like waves. Let it scour their sharp edges until they were as smooth as sea glass.

Caroline watched his elegant hands move across the ivory keys. Long fingers coaxing forth strands of melancholy sound, spinning them into something achingly sweet. She thought of where those hands had touched her skin only hours before, mapping her with reverence. The memories echoed through each mournful note.

She could see Julian's fingers tremble. His knuckles stood out in sharp relief, skin pulled taut over bone. The veins on the backs of his hands flexed with each note, delicate traceries that captivated her. He had musician's hands. Graceful and strong. Hands that knew every inch of her.

Without turning, Julian asked, "Did I wake you?" His playing never faltered despite the distraction.

"I don't mind." She drew closer, bare feet soundless on the carpet. "It's beautiful."

And it was. Achingly so.

A noncommittal grunt. "My technique is rusty."

"It sounds flawless to me."

As his fingers dropped from the keys, silence swelled to fill the void. Still, Julian did not turn.

"You're thinking very loudly over there," Caroline said gently. "What's troubling you? Is it Richard?"

"It's nothing." He did not stir from his perch. "Just an old piece I was trying to remember."

"It sounded like a lament." And like a love song for something lost. For apologies left unspoken.

Another broken chord, almost a sigh. "I wrote it for Tristan and Grace." His voice dropped. "And for you. After."

*After*. A single word encompassing all the sprawling years. Since the ground crumbled beneath their feet. Since the slow undoing.

Since the strangers they had become.

Grief pierced Caroline once more, sharp and unexpected. She had thought herself inured, calloused from years of sorrow worn smooth. But the wound gaped as fresh as ever – bloodless yet still so quick to sting.

She thought of eight years wasted, eight years they could never regain. A wall of regret had risen brick by brick until she could scarcely see him on the other side. Until all that remained were two hollowed-out people circling in orbit, neither daring to draw too near.

She fought to keep her voice steady. "Play me the rest. I want to hear it."

Silence swelled around them, deep as the darkness between stars. For a heartbeat, she thought he meant to refuse.

But then he shifted on the stool in silent acquiescence – an invitation for her to join him.

Caroline crossed the floor, silk slipping softly at her legs. The old wood creaked faintly beneath her as she settled at the piano beside her husband. His fingers returned to the keys.

The melody moved through her, low and soft, then climbing, pleading. Speaking of grief, chances lost, chances still waiting, just out of reach. It crested inside her chest, receded like the tide, and then swelled again. A lament to love smothered too soon.

Unable to stop herself, she reached out and let her hand hover just above his thigh. *Shall I touch you? Comfort you?*

Before doubt could take hold, Caroline pressed her palm to his leg.

The notes fractured, faltered. Julian's focus slipped from the keys as her hand stayed in place, trembling with possibilities. With words left unspoken and memories beaten smooth. She held her breath, her heart crashing against her ribs. Waited for him to pull away, to slip back behind cold marble. Behind locked doors and hollow vows.

But Julian remained still beneath her touch. Slowly, by increments, the tension leached from his body. Only once he had mastered himself did the melody resume, low and sweet. His fingers moved across the piano keys, coaxing forth notes like strands of glass, fragile and thin. They cut into her soul, deeper with every repetition.

*Flay me open*, she thought. *Lay my sins bare*.

As the final notes faded, they sat in silence. He did not pull away. Did not retreat, as he had done for so long. And neither did she. The space between them rang hollow with all their unspoken truths.

His fingers curled into fists on his thighs, knuckles sharp beneath the skin. At last, Julian turned towards her. Someone haunted and far removed from the boy with ink-smudged fingers who had shared secret smiles with her as they passed notes across a crowded ballroom lifetimes ago.

"Come here, duchess," he said softly.

Reaching out, he drew the silk robe down her shoulders. It slithered to the floor between them, baring more of her shivering skin to the shadows. To him.

"I want to see you. All of you." His breath gusted hot against the shell of her ear.

Caroline did not pull away. Did not move at all save for the agitated rise and fall of her chest. She held still, pulse thundering, as Julian's gaze moved over her. His hands followed in slow, burning trails, fingertips skating up her thighs. They traced her hips, her waist, skimmed the undersides of her breasts with reverent restraint. Every hollow and ridge was mapped beneath those elegant hands. Following the paths charted into muscle and memory.

Caroline shifted to straddle him. Even through the thin linen of his trousers, she felt him harden against her as the slick heat of her core settled against his cock. The exquisite pressure made her dizzy, nerves singing as she slid over that thick hardness.

Julian's fingers constricted on her hips, a broken noise tearing from his throat. For endless moments, they remained suspended, frozen in torturous possibility, breaths crashing loudly between them.

Tilting her face up, she ghosted her parted lips along his frantic pulse. Felt it leap beneath her teeth when she whispered, "I've never been with anyone else. Just you."

A secret spilled to soothe old wounds. Somehow, to stitch their tattered edges back together.

His arms tightened. "Not even Grey?"

"No." Her lips moved against his skin. "I couldn't bring myself to let Richard touch me. I felt… nothing for anyone after you. Just empty inside. And that made me hate you more."

Julian tensed, but his arms stayed locked around her. She inhaled slowly, the air burning in her lungs.

"So I asked Richard if I could paint him instead. If I couldn't give myself to someone new, I wanted my art back. To replace the memories of you." Silence rang out, hollow as a rotted tree. "And if you saw my paintings, I wanted you to hurt the way I did. God, Julian, I hurt so much I barely knew myself."

It was so loud, a howling in her chest.

"Shhh." He stroked her hair. "It's all right." The words breathed warmth across her scalp, her temple. "I know, sweetheart."

"You asked me to forgive you eight years ago," she whispered. "But I never asked you to forgive me back." Her lungs ached. "I'm sorry, Julian. For everything I said to you."

He stilled. In the silence, she leaned in and brushed her mouth to his in the softest plea. When he did not retreat, she kissed him again, firmer. Harder. Parted his lips beneath her own and tasted smoke and brandy and the velvet slide of his tongue stroking hers.

He kissed her deeply then. With bruising force, as if he could scour away the bitter years, the regret. Kissed her until she knew nothing but this. Until the jagged pieces between them melted and blurred into something smooth. Something that did not draw blood with every caress.

"There's nothing to forgive," he told her.

She kissed him again. He had always felt like coming home. Her body remembered, even after all this time – like their own language, wordless and wild.

Julian's mouth slanted over hers again and again until she was dizzy and desperate for him. His hands slid down to grip her hips, then lower still to cup her backside almost roughly.

She rocked against him. Craving more. Needing him inside her, claiming every part that was his. She started to reach down, to free the hard length of him straining beneath the trousers. Take him in hand—

But Julian tore his mouth away with a curse. Grasping her tight, he stilled her movements. They stayed locked together, bodies trembling with need, a thin sheen of sweat blooming across heated skin.

"Not here," he rasped.

With infinite care, he eased Caroline back, then lifted her into his arms. He carried her from the music room down the darkened corridors to the bedchamber. He lay her down on the bed – this bed she had too often found cold and lonely without him, an elegant tomb.

She watched his silhouette as he removed his clothes, each layer peeling away as if he were stripping barriers between them. Then Julian followed her down into softness, weight braced on rigid arms. His gaze searched her face, gleaming even in the darkness. Then his mouth found her throat, her collarbone. His tongue teased her nipple before sucking firmly, wringing a sharp gasp from her.

When his lips trailed even lower, tongue dipping briefly into her navel, a shattered moan tore from her.

"Please—" Her fingers twisted in his hair, urging him lower still.

Julian's hands gripped her knees, easing her thighs apart. Their gazes locked, his eyes quicksilver in shadow.

Then his mouth descended to her aching core. Caroline's back bowed at the first stroke of his tongue. He devoured her as she writhed, one strong arm pinning her hips in place. He slid two fingers deep inside her, stroking tight nerves only he had ever touched. Pressure coiled at the base of her spine, tighter with every thrust. She rocked into his mouth, his fingers, chasing the precipice.

But just before she tumbled over the edge, Julian withdrew. Leaving her empty, throbbing. She barely had time to drag in a protesting gasp before he was above her, pressing her thighs wide. Poised at her entrance, the hard length of his cock nudging her.

Slowly, by increments, Julian sank into her. They froze, gazes locked, as her body stretched and yielded around him. Then Caroline dragged her palms down the sweat-slick plane of his back, feeling the ridges of his muscles, every dip and valley. Tracing the maps carved into his skin.

"I want you to stay," she breathed, lips shaping the plea against his parted mouth. "Don't go back to your townhouse after your tenant leaves. Don't board your ship to Italy. Stay here."

*With me.*

He kissed her, long and slow. When he pulled back, his words were warm across her cheek. "Shall I live here now, my duchess?"

"Yes. With me." She twined her arms around his shoulders, urging him deeper with her hips.

Julian's restraint shattered. He claimed her with powerful thrusts that stole her breath, spoke of possession and need.

*Mine*, each thrust seemed to say.

*Yours*, her body answered back.

*Ours.*

The force of his claim pushed her up the bed into the pillows. Caroline arched into each devastating plunge, craving more.

Needing him deeper. Harder. Needing him to carve himself into her bones, her blood.

"I love you," he whispered.

He crushed her lips beneath his just as his fingers slipped between her thighs, working her sensitised flesh in tight circles. Euphoria crashed through her, every nerve ending sparking white hot. Seconds later, Julian went rigid above her with a rough curse, finding his own release.

Afterwards, they collapsed together in a tangle of limp, sweat-slick limbs. Julian gathered Caroline against him, her back against his chest.

She lay awake long after his breaths deepened into sleep. Focused on the steady thrum of his heart, willing the minutes to slow.

# 23

The early morning light did little to penetrate the heavy mist that clung to the London streets. Julian stared out of his study window, hands clasped behind his back. Restlessness clawed beneath his skin, fraying what remained of his control.

*I've never been with anyone else – just you.*

God, but Caroline's whispered confession the night before had wrecked him. How long had he stared at her paintings from afar and imagined her finding pleasure in another man's arms? Thought that if he saw her again, he would find their marks etched into her flesh?

But she had stayed his, waiting among the ruins they had made. After everything they'd endured. Everything he'd done.

Emotions strained against the ruthless composure he wore like armour. He'd come too close to losing her again, and there were still threats lurking. He wouldn't – couldn't – risk Caroline's safety. Not when they'd only just begun piecing their broken marriage back together.

A quiet rap on the door jolted Julian to the present. His butler glided into the study. "Mr Wentworth is here to see you, Your Grace. Shall I show him in?"

Julian gave a curt nod, reining in his unruly thoughts and donning the remote mask of the Duke of Hastings once more.

A moment later, Wentworth strode in with a leather satchel beneath one arm, his features etched deep with hollows that had not been there the day before. Dark circles ringed his eyes – proof of little sleep.

"Apologies for the early intrusion," Wentworth said in greeting. He looked like a man on the ragged edge of exhaustion and temper. "You're looking better than you were at Charing Cross."

"I should hope so." An understatement, considering Julian had nearly had his brains splattered across the train platform.

Wentworth held up a slip of paper between his fingers. "This arrived an hour ago by private courier. Addressed to you, not even coded. A personal bloody love note addressed to you from our bomber." He slapped it down on Julian's desk. "The bastard was watching us at Charing Cross, and now he knows the Duke of Hastings decoded his deranged letters. Apparently, you've impressed him."

Julian tensed. If Edgar Kellerman was sending these vile missives, the man now knew he and Caroline had attended that sham investment party under false pretences.

"Anything else?" he asked. "Beyond gloating at evading capture, I mean?"

"Says he looks forward to your next meeting." Wentworth's jaw hardened. "The implications being he has plans involving you."

"Wonderful," Julian said dryly. "I'd ask if you want tea, but I suspect a brandy might be in order."

"Double. I've been awake for thirty-six hours questioning our man from the tracks."

Julian poured him two fingers of brandy, and Wentworth took a bracing gulp. Clearly, they were both barely clinging to civility today.

He glanced at the abraded and bloody knuckles Wentworth hadn't even attempted to hide. "I see interrogation went about as well as expected. Did he tell you anything?"

They were interrupted by a creak outside the study. Familiar footsteps padded closer before Caroline appeared in the doorway. His duchess wore a pretty muslin day dress, her blonde hair falling around her shoulders in messy waves that spoke of recent activities best kept private. She practically radiated sensual contentment, the subtle glow on her skin making it impossible to look away. He knew that beneath the neck of that dress, he'd left marks all over her body.

*Get it together, man. Wentworth's still in the bloody room.*

"I hope I'm not intruding." Caroline's voice emerged rough around the edges, smoke and silk that stroked over his skin. "The maid said we had an unexpected guest."

Wentworth stood from his chair, inclining his head in polite greeting. "Good morning, duchess." He took her hand and kissed the air over her knuckles. "Forgive the early intrusion."

"How kind of you to say," she said. "But I rather suspect you didn't come calling at this hour for pleasantries."

Amusement flickered over Wentworth's features. "I'm afraid not." He made no move to speak.

Julian sat back in his chair. "I feel obliged to remind you that without my wife's invaluable assistance, you would have more dead aristocrats on your hands and no one in custody. So if you've come to talk business, say it in front of her."

Wentworth returned to the wing chair, every line of his body betraying bone-deep exhaustion beneath the veneer of crisp efficiency. "Duly noted. My apologies, duchess. It's not personal. I'm afraid we've had another development related to the train station incident that requires discreet handling."

"I see." Caroline crossed the room and perched on the arm of Julian's chair. He had to lock every muscle to keep from tugging her onto his lap. "Must be imperative if you're here before breakfast."

"The bomber made contact expressing… let's call it admiration of Hastings' skills decrypting his codes at the train station."

"How flattering," Caroline said. "Murderous villains everywhere salute my husband's intellect. Because, of course, he solved the missive all on his own, with no help whatsoever."

Wentworth smiled at that. "Well, now he thinks the Duke of Hastings has accepted the gauntlet thrown down."

Julian couldn't stop himself from brushing his thumb over the back of Caroline's hand in a tender caress. "The interrogation, Wentworth."

"Got him to admit the identity of the man who hired him before he choked on his own blood. Beg pardon, duchess." Wentworth flashed Caroline a wry smile before continuing. "He described the man who hired him as 'a tall gent with dark hair and moustache, dressed in fine broadcloth and money to burn.' Paid him three hundred quid up front to sabotage the train. Used the name William Bell." Wentworth leaned forward, keen eyes fixed on Julian. "I know that look, Hastings. What are you keeping from me?"

Julian's jaw tightened. "I don't believe William Bell is real. You should investigate Edgar Kellerman."

The other man's expression remained neutral, but Julian glimpsed the sharpening of interest in his gaze. "The financier hosting lavish parties all over town? Popular fellow these days. What makes you suspect him?"

"A hunch. I've observed some inconsistencies that don't sit well with me."

The spymaster tapped out a rhythm against his chair. "A hunch and inconsistencies hardly constitute evidence worthy of the Queen's Bench, duke."

Julian forced himself to take a slow, steadying breath. "Then humour me. Discreetly look into his affairs here in London. I'm not asking you to arrest the man outright. Just apply that relentless tenacity of yours."

"I'll consider it." Wentworth looked up at Caroline. "Duchess, your input?" He sipped his brandy, watching her with interest.

"Hastings and I attended one of Mr Kellerman's parties, and it struck me that if an outsider wanted access to the movements of the *ton*, being a financier is the perfect disguise. Not to mention the gossip he'd overhear. The ladies mentioned he'd appeared in society just last year after some time abroad. No one knows anything about his origins."

"Cleverly reasoned," Wentworth said with an approving nod.

"He wears a signet ring," Julian said, plucking the drawing out of a drawer. He passed it to Wentworth. "Does that motif strike you as familiar?"

Wentworth examined the image. "This is incomplete?"

"I didn't get the best look at it."

"It's familiar," Wentworth said. "You think Edgar Kellerman is another alias, like William Bell?"

"Yes," Julian said. "Look into the backgrounds of the noblemen targeted so far and see if they have any unusual connections in common."

Wentworth gave a curt nod. "As you say. I'll make some quiet inquiries." With a hint of wryness, he added, "My talents do extend beyond shooting and skull cracking, believe it or not. On occasion." He cleared his throat. "But I've another matter to discuss. You both should brace for rather intense public scrutiny in the coming days. Word came this morning that Her Majesty wishes to honour the pair of you for services after the theatre bombing. You ought to receive an invitation today."

"You can't be serious," Julian bit out.

"Oh, she's quite adamant. The queen loves a dramatic tale of courage and sacrifice." Wentworth gave an apologetic grimace. "Saving your duchess from the blast, tending the wounded, tracking down the culprit – it has all the makings of high drama."

Julian and Caroline exchanged a look. The gossipmongers at the theatre had been bad enough, but a royal ball was the equivalent of a wolf's den – yet refusing the invitation was unthinkable. No matter how graciously worded, the queen's requests were commands to be obeyed.

"Is that wise?" Caroline asked Wentworth. "After the bombing?"

The spymaster took another swallow of brandy. "No. But if you've a mind to tell Her Majesty so, I wish you the very best of luck. But it might be wise if you both pretended to go on as normal so Kellerman doesn't catch the scent."

"We'll go," Julian said with a sigh.

He escorted Wentworth out shortly after, then prowled back to the study doorway, where Caroline waited. Taking in his coiled frame as if she could read his thoughts.

Perhaps she could.

Julian tangled his hands into her hair, pressing his mouth to hers in a bruising kiss. She moaned into his lips, "Are you worried about—"

"Not now." His voice was rough as he backed her against his desk.

Caroline gasped as the edge of the desk dug into her lower back. "But—"

He turned to nuzzle her cheek, breathing in her familiar scent. "On the desk, duchess. I don't want to think about anything except you right now."

# 24

A fortnight later, Julian tugged at his cravat, the starched linen like a noose around his throat. He cast another glance out of the carriage window as their coach rumbled through the rain-washed streets towards Buckingham Palace.

Apprehension roiled in his gut. He'd visited Edgar Kellerman's offices just that morning, only to find the place shut up tight as a nunnery. Not a whisper or scrap of evidence remained. And still no word from Wentworth.

Somewhere out there, a killer plotted his next move while Julian prepared to play the fawning sycophant beneath the chandeliers.

*Bloody fantastic. Why not add disembowelment to round out the festivities?*

Beside him, Caroline drew a muted, trembling breath. To the outside world, the Duchess of Hastings presented the picture of polished nobility. But Julian glimpsed the cracks in her genteel façade – the faint tremor in her gloved fingers, the crease of worry between her brows.

He reached over to cover her restless hands with his own. "Just two hours of meaningless pleasantries at most. Smile, greet the queen, have some wine. The usual nonsense."

"While the most powerful woman in the country stares us

down like a governess ready to rap our knuckles if we misbehave," Caroline said.

Despite the circumstances, Julian's lips twitched. "Think of Her Majesty in her nightdress. It always humanises the grandeur."

Caroline cast him an arch look, though he noted some of the tension around her eyes had smoothed away. "You want me to imagine our queen in her undergarments?"

He lifted a shoulder in a shrug, keeping his tone light. "She's still just a woman. Puts her skirts on one leg at a time like any other lady. But say the word, and I'll whisk you behind a potted palm to catch your breath."

Her darting glance held a spectre of panic. "If anyone asks about the bombing—"

"Lie through your teeth."

"Truly?"

"Absolutely. Tell them you carried me over the rubble in your dainty arms after I swooned from manly vapours."

She cut him a glare. "They thought *I* was the one who fainted, duke."

"Then I'll tell everyone you saved a basket of kittens," he replied.

"Make it a dozen orphans, three puppies, the Crown Jewels, *and* a basket of kittens," she added. "Might as well make it good."

"That's my audacious girl," Julian said, kissing her knuckles.

The line of her shoulders eased just a fraction beneath his lingering touch. She was still too tense and braced for disaster – but they would get through this farce with fortitude and wine. Plenty of wine. He just needed to keep her smiling.

A liveried footman opened the door as the carriage drew up outside the palace. Raindrops speckled the white marble stairs. As Julian handed Caroline down, voices and raucous laughter bled from the palace's illuminated façade. The muted strains of the orchestra provided a counterpoint to the swelling din.

Inside, the grand reception hall gleamed, polished to a high shine. Liveried footmen stood posted along the red carpet runner that guided guests towards the ballroom's vaulted splendour. The mingled perfume of rare hothouse blooms filled the air beneath the blaze of a hundred chandeliers, turning the mirrored walls into dazzling facets of light.

They joined the elegant queue of guests waiting to be announced. Despite the exaggerated deference, curiosity burned behind the polite smiles turned their way. Julian clenched his jaw as yet another gawking matron eyed Caroline's stomach with interest.

"Why do they keep staring at my midsection as if they expect a baby to pop out and do a jig?" Caroline asked.

"Looking for proof we've produced an heir in weeks, I suspect," Julian said in irritation. "Would you like me to scare them off?"

"I think we're meant to be the toast of the *ton* tonight, not a spectacle." She fidgeted with her gloves. "Really, it's odious."

"Just remember, picture their undergarments."

She sputtered a laugh. "*Julian*."

"That dowager over there, for example." He tilted his head discreetly towards a jewelled matron. "Go on, give it a try. Or picture her stark naked. That ought to help."

"Thank you," she said dryly. "Now that image will be seared into my memory for all eternity."

"You're welcome, duchess."

Any response she might have made was lost as the announcer's voice rang out, "Presenting His Grace, the Duke of Hastings, and Her Grace, the Duchess of Hastings!"

Drawing a bracing breath, Caroline tucked her hand into the crook of his elbow. Together, they moved into the crowded ballroom. Hundreds of eyes turned their way, raking over them in frank assessment. The whispered speculation began.

*"... does she look peaked to you?"*

*"I heard she fainted dead away at the theatre..."*

*"... had to be carried from the wreckage."*

On and on. No detail escaped their notice. The hungry eyes

assessing Caroline with such vicious interest made Julian want to don the coldest, most ruthless ducal mask.

He squeezed Caroline's trembling hand. "Steady," he murmured. "We've braved far worse."

As they moved through the sea of jewelled silks, the crowds parted before them. Polite smiles now graced the faces of those who had just been whispering behind their fans seconds earlier. Julian inclined his head in a show of courtesy.

At last, they approached the throne on the dais at the far end of the ballroom. Queen Victoria watched them with sharp interest, taking their measure.

As one, Julian and Caroline sank into deep bows before the queen. "Your Majesty," Julian said. "Thank you for this honour."

The queen tilted her head in acknowledgement. "I wish to convey my appreciation for your heroic actions. You showed great bravery in the aftermath of that dreadful attack, duke. And, duchess – how valiant of Hastings to rescue you, my dear."

At his side, Caroline's fingers clamped around his wrist with the tenacity of a barnacle. He could practically hear her teeth grinding.

"Yes, quite," Caroline said.

Julian drew himself up straight. "Merely doing our duty, ma'am."

Beside him, Caroline muttered through clenched teeth, "I need to take cover behind a potted plant. Now."

Julian's mouth twitched.

After suffering through a few more agonising pleasantries, the queen nodded in dismissal. Julian seized Caroline's arm and hustled her away before she combusted on the spot.

As they retreated, Julian's gaze snagged on a familiar figure lurking in one of the shadowed alcoves. Mattias Wentworth lifted his glass in a subtle salute, all polished congeniality stripped from his features, leaving only icy purpose. Unease slithered down Julian's spine.

"Come with me," Julian murmured to Caroline. He wanted to confer with Wentworth beyond the reach of curious ears.

"Talk," Julian bit out without preamble. He kept his voice soft. Those nearby didn't need to overhear. "What news?"

Wentworth looked like hell. Jaw unshaven, eyes bloodshot and bruised. "Gone to ground. Slithered right out of our grasp, the slippery fuck."

Julian's hands jerked with the urge to crush something. Preferably Edgar Kellerman's smug face. "How the devil did he evade you?"

"Wasn't through lack of trying on my end." Wentworth slugged back more brandy. "I looked into him, and your instincts were right. Edgar Kellerman didn't exist before his sudden appearance in society. I couldn't prove the murders, but I had enough evidence to pin him on swindling aristocrats. When the lads and I went for the arrest, he was gone. Nothing disturbed or ransacked, didn't leave in a hurry. Appears he simply walked out the front door whistling a merry tune. Which means the bastard caught wind of surveillance somehow. He left because he wanted to leave."

Julian fought to keep his snarl of frustration leashed behind his teeth. This had disaster bleeding all over it.

He glanced around the glittering ballroom. The graceful orchestral strains seemed to mock him. How many here tonight might have their names on some aristocratic hit list?

"He can't have gone far," Julian said, knowing the reassurance rang hollow. "Not without funds. Arrangements."

"Agreed. I have agents scouring every station and port," Wentworth said. "We'll find him."

Out of the corner of his eye, Julian noticed Lady Amesbury drifting closer, shamelessly attempting to eavesdrop. He gave her a cold glare, and she darted away.

"We'll speak later in a more private setting," Julian said.

"You'll hear from me soon." Wentworth finished off his brandy in one long swallow. "And Hastings – watch your back. You're a target now, too."

Then he slipped into the crowd of aristocrats.

# 25

The opening notes of a waltz swept through the ballroom. Caroline resisted the urge to adjust her gloves or fiddle with the diamond drops dangling from her ears. Instead, she donned the mask she'd perfected – the consummate duchess. Poised. Controlled. A portrait of calm on the surface.

"Shall we have a dance, duchess?" Julian murmured at her side. He held out one gloved hand.

*Just one dance. You can endure one dance*, Caroline told herself, slipping her hand into his.

He pulled her close, and the ballroom and all its glittering occupants faded away as they began to dance. The whispers and assessing glances melted into insignificance until nothing remained but the two of them, suspended in their own private orbit.

Julian led them flawlessly through steps ingrained in muscle memory, so attuned to the changes in Caroline's body – the hitch in her breath, the tension singing through her limbs. Her thoughts drifted back through the years to another dance beneath endless blue skies. Just a wild, barefoot girl dancing with a boy in the meadows. No titles, no expectations, only possibilities.

She risked a glance upward, taking in his remote patrician

features and pale eyes. To the rest of the ballroom, he wore his distant mask, the consummate duke – cold and untouchable.

But not to her. Never to her.

"You dance as flawlessly as I remember," she managed.

His voice was smoke against her skin. "As do you. Just the same as always."

A wistful smile teased her lips. "That's not true, and you know it. I was all tangled feet and clammy palms back then. I couldn't stop stepping on your poor toes."

"Understandable, given your tendency to dance barefoot through meadows. All that wild spinning can't have helped matters."

The shared memory kindled a spark of warmth. She pictured his hands at her waist beneath sprawling oak branches, spinning faster and faster until they tumbled breathlessly into the grass. Her body tingled everywhere they touched. She had ached for more even then, before she understood this clawing need.

So many possibilities lived in every touch since he'd walked back into her life weeks ago. When he worshipped her body until she came undone beneath his hands.

She never wanted that to end.

"Where did your thoughts wander off to just now?" His voice pulled her back to the present. When she stayed mute, he made a rough sound of understanding. "Not so very proper thoughts, then. Well, my imagination is vivid. Care to share?"

Caroline fixed her gaze at a point beyond his shoulder, watching the other couples twirl by. "Admiring the architectural details. The crown moulding is just exquisite."

His low laughter teased her. "You're a dreadful liar, Linnie. I see you blushing and want to hear every improper thought you've ever had."

Whispers surrounded them at the unfamiliar sound of the duke laughing. "You're causing quite the scandal," she murmured. "What will they think, seeing the Duke of Hastings laugh?"

The possessive hand at her back urged her closer as they moved in effortless synchronicity. "I suspect they'll think I'm besotted with my wife," Julian said. "And they wouldn't be wrong."

The confession shattered the last remnants of her composure. Without thinking, she tipped her face up to his.

His arm tightened almost painfully around her waist. Her poise was burning away, reduced to a pounding heart and visceral need. She stared into familiar eyes gone hungry, feral. On the razored edge of losing control. That same madness fraying the ends of her own restraint.

"Careful," he warned, voice rough. "Any closer, and I won't be able to resist kissing you senseless in front of all these fine people. Think of the scandal we'd inspire. Her Majesty may banish us from polite society for depravity."

Caroline sucked in an unsteady breath, drunk on his nearness. She wanted nothing more than to close those last few inches between them. "Then let's finish this dance and go home."

The answering flare in his gaze promised retribution. "Can't leave before the queen. Proper protocol. But at home, I fully intend to punish you for tempting me so shamelessly."

Molten heat pooled low and aching between her thighs at the promise in those words. She wanted him wild, wanted that iron-clad control stripped away. Again and again, until thought fractured.

Reckless, she leaned in. "However will you discipline me for my depraved behaviour?"

Something dangerous sparked in Julian's face. "When we get home, you're to walk straight to my study and bend over my desk. Spread your legs and await your punishment." Julian's heavy-lidded stare drifted lazily down the length of her body before returning to hers, full of dark vows. "Then I'll rip that gown off and mark you up until every inch is claimed as mine."

"You're a wicked man, Hastings."

Now Julian smiled, and she understood why he never did

so in polite company – it was devastating. Full of promise and sinful pleasures in the darkness. Around them, feminine gasps and whispers broke out.

"My duchess," he purred against her ear, "I can't wait to show you how wicked I can be."

Anticipation shivered down her spine. She could feel his predatory focus as the waltz finally ended and he guided them from the dance floor. Caroline was acutely aware of Julian's warmth, their shoulders brushing intimately as they walked.

A flash of movement in the corner of her eye made her falter. There, across the glittering ballroom – a familiar face.

Edgar Kellerman.

His eyes fixed on Julian. And clutched in his hand as he stepped from behind a pillar was—

"Julian!" She shoved him out of the way.

For a breath, the opulent ballroom froze.

Then, the deafening crack of the gunshot splintered the air, and pandemonium erupted. Screams and shouts echoed as ladies grasped their escorts in panic. Men bellowed in alarm, heads turning to locate the threat.

In the chaos, Caroline's ears rang. She looked down slowly to see crimson spreading across the emerald silk of her gown. When she lifted her hand, it came away slick with blood. Some distant part of her registered the sting of pain, but deeper than that, underneath, was an icy numbness circulating through her limbs. Her legs folded, dress pooling on the polished floor.

Strong hands caught her before she hit the ground. "Linnie? Oh, God." Julian's face blurred above hers as he applied pressure to the wound. "Linnie," he choked out.

His voice sounded muffled as though coming from underwater. Caroline tried to respond, but all that emerged was a wet choking sound. She could taste iron on her tongue.

As the ringing in her ears faded, she could just make out Julian's commanding shouts. Then, the darkness finally claimed her.

# 26

The cacophony of screams rang in Julian's ears, his focus narrowed to the growing crimson stain spreading across Caroline's emerald gown. His hand pressed to the wound.

"Linnie." His voice scraped raw and broken from his throat as he searched her ashen face. "Someone fetch a doctor!"

Around him, chaos reigned. Voices raised in panicked cacophony – useless, all of them. Milling sheep with no capacity to help.

Julian's focus homed in on the footman slipping away along the perimeter. Livery granting him anonymity amid the tumult as he ducked through the servants' entrance to escape.

Edgar Kellerman.

Rage ignited in Julian's gut, white-hot. Kellerman had hidden himself among the staff, posing as a harmless attendant until he had a clear shot.

*Me. This is meant for me.*

He tracked movement along the perimeter – Wentworth and two men breaking into pursuit of the hidden assassin. But Julian couldn't stay to witness the hunt, not when Caroline was slipping further away.

Her fading heartbeat fluttered beneath his palm, rapid as

hummingbird wings. Each frantic beat pushed more blood through his fingers.

So he gathered her against his chest and began carving a path through the melee. The brocaded silks and embroidered satins blurred around Julian as he moved, the world reduced to the fragile weight in his arms. He cradled her closer.

When one onlooker stretched out a tentative hand as though to touch Caroline's hair, Julian bared his teeth in a feral warning. He was willing – no, *eager* – to kill anyone who so much as looked at her right now.

She was his.

"Bring the carriage," Julian snapped at a waiting footman. "Then find a surgeon. Now. I don't care what it takes."

The footman gave a jerky nod. "Right away, Your Grace."

After an eternity, the carriage arrived in a splash of mud. Julian slid inside, clutching Caroline tight in his lap. He cradled her against his chest, willing her to take just one more laboured breath.

The alternative was a yawning void threatening to swallow him whole.

Unthinkable.

As the carriage jolted forward, Julian grasped her limp hand between his. Her delicate fingers remained slack and cool within his hold. He chafed the chilled skin, trying to rub warmth back into her.

"You'll be all right, sweetheart," he rasped. "Just stay with me."

Only the creak of leather and rattle of wheels answered him. No hitched breath or twitch of her fingers. Caroline remained motionless in his arms, blood dripping onto the carriage floor.

Julian couldn't tear his eyes from her face – kept tracing the pale curves and elegant lines over and over, searing them into memory. Desperate to catch any faint flutter of her lashes, any hitched breath.

When the coach rolled to a halt before Stafford House, Julian gathered her into his arms and staggered up the front steps through the downpour. The staff stood waiting in the marble hall, features pale and stricken at the sight of their mistress.

Without a word, Julian carried Caroline down the shadowed corridor to her bedchamber – their bedchamber. The one they had only just begun sharing again after so many years apart.

He laid her on the pristine bedding. Arranged the pillows beneath her head as though she were sleeping. As though she might open her eyes at any moment.

Only then, in the quiet stillness of the room, did the stark reality crash down with crushing force.

Caroline was dying.

Julian's chest constricted, ragged breaths too loud in the quiet room. His vision wavered as he stared down at her, eyes burning.

He'd just held her in his arms an hour ago as they danced. Playful. Vibrant. Whispering things that left him aching with wanting.

Now she was still. Fading by the second.

When footsteps sounded in the hall, Julian's head jerked up.

The surgeon entered, leather satchel in hand. "Your Grace. Let me see what I can do for her."

He assessed Caroline briskly, easing her blood-soaked gown aside to study the wound. Julian observed from the corner, tension threading through every rigid line of his frame.

After long minutes, the surgeon stepped back. "The ball passed clean through her side. She's lost a significant amount of blood."

Julian dragged a shaking hand over his face. Forced himself to rasp the question that might shatter him. "What are her chances?"

"She wasn't hit anywhere vital, but she'll need to fight off infection." He shook his head. "We must worry about the fever more than the damage the bullet did. I'll give you what you need to keep her comfortable."

Julian nodded, incapable of speaking around the jagged shards lodged in his throat. He resumed his vigil at Caroline's bedside. The surgeon took his leave with murmured condolences. Alone again amid the swelling silence and shadows. Nothing left to do but wait. And pray.

Soft footsteps in the doorway roused him from his grim thoughts. Caroline's maid bobbed a quick curtsy, face wan.

"Begging your pardon, Your Grace. But Mr Wentworth is asking for you downstairs."

Leaving Caroline's side tore something vital from Julian's chest. But he forced himself to follow the maid to the ground floor drawing room.

Wentworth paced before the fire, features etched with grim lines.

"Tell me you have him," Julian said as he strode in. "Tell me you caught the bastard."

Wentworth's jaw clenched. "He had a bomb waiting outside the palace. My men had to choose between pursuing him or saving innocent lives."

Blinding rage roared through Julian's veins. His hands flexed with the urge to wrap around Kellerman's throat and squeeze. "So you let him get away. He's out there somewhere while my wife – *my fucking wife*, Wentworth – is upstairs dying from a bullet meant for me."

Wentworth's expression wavered. "Her prognosis?"

"Too soon to tell." Julian sucked in a raw breath, grappling for some semblance of control before his fury shattered him. "But if she dies, I'll paint the city with that bastard's guts. Understand me?"

Wentworth scrubbed a hand over his face. Began wearing out the rug again beneath his boots. "I'll find him, duke. Her Majesty has every resource looking. We'll scour London brick by brick if we must."

"See that you do. In the meantime, I'm returning to my wife's side. Send word immediately if you have news."

"Of course. I hope your wife pulls through, Hastings."

Back upstairs, Julian braced himself before entering the bedchamber. He focused on the figure in the bed, still motionless amid the pillows, her blonde hair spilling across the linen. Still balanced on the knife's edge.

Crossing to the bed, Julian sank into the chair beside her. Gently took her hand between both of his. He clung to the solidity, the anchor keeping his fraying thoughts from slipping their moorings.

"Linnie." Her name scraped raw and jagged from his throat. He traced the delicate blue veins beneath her translucent skin, felt her faint pulse. "I love you."

Julian lifted Caroline's hand and pressed his lips to her knuckles. Inhaled the scent of her. This hand he'd held countless times, from barefoot in sunny meadows to gilded ballrooms. These beautiful fingers that drew him. That touched him.

He wanted her to wake up and touch him again.

*Please. One more breath. And then another.*

"Come on, sweetheart," he whispered into her palm. "Just open your eyes."

Julian traced the sharp angle of her cheekbone, then the graceful bow of her lower lip. Soft. Still warm. Lips he ached to kiss again.

*Wake up.*

But she remained motionless amid the pillows. The only sound was her shallow breaths, growing fainter.

# 27

Julian had lost track of the hours and days, keeping grim vigil at Caroline's bedside.

She burned. The fever ravaged her body, leaving her wrung out and restless beneath the linens. Her skin was dry beneath his hand as he bathed her flushed cheeks with cool water.

When the dreams tormented her, Julian administered a few drops of laudanum, hoping to ease her torment. But the tonic only pulled her deeper into delirium, her lips moving as she whispered to ghosts.

Even in the throes of fever, he refused to relinquish her hand, his thumbs tracing the veins and delicate knuckles. Imprinting the precious topography to memory.

How often had he traced that elegant sweep of brow and cheekbone? His fingertips knew her features better than his own. Every nuance was inked into his bones, imprinted on his soul.

When they were young, he'd spent hours studying her as she sketched his nude form. Always more brazen with charcoal in hand, her tongue caught between her teeth in endearing concentration. Blushing the entire time. And later, after they married, he had mapped her in return – each freckle and contour – with hands and lips.

Those days were stained by the years of bitter silence that

followed. But they had rediscovered tenderness amid the wreckage left by grief and loss.

Until Kellerman's bullet had torn through her flesh, ripping that progress to shreds.

And now Julian watched her fight for each shallow breath. His days had distilled to the routine of wiping her brow, administering drops of tonic, begging her to hold on.

The hours crawled by as the mantelpiece clock marked their sluggish passage. One chime. Two. Five.

As dusk swallowed the sickroom, a faint whimper fractured the silence. Julian dragged his bleary focus from his ledgers. Setting aside the pen, he grasped Caroline's questing hand.

"Shhh. I'm here." His rasp of a voice still startled him. How long since he had uttered more than a few hoarse words?

Tonics hadn't eased her distress. Her slender frame thrashed and convulsed as the fever took fresh hold. Julian filled a cup from the pitcher and gently lifted Caroline's shoulders.

"Drink this," he coaxed. "Come on, my duchess."

After a few unsuccessful attempts, he managed to work some water down her parched throat.

As the night stretched on interminable and bleak, he waited for some sign the medicine had pierced the muddled haze of her mind. Some small mercy granting respite from her torment.

When the big clock downstairs struck four miserable times, Caroline's restless thrashing finally eased. The lines marring her brow smoothed somewhat. The harsh rasp of her breath softened, losing its frantic edge. Julian exhaled as some of the panic choking him loosened its claws.

"That's better," he said, even as exhaustion blurred the edges of his vision.

Still, Julian fought the pull of sleep – just a few more minutes basking in the sight of her peaceful in repose.

"Julian."

His name on her lips, faint as a sigh – yet it fractured the silence as sharply as any gunshot. Julian jolted upright, alert.

Caroline had not spoken more than a few delirious words since the night he'd carried her broken body home. Now she called to him across some vast divide, soft and plaintive. The sound carved out a jagged hollow inside his chest.

"Julian."

His name. She called his name this time – not like in Edinburgh. Trusted him at that moment.

The hours crawled by, broken only by the relentless chime of the clock.

*Stay with me. Open your eyes, Linnie.*

Soon, the first delicate rays of sunlight washed the room in watery gold. Still locked in a restless sleep, Caroline sighed and turned her face into Julian's throat. Her lips grazed the frantic pounding of his pulse. With infinite care, Julian settled her back against the pillows once more. He remained curled around her, unwilling to relinquish the exquisite intimacy of sharing breath.

When he next woke, it was to find Caroline shifting in his arms. Her lashes fluttered, gaze dragging itself into focus. Meeting his.

"Hello, my duchess," he rasped. "I'm absolutely furious with you."

Her chapped lips lifted faintly. "And why... is that?" she managed.

"Because you took that bullet for me." His eyes scalded as he stared down at her, throat raw around the confession. How many nights had he wondered if he would hear her voice? "Never frighten me like that again."

"You would have done the same for me," Caroline replied weakly, brushing her fingers along his stubbled cheek. "You ran into a fire for me in Edinburgh. Shielded my body with yours during a bomb." Her voice was faint. "If you took a bullet for me, I fear the ladies of London would be at my door, falling over themselves to steal you."

A strained noise tore from Julian's throat. Then he captured her lips in the softest kiss, pouring every shred of longing and relief into the contact. He gentled the pressure, terrified of causing her pain. But Caroline made a noise of protest, tangling her fingers in his shirt to keep him close.

So Julian melted into her once more. Let her mend the fissures that had cracked him wide open in her absence.

"I love you," he said. His fingertips traced down her throat, reassured by the rhythm of her pulse. "Rest. I'll be here when you wake."

In the following days, Caroline regained some fragile strength as the fever released its claws one grudging inch at a time. The deathly pallor of her skin gave way to a healthier glow, bringing some comfort to Julian's fraying sanity.

One afternoon, when he returned upstairs from conferring with the doctor, Julian found her sitting at the edge of the bed, wrapped in a robe and attempting to stand on wobbly legs.

"What are you doing out of bed?" he snapped, striding over to grip her shoulders before she could topple to the floor. "Get back under the damned covers before you collapse."

"You're hovering, Julian."

"You were at death's door a handful of days ago. So yes, I'll bloody well hover until you don't look ready to faint." He tried gentling his tone, thumbs sweeping over her shoulder blades. "Back in bed."

"Bedrest accomplishes nothing. Help me walk."

Christ, this woman would be the death of him.

Caroline tottered the length of the room on his arm with halting steps. They managed a complete circuit before her limbs gave out, but the small victory made her smile.

As Julian tucked the linens around her, Caroline clutched at his wrist with sudden urgency. "Bring me the sketch you made of Kellerman's ring."

Julian tensed. "Did you remember something?"

"Maybe." She shook her head. "Let me see it again."

He went to his study and rifled through the sheaf of

cryptograms and drawings until he located the crumpled page, then returned to his wife's side.

Caroline's blue gaze sharpened at the sight. "There." She traced the small leaf in his drawing. "This is not part of the crest. This motif is a signature."

Understanding crashed through Julian. "You recognise it?"

Caroline gave a faint nod. "It matches a ring my late father once owned. All his friends had the same – a group of privileged men engaged in drinking, gambling, and debauchery." Her brow creased. "One was tried for treason, but the details escape me now."

"Did this group have a name?"

She paused, considering. "Yes, but I was a child. Between the scandal and his gambling debts, we left London for our countryside property near your father's estate. My father sold off the ring."

"You're certain of this?"

Caroline nodded. "Yes. The signature belongs to Aurelius Van Derlyn on Albemarle Street."

He pressed a fierce kiss to her knuckles. "Well done, duchess."

# 28

The shop's polished brass bell gave a light tinkle as Julian stepped across the threshold, the door clicking shut behind him with a soft thud. His sharp gaze swept the interior, taking in the velvet-lined cases and shelves laden with glittering wares that beckoned beneath the late morning sun streaming through the front windows. An ostentatious display of wealth, each piece exquisitely wrought.

The proprietor glanced up from an account book, eyes blinking wide behind spectacles perched on a hawk-like nose.

"Your Grace. To what do I owe the honour?" The jeweller executed a quick bow.

"Mr Van Derlyn." Julian inclined his head in polite acknowledgement. Beside him, Wentworth offered no greeting.

Julian's smile held all the warmth of a dagger point. "I've come about a piece my wife's late father owned. A ring you crafted some years ago. It bears a motif on which I'd like some information."

The proprietor swallowed, but his tone remained pleasant. "Of course, Your Grace. Happy to be of service regarding any of my creations." His shrewd gaze flickered from Julian to Wentworth, no doubt noting the latter's ill-concealed impatience. When his gaze cut back to Julian, they held a glint of wariness. "How might I assist you gentlemen today?"

Julian withdrew the hastily sketched crest from his pocket and unfolded it on the gleaming counter. One finger tapped the small motif Caroline had identified as the jeweller's signature.

"Have you sold any pieces bearing this addition to the design?" Still polite, still mild. As if they spoke only of the weather or the day's newspaper headlines.

As if Julian's heart wasn't pounding out a demand for retribution.

Van Derlyn adjusted his spectacles with a trembling hand before visibly gathering himself. "I create bespoke pieces, Your Grace. My work is quite exclusive, as I'm sure you and the duchess appreciate. Client confidentiality—"

Julian didn't let him finish. He braced his hands flat on the counter and leaned in. "I admire discretion as much as any patron of your fine establishment, Mr Van Derlyn," Julian said, still polite. "However, a matter of some urgency has arisen, you see. My wife's health, as it happens."

Something shifted behind the jeweller's eyes. His thin lips flattened.

"She took a bullet meant for my heart. Do you know what that does to a man, Mr Van Derlyn?" Julian's voice dropped to a lethal purr. "It fills his thoughts with visceral and imaginative ways to dismantle those responsible. Piece by piece."

Van Derlyn's throat worked. "I... see. You have my deepest sympathies, Your Grace. Forgive my hesitation, but you understand, matters of discretion—"

A muscle ticked in Wentworth's rigid jaw. His fingers drummed a staccato on the display case. The sound rang in the tense hush. Sharp. Impatient.

"Let me be frank, Mr Van Derlyn," Wentworth said in clipped tones. "A wanted criminal remains free, courtesy of your silence. If you refuse to help, I'll find any means in my power to ruin you. If the next bullet finds its mark in the duke's heart, I'll hold you accountable, and I will bury you." He braced his hands on either side of the open ledger. "Now. The crest."

With a last helpless glance at Julian, Van Derlyn capitulated. "It belonged to the members of the Scarlet League," he admitted. "The Earl of Wyndham was a member."

Wentworth's threatening posture relaxed into geniality once more. "There. That wasn't so difficult, was it?"

*Wyndham*. The name tugged at a memory. The earl had faced treason charges over military intelligence leaked during the Crimean War, if memory served correctly. His family was stripped of honours and sentenced to disgrace. Rather than accept the harsh verdict, the earl had fled into exile with his young son.

The son.

Theodore Warrington.

The aristocrats targeted had all been involved in the Wyndham investigation – all part of the same group as Caroline's father. This was personal, not profit. A vendetta decades in the making, with Warrington hunting down the men he held responsible for his family's destruction, leaving the Wyndham heir penniless.

Julian wrenched his thoughts back to the present. "Thank you for your help, Mr Van Derlyn," he said, folding the paper and tucking it inside his coat. "I apologise for disrupting your morning, but as you can understand, time is of the essence."

The proprietor tugged at his cravat. "Of course, Your Grace." He hesitated before adding, "Do pass along my regards to the duchess for a swift recovery."

With a final brusque nod, Julian turned on his heel and left the shop, Wentworth falling into step beside him. The humid air closed over them as they emerged onto bustling Albemarle Street.

"The name is familiar from old case files before my time at the Home Office," Wentworth said. "Wyndham went into exile with his son well over twenty years ago."

"It explains why Kellerman emerged in society a year ago with genteel manners that belied his upbringing," Julian murmured. "I imagine he's been plotting for years."

"I'll go into the old records, find out who gave up their silence on Wyndham."

Despite Wentworth's assurances, frustration nagged Julian. Every minute wasted was another which Kellerman might use to disappear into some fetid bolt-hole and plot fresh attacks.

No. Julian refused to squander another moment.

Instinct shrieked at him to tear apart London stone by stone. But the logical part of his mind understood he would make little progress without proper intelligence. He lacked Wentworth's shadowy networks of informers and spies.

"Keep me informed of any developments," Julian said as they halted at the street corner where their paths diverged. "I want to be included when your men locate him."

Wentworth gave a grim nod. "You know I will. I owe the duchess a personal debt."

With a final terse nod, Julian left Wentworth and took his carriage home. Soon, Stafford House rose before him, all pale stone and imposing columns. He took the marble steps swiftly, boots rapping out a crisp staccato.

He opened the bedroom door only to find it empty, the rumpled bedsheets glaring back at him. Stifling a spark of panic, he moved to the adjoining room, her art studio. Relief coursed through him at the sight of Caroline seated at her easel, lost in concentration as her charcoal danced over the page. Late afternoon sun bathed the room in warm golden light, catching on the pearl combs pinning back her unbound hair. She looked fragile sitting there.

"Any developments?" She spoke without turning, still wholly absorbed in her sketch.

"You're meant to be resting," he growled, torn between sweeping her up bodily to deposit her back in bed or kneeling at her feet to worship her.

"And you're supposed to be telling me what you learned." She didn't even turn, the minx. Just kept dashing charcoal over paper. "Honestly, drawing in an armchair hardly qualifies as a strain."

"Need I remind you that you took a bullet less than a fortnight ago? Most people lack the fortitude to brave a gunshot wound with such nonchalance."

No, she was entirely singular. And the most troublesome creature he'd ever had the misfortune to love with his entire damn heart.

"Need I remind you that we have an assassin to catch?" She gave him a pointed look. "So, if you've finished clucking over my health, tell me what you discovered."

Julian moved to stand beside her, resting a hand on her shoulder. Such delicate bones beneath his palm. Deceptive, like the steel in her spine.

"Your father was part of a group called the Scarlet League – along with the Earl of Wyndham."

She paused her sketching. "I recall now. Wyndham gave intelligence to the Russians during the Crimean War. The earl was stripped of title and fortune and exiled in disgrace. Forced to drag his small son into impoverished obscurity."

She took a bracing breath before continuing. "Some believed my father was part of the plot, though nothing could be proven. We left for the country to escape the scrutiny. Our limited means could not withstand the relentless gossip."

"Wentworth will quietly investigate which aristocrats informed on Wyndham and see how many targets there are. His son, Theodore Warrington, was my age when they were exiled. Kellerman must be his alias."

Caroline's chin lifted, eyes flashing. "But who took the earl's son under their wing when he returned to London to orchestrate his vengeance? Someone must have aided him, may even stand to profit from his swindles. I wonder..." She trailed off, clearly following the thread of an idea. "The landlord for Mr Kellerman's offices must have a record of any business partners. We'll question him."

Julian froze. "We?" he repeated.

"Of course, we. I'm injured, not useless."

"You're reckless, disobedient, a danger to my sanity, soon to tear open your slowly mending wound..." He ticked the points off on his fingers.

She drew herself up. "I'm more charming than you and apt to get answers. I can ask Richard what he knows about the landlord."

Julian ground his teeth. He was relieved Grey and Caroline had never been intimate, but that didn't mean he liked the man. "We're not involving Grey. And we're not involving you."

"Richard collects blackmail material like some people collect debts, and he's still in town. All I have to do is ask him for the name and details of the landlord for the offices on Threadneedle Street." She examined her fingernails. "And I could give you this information if you let me come along."

His jaw went hard, knowing she was right. "Fine."

"Good." She tapped her charcoal against the canvas. "And we won't go as the Duke and Duchess of Hastings. Kellerman ran off once because he was alerted to Wentworth's men closing in."

She was too clever. "No risks, Caroline."

He clenched his jaw so hard it was a wonder his teeth didn't crack. She was the most maddening, stubborn, vexing—

"While you stand there fuming, be a darling and disrobe for me, will you?" She gave him a look over her shoulder. "I've gone much too long without sketching your form properly. You're utterly glorious when you brood."

With a long-suffering sigh, Julian began unbuttoning his shirt. "You're impossible."

"Mmhm, yes, I know." She made a motion with her hand. "Trousers off."

"You're going to pay for this later, once you've fully recovered," he warned.

Her lips curved. "I certainly hope so." Caroline turned back to her easel. "Do try to look imposing. I'm drawing you as Hades."

He bit back a smile, settling onto the divan.

# 29

The cobblestone street glistened as Julian and Caroline approached the unassuming brick building. A small wooden sign creaked beside the entrance, identifying it as the offices of Talbot's Property Management.

"You are not to use Grey's information until I give the word," he murmured.

Caroline resisted the urge to roll her eyes. "Of course. I'll let you and your charming manner do all the talking."

He did not look amused.

The bell above the door announced their arrival with a cheerful jingle that seemed out of place in the dreary office. Ledgers and documents perfumed the air with the tang of ink. The man seated behind the narrow desk glanced up from his scribbling.

"Good day. How might I be of service?"

Julian flashed a smile. He looked like a wolf baring its teeth – a man unaccustomed to feigning charm. "Mr Talbot, I presume? My man of business wrote to you yesterday to arrange this meeting. Alexander Heyward, at your service. And this is my wife, Mrs Heyward."

"Ah, yes, of course." The clerk cleared his throat. "I did receive word you had expressed interest in leasing property.

My apologies for the cramped office. We're in the process of expanding."

Julian waved away the stammered explanation with careless aristocratic grace. "Think nothing of it. I'm certain you'll soon have premises to rival the finest in the City."

"You're too kind, Mr Heyward. Now, how might I assist you today?"

"My wife and I only just arrived in London after some years abroad. We're eager to make a few smart investments." Julian flashed an easy conspiratorial smile. "I'm determined to avoid the follies many family fortunes are squandered on. Lavish country homes sitting empty eleven months of the year and so forth." He gave a careless shrug. "I prefer pursuits with more lasting rewards. Wouldn't you agree, my dear?"

Caroline fluttered her lashes up at her husband and nodded.

Julian patted her hand indulgently before redirecting his attention to the clerk. "You come highly recommended for your discretion and shrewd eye. I understand you've placed several gentlemen in excellent business premises. I spoke to one recently—" He paused and glanced at Caroline. "Remind me of his name again, darling? Began with a K, if I recall correctly."

"Mr Kellerman, dearest," Caroline supplied sweetly.

"That was it. Kellerman. The offices on Threadneedle Street. But I noticed his establishment appears to have closed up. Did he have a partner I might speak with, sir?"

At the casual mention of that name – Kellerman – disquiet flickered over Talbot's face. His reaction betrayed him before he could school his features.

"He did, but I'm afraid client confidentiality prevents me from divulging details of their holdings or arrangements," Talbot hedged.

Tension coiled through Julian's imposing frame. To an outsider, he appeared at leisure, but Caroline noted the restless tap of his fingers against the scarred wooden desk. Betraying his impatience. Julian was unaccustomed to being denied, especially with lives at stake.

"Naturally, discretion is expected." Julian nodded. "However, I'm prepared to pay handsomely for your expertise and, shall we say, insights, regarding Mr Kellerman's recent business. Combined with your good counsel on properties available for our ventures, I'm certain we'll establish a mutually profitable rapport."

When Talbot still hesitated, Julian added, "One hundred pounds. Provided you can share further details on one particular office location." His tone remained conversational, as if they were enjoying a talk over port and cigars.

Before Talbot could stammer out another excuse, Caroline stepped forward. "Might I trouble you for a glass of water while you gentlemen talk business? All this dreary chatter is quite taxing for my poor mind."

"Ah, yes, of course." Mr Talbot rose, all but tripping over his feet to escape the tension. "Right away, Mrs Heyward."

As soon as the clerk had scurried from the room, Caroline rounded on Julian. "You're terrifying him, and it's getting us nowhere. We'll need a new approach. For now, you're just a gentleman without the backing of a dukedom behind the name."

Julian's eyes narrowed. "Are you asking permission to take over?"

"Of course," she said. "I've memorised Richard's entire dossier. Just watch."

When Talbot returned and presented Caroline with a murky glass of water, she fixed him with her most imperious stare. The full force of her will bent solely on breaking the man.

"The details about the offices leased by Mr Kellerman," she bit out sharply. "I want them now."

The clerk recoiled as if she had struck him. "Madam, as I explained to your husband—"

"The discretion you're so determined to uphold does not extend to concealing the movements of wanted men. Should anyone learn you let offices to a swindler bleeding aristocrats dry, I suspect it would be rather damaging for business." Caroline arched a brow. "A rather grubby corner you've painted yourself into, Mr Talbot."

Talbot took a hasty step back, wringing his hands. "I must ask you both to leave."

Caroline bared her teeth in a ruthless smile. "Of course. But first, allow me to paint you a picture of what happens next if you withhold the information we require." She paused for effect. "I will pay a visit to Mrs Talbot," she continued silkily, "and share every sordid detail of your proclivities. The pretty young actress you fritter away your wife's allowance on. The nights spent fumbling with prostitutes when you fail to come home. And should you need further motivation, I'll remind you that your gambling debts would be ruinous without your clientele. Imagine what Mrs Talbot would say about a husband at risk of going to the debtors' prison."

She stepped nearer, backing Talbot up against his desk until he shrank from her. "If you keep that information, I'll dig up far more shocking tales to share. I'm a woman of resources, and I don't enjoy wasting my time." Caroline rested her hands on either side of Talbot's desk. A lioness closing in for the kill. "Now. Tell me about Kellerman's business partner. Or by this afternoon tea, I'll be taking Mrs Talbot into my confidence." She held Talbot's terrified stare, watching beads of perspiration slide down his pallid face as he sputtered wordlessly.

When Talbot finally found his voice, it trembled. "The offices on Threadneedle were leased by a Bartholomew Pritchard on behalf of Mr Kellerman."

Triumph fired through Caroline's veins.

"Pritchard," Julian said. "Describe him to me."

"Mid-forties, sturdy build. More like a dockworker than a gentleman, despite the fine clothes." Talbot mopped his damp brow with a trembling hand. "Had a mean scar. Like he's been in fights."

"Where does he live?" Caroline asked sharply.

"I don't know. But I hear he frequents the Brimstone in the East End."

The Brimstone. She knew it well. Its owner funded several of her charitable causes.

"Please." Talbot grasped the edge of his desk until his knuckles blanched. "Don't tell my wife."

"Thank you for your cooperation," she said, ice in every syllable. "We're finished here." Pausing in the doorway, she speared Talbot with one last glare. "Speak a word of this meeting to anyone, and I tell Mrs Talbot everything. Good day, sir."

Outside, Julian helped Caroline into the nondescript carriage waiting at the curb. As soon as he had settled onto the seat beside her, he dragged her into his lap, claiming her mouth in a fierce kiss. "Watching you dismantle that fool was astonishing. Terrifying. And—" He groaned. "Christ, it was arousing," he muttered.

Breathless, Caroline braced her hands on his shoulders to steady herself. The heat of his stare seared her, raw desire pulling taut between them.

Julian cradled her face between palms. "If you demanded I cut out my own heart right now, I'd place it in your hands without hesitation. To do with as you please."

She turned her cheek into his palm, brushing her lips to his wrist. Feeling the wild staccato of his pulse.

When she found her voice, the confession fell raw and honest between them. "I already have your heart, don't I?" she whispered. "I'm craving something else entirely." Her nails raked through his dark hair, wringing a rough noise from Julian's throat that vibrated against her chest.

"As soon as you've healed, I'm going to strip every stitch of clothing from your body." His voice was gravel and smoke. "Tie your wrists and take you hard until you've spent yourself from pleasure. But don't start something we can't finish yet."

Sighing, she said, "Is that your way of reminding me to focus on Bartholomew Pritchard?"

"Only for now." He kissed her cheek. "He must have money to play those tables. Men only go there to bet deep."

Caroline idly traced her fingertips along his nape as she theorised aloud. "Perhaps he's a swindler himself. An old mentor teaching his protégé the tricks of the trade, in exchange for a share of aristocratic spoils. It would be easy to overlook a few murders if he's profiting handsomely. We'll visit the Brimstone tomorrow night."

"I won't be able to go under an alias," he pointed out. "All the aristocrats will know me."

"Nicholas Thorne and Alexandra Grey are patrons of a few of my charities," she said, referring to the club's owner and his wife. "I'm familiar with their staff. I'll disguise myself as a serving maid. Try to find out where Mr Pritchard lives. He might be harbouring Kellerman."

"I don't like putting you in danger." Julian traced her lower lip with the edge of his thumb.

"I could say the same about you," she replied.

# 30

The servant's cap did little to tame the riotous wig of ink-dark curls spilling over Caroline's shoulders. She adjusted it with gloved fingers, tucking a few stray locks beneath the brim. Her cloak concealed her daring obsidian gown and the item hidden within its voluminous folds – a demi-mask crafted of black silk and lace to shield her identity.

These were her weapons tonight, not satin and diamonds.

A knock preceded Julian's entrance, and Caroline met those frost-coloured eyes in the mirror as he filled the doorway. Broad shoulders stretched the fine fabric of his evening kit.

"Where did you get that cap?" His gaze moved over her, no doubt cataloguing each detail.

Caroline turned to face him, offering a coy smile. "It's on loan from one of the maids."

In two swift strides, he had her backed against the armoire, palms planted on either side of her head. He towered over her, all imposing height and lean muscle. The scent of spice and smoke enveloped her. Caroline inhaled sharply as his hard body pressed to hers.

"Tell me," Julian said, his voice dropping to a silken caress that set her nerves alight. "What do you have on under the cloak?"

Caroline smiled up at him, doing her best to affect innocence. "Betsy's uniform, of course."

His hands slid lower, palms skating over her hips through the concealing cloak. His touch was pure temptation.

"Would you care to play at servant and employer sometime? I suddenly find myself longing to discipline you."

Oh, she just bet he did. Imagination supplied several vivid ways he might choose to chastise her later.

"I think that could be arranged," she said. "Would 'Your Grace', 'my lord', or 'sir' please you more?"

"Mmm. I've never been a 'sir'. It holds an undeniable appeal." As punishment, he nipped at her jaw, just sharp enough to sting. Caroline gasped as the brief flash of pain melted into molten pleasure. "We could stay in tonight," he suggested, voice rough with want. "Play out that naughty fantasy right here."

Oh, she burned to take him up on that tantalising offer, to stoke the smouldering desire that arced hot between them.

But duty called tonight.

Caroline reached up and patted his cheek. "As delightful as that sounds, we have an assassin to catch."

Julian released her with a soft huff of frustration. He offered his arm, and they descended the grand staircase to the carriage waiting below.

Inside the darkened interior, Caroline smoothed her clothes as she fought to slow her racing heart. She only hoped her disguise would prove distraction enough for Bartholomew Pritchard.

When the carriage slowed to a halt, her husband turned to her. Tension radiated from him in palpable waves. "You'll stay with the staff tonight," he instructed. "Don't speak to the patrons or do anything reckless to put yourself in harm's way. The moment you discover anything about Pritchard, you return to the carriage to wait for me. No unnecessary risks, do you understand?"

She gave him a teasing smile, hoping to ease his concern. "Only the necessary ones."

His mouth flattened into a grim line, clearly unconvinced.

"Somehow, that does little to reassure me. Need I remind you that you took a bullet weeks ago?"

She waved a hand dismissively. "Maybe I'm impervious to bullets now. I might even catch them in my teeth."

"Promise me you won't attempt to catch any projectiles tonight. Not with your teeth or any other part of your anatomy."

"No bullets," she promised. She knew Julian only lectured because he cared. Because the memory of her injured and bleeding still haunted him. "No unnecessary risks. I'll go around back and alert the staff I'm here."

Her boots clicked out a rapid staccato on the cobbles as she hurried to the servants' entrance, stripping off her cap and donning the demi-mask she'd hidden in her pocket.

She knocked. Caroline listened to heavy footsteps approach from within, the bolt scraping back. The weathered door swung inward to reveal Leo O'Sullivan's imposing silhouette.

Rumour held the club's factotum had once killed a man with his bare hands. Violence lurked in him, coiled tight and leashed. He had the golden good looks of a fallen angel – beautiful, but remote.

Squaring her shoulders, she offered him a smile. "Mr O'Sullivan. How lovely to see you."

He sighed, clearly unenthused by her presence. "As I've said a thousand times, the ladies from Maxine's go to the front—"

"And what about the Duchess of Hastings?" Caroline interjected before he could dismiss her.

He raked her with a look, taking in her disguise. "Her Grace forgets whatever mischief brought her here and goes home. Now."

Mr O'Sullivan moved to shut the door, but Caroline slapped a hand against the scarred wood to stop him.

"I don't think so. I've come on urgent business regarding a gentleman who gambles here. Bartholomew Pritchard." She leaned in closer and lowered her voice. "Might we speak inside where prying ears won't overhear? I'd hate for whispers to reach Lady Alexandra about your discourteous treatment of a duchess."

There wasn't a soul in London not terrified of Richard's sister.

"Christ," he muttered, stepping back and letting her slip inside. "Fine. Get in before someone sees you skulking around."

"My apologies for barging in unannounced," Caroline said. "But surely you've heard of the recent attempts on my husband's life?"

O'Sullivan's stern gaze flicked over her once more, slow and assessing. "Word is you took a bullet for the duke."

"I did." She reached for the top clasp of her cloak, working it free. "The duke is already inside looking for Pritchard. I suspect the man has information about the culprit, and while Hastings is skilled in many areas..." She flashed a wry smile. "I believe I would fare better convincing Pritchard to share what he knows."

The cloak dropped to her feet. She heard the sharp inhale, saw Leo's gaze skim down over scandalous curves barely concealed by silk. Watched faint colour stain his cheeks as he averted his eyes to the ceiling.

She allowed herself a small, satisfied smile at having rendered the unflappable Leo O'Sullivan speechless.

"This." He waved a flustered hand at her state of undress. "This was your cunning plan?"

"Come now. I make a flawless fallen woman. I'll blend in with the ladies of the night in your club."

O'Sullivan dragged a palm over his face. "Jesus wept. You'll cause a bloody riot. Thorne will roast my bollocks on a spit when he hears of this, and then your savage beast of a husband will carve what remains into a souvenir."

"You have such a flair for the dramatic, Mr O'Sullivan. I'm touched you feel so protective of my honour."

"I don't give a damn about honour," he said. "But I'd like to keep my bollocks, if it's all the same to you. Does your husband know you're here prancing around dressed as a doxy, making demands?"

"He thinks I'm dressed as a maid. He would have forbidden me to come otherwise."

"A sensible man," O'Sullivan muttered. "I can't, in good conscience, be party to the Duke of Hastings' wife parading around a gambling hall dressed like... you."

"Well, it's a good thing I'm not asking your permission." She turned and peered down the dim hallway, contemplating. "Of course, I could always invite Lady Alexandra to accompany me—"

"Good God, no." He dragged both hands through his hair before spearing her with a stern look. "You'll stay by my side. No exceptions, understand?"

Muttering under his breath, O'Sullivan turned and strode back down the cramped staircase into the bowels of the club. Caroline hastened after him. As they navigated down into the pulsing heart of the club, raucous sounds filtered up – shouts and gritty laughter, the clink of glasses and slap of cards. The cloying stale air was choked with expensive cigars favoured by aristocrats.

At the base of the stairs, Leo turned back with a warning look. "If your husband murders me, I will haunt you until the end of time. Stay close. And for the love of God, try not to get us both killed tonight."

She took his arm. "I make no promises."

He led her through a stained oak door into pulsing chaos – the press of bodies hunched around card tables, the heady aroma of liquor and tobacco choking the air. Scantily dressed women draped themselves on laps, pouring amber liquid into waiting glasses. Entwined limbs and bared skin abounded in shadowy corners.

O'Sullivan kept them along the periphery, navigating through the crush of patrons towards the back rooms. But Caroline felt the heavy weight of assessing male eyes tracking her. Heard their lewd laughs and jests, the crass whispered speculation regarding what they wished to do with her. She kept her gaze fixed straight ahead, spine stiff beneath their scrutiny.

Her instincts prickled in warning an instant before she saw him. Julian sat at a hazard table against the far wall, an untouched glass of brandy near his elbow. He appeared relaxed, long legs stretched out casually before him.

As if sensing her attention, his piercing blue gaze found hers across the crowded room. She watched him catalogue each scandalous detail of her attire, mentally stripping away the flimsy barrier of her dress. Fury warred with lust in the harsh lines of his beautiful face.

She almost smiled. Oh yes. Later, he was going to punish her thoroughly for this little deception.

"Which one is Pritchard?" she asked O'Sullivan under her breath, dragging her attention back to the task at hand.

"The one in the grey coat at your husband's table."

Caroline followed his subtle gesture. Pritchard sat with his back to them, broad shoulders hunched as he stared at his cards. An unlit cigar dangled from his lips.

"Does he often bring women home from the club?" she murmured, watching Pritchard leer at the serving girl leaning over his shoulder. His hand reached out to slide low on her hip, proprietary. Claiming. The girl flinched almost imperceptibly.

O'Sullivan cut her a sharp glance. "No decent woman would tolerate his vile appetites for long."

"So, he doesn't often bring women home, then?" Caroline clarified.

"Yes, he does," O'Sullivan bit out. "But you're not going anywhere near the blackguard, so it hardly matters."

She flashed him a coy smile. "I'd like a drink first."

With a muttered oath, O'Sullivan signalled the barman to bring them two glasses. The man wiped his hands on a rag and thumped the drinks down. O'Sullivan slid coins across the bar in payment before nudging her elbow.

"I'll not have you swooning halfway through this farce. Just enough to take the edge off, understand?"

Caroline slid him a playful look and lifted her glass, allowing the barest sip to wet her lips before setting it back down. Warmth trickled down her throat, mingling with the heady taste of nerves and anticipation already intoxicating her. She felt powerful tonight. Reckless. The realisation made her want to smile, sharp and dangerous.

"Well, if you'll excuse me," she said, turning away, "I have information to extract."

Before O'Sullivan could seize her elbow again, Caroline strode with purpose towards Bartholomew Pritchard.

# 31

Julian stared down at his cards. The Queen of Hearts smirked up at him, taunting. He resisted the urge to crumple her in his fist. Christ, he needed to focus. Lives depended on the information he aimed to extract tonight. But at that moment, most of his blood had rushed decidedly south, leaving scant capacity for lofty thoughts of queen and country.

All because of the vixen across the smoky gambling hall.

His wife.

When she'd first sauntered through the doors on Leo O'Sullivan's arm, Julian had barely stopped himself from dragging her from the room. Never mind that such a display would draw the attention they wished to avoid. Never mind that she'd gut him for attempting such high-handed tactics before a crowd of ogling dandies.

In that heated moment, none of those practical considerations mattered. Only the primal urge to remove her from the view of so many prying eyes. To conceal all that skin from their hungry stares.

*Mine.*

The thought clawed at his throat. With effort, Julian wrenched his fevered gaze back to his cards. But the words remained, pounding through his veins with each furious beat of his heart.

Christ, he hardly recognised her. She was masked and spilling out of an onyx silk dress, swathes of flawless skin exposed. Except that he knew, beneath the gown, she bore the injury meant for him. His wound. The one he'd traced just this morning with trembling lips, reminding himself of how close he'd come to losing her.

His wife possessed a talent for provoking both savage and tender urges within him, often with minimal effort. Even with her features obscured behind an ornate black mask, Julian would know her anywhere. Seeing Caroline in that intoxicating scrap of silk tested the bounds of his sanity. Skin meant only for his eyes, his hands. His marks.

"Trouble in paradise, Hastings?"

The sly taunt wrestled Julian's attention back to the table. To the circle of gentlemen watching him over their fanned cards, sharp with speculation.

Julian flicked a pointed glance towards a man groping a giggling tavern maid. "Nothing I'd care to discuss in present company. Just appreciating the varied amusements Whitechapel has to offer this evening."

"We all get restless for variety, duke. Nothing to be ashamed of." The Viscount Brandon chortled.

"Of course." Julian watched his wife across the haze. "What man doesn't?" he replied. He tossed back the rest of his drink, relishing the burn. But it did nothing to dull the fierce longing rising within. "Now, I believe you owe the pot unless you're bluffing, Brandon."

Grumbling, Brandon tossed his cards down to reveal a losing hand. The younger peer pushed a pile of notes towards him as he stacked his winnings. All the while, Julian's senses remained trained on his wife. Laughing at remarks that likely concealed groping hands. Submitting her graceful neck to their ogling regard.

When Caroline turned those beautiful, shrewd eyes on Pritchard, every man at the table perked up. Jackals scenting prey, eager to move in for the kill. Ravenous. She was exquisite and lethal and not theirs to touch.

Fury and lust warred within Julian. He wanted to gouge out their leering eyes, to stake claim to what was his. The most primal parts of him strained at their tethers, the urge to rip into them was a madness in his blood. The stoic duke hanging on by a thread, always thinly veiled beneath a veneer of civility that she – only she – tore to shreds.

And now she approached the table in a rustle of silk, scent wrapping around him – an invitation in her gaze.

"Good evening, gentlemen," she all but purred.

The men's reactions were instant, visceral. Their focus homed in on her, to the exclusion of all else. Drawn forward by some primal magnetism. The game, the cards, the coins – all forgotten.

Because his wife was magnificent.

Only Julian remained as still as stone. Outwardly bored, an aristocrat inured to feminine wiles. He forced a flat tone. "Out for a night of sport, madam?"

*I am going to punish you later.*

*I am going to pleasure you until you can't move from my bed.*

"Out looking for a bit of trouble tonight. And I believe I've found it." Her full lips curved.

Julian's muscles coiled tight. He focused on keeping his breathing even despite the fury clawing his insides. Chaos always followed in her wake. She was chaos herself.

His chaos.

One sly, sidelong glance through lowered lashes ensnared Pritchard instantly. "What about you, sir? Are you feeling adventurous this evening?"

Pritchard's grin turned wolfish. "Always ready for a bit of sport, me."

He hauled her onto his lap. She let out a breathy squeal, settling on his knee as if she belonged there. His arm curled around her waist, moulding her against his chest.

Only Julian noticed the way she hid her pain as Pritchard jostled her wound.

He wanted to punch something.

"A lost little lamb, are you, sweet?" Pritchard murmured, bringing one hand up to toy with the beaded edge of her mask. His fingers then traced lower, grazing the exposed swells of her breasts in an intimate caress.

Julian gripped his cards, crumpling the edges. The painted faces blurred.

Caroline laughed, arching into the crude embrace. "Oh, not a lost lamb at all, sir. I know precisely what I'm doing this evening."

"Do you now, lovely? Then I mean to have you. Over and over until you can't walk straight."

*Over my dead, rotting corpse.*

Another husky laugh escaped her lips. "That sounds like my idea of trouble. But are you sure you can afford me?"

His smile widened. "Darling, my recent ventures could keep you dripping in rubies."

Good God. She'd just got him to admit his money was recent.

Caroline bit her lip and released it slowly. "Is there a place we can continue this conversation in private? After you gents finish your card game?"

The table had fallen silent as the drama unfolded, all pretence of gaming abandoned. The men watched the debauchery play out before them with keen interest.

As Caroline insinuated herself deeper into Pritchard's embrace, Julian considered the many advantages of murder versus a lifetime in gaol. He pressed his tongue to the roof of his mouth and inhaled through his nose, clinging to a fraying thread of control.

Pritchard gazed at her heaving breasts as if ready to devour her whole. "I've a mate with a set of rooms close by. Discreet, like. He'll shove off until I'm through with you." Another suggestive caress. "A pretty little treat like you might earn herself a few shillings extra if you take my meaning."

She laughed again, husky and low. A private sound meant only for him. "With such a generous offer, how could any girl resist? How close is it?"

"Osborn Street, love," he said. "Just above the Hound and Hare. No more than five minutes."

"Perfect," she whispered with a brilliant smile. "How soon until you're finished here?"

Even amid his red haze of fury, Julian admired how easily she'd extracted information he might not have learned even after plying the blackguard with drink.

"Lads," Pritchard announced, "deal me out. I find myself suddenly very preoccupied." He lowered his face to her exposed cleavage.

Julian laid down his cards. Yes, he was absolutely going to murder this man – and enjoy it.

Pritchard made to stand, no doubt meaning to hustle Caroline to his seedy rooms.

O'Sullivan finally intervened. The Irishman yanked her off Pritchard's lap and eased her back a pace. "Leave off. This one's spoken for tonight."

"She said she was leaving with me," Pritchard spat.

O'Sullivan's glare was lethal. "And I just said she's spoken for. If you value your jaw remaining in one piece, you'll either sit back down or get the hell out."

Pritchard cleared his throat and sat, clearly in no mood to take on a former bare-knuckle fighter over a woman.

"That's what I thought," O'Sullivan said. To Caroline, he murmured, "Come with me. Now."

Pritchard growled out a protest, but O'Sullivan had already pulled her into a side room. Safely out of reach.

Thank God for Nick Thorne's factotum. He'd saved Pritchard from getting his neck snapped.

But fury and possession continued seething beneath Julian's skin – a raw-edged madness he'd leashed. It would no longer be restrained once they were behind closed doors without the constraints of duty or appearance.

After waiting several torturous minutes for decorum's sake, Julian turned from the card table.

He stood, the movement fluid as a blade pulled from its sheath – nothing to suggest the reckless violence roiling just below the surface.

"My apologies, gentlemen. Another hand will have to wait."

The mask of civility slipped further with each step, the gentleman receding as the feral creature within clawed closer to the surface. *Mine*, it growled, the word etched by razor claws across his mind. So close now, the object of his hunger. *Mine, mine, mine—*

Julian shoved open the door.

O'Sullivan and Caroline were locked in a heated debate that ended as they both turned. Whatever she read in Julian's stark expression made her straighten in comprehension. In unspoken challenge.

*Good*, he thought. *Let her see. Let her reckon with the consequences.*

"You—" Julian speared O'Sullivan with an arctic glare promising retribution. "Are lucky you still draw breath." His focus shifted, raking his wife with a look that coloured her cheeks. "You. Outside," he bit out. "Now."

He didn't wait for her response. Just grasped her wrist and yanked her through the rear door. Outside, the bracing air did nothing to cool the fever beneath his skin. Spying their carriage, Julian bundled her inside.

"Home," he barked at the driver. "Take the long route."

Julian followed her into the concealing dark and pulled her into his lap. The space was reduced to mingled breaths and pounding hearts, two bodies straining in the carriage's confines. Her nails raking his back through his shirt and waistcoat might have been pleasure or pain. Both. Neither. A provocation urging him closer to that seductive loss of control. She was his most tempting sin given flawless shape.

*Mine.*

"You're meant to be healing." He dragged his teeth along her pulse, then soothed the sting with his tongue. "Not letting scoundrels paw at you. That wasn't what we agreed on tonight."

A breathless laugh escaped her. "Let me worry about what I'm meant to be doing. And I got the information we needed, didn't I?"

Julian sucked in a harsh breath as her leg slid up his thigh, blissful pressure on his aching arousal. He tore the wig from her hair and twined his fingers through the blonde strands beneath, giving them a sharp tug.

"You are a menace." The words escaped through clenched teeth.

Here in the shadows, stripped of disguises, they were laid bare. Two primal creatures, raw edges exposed.

He would ruin her and remake her in a thousand different ways, mark her so deeply that no one could look at her without witnessing his claim etched into her bones. No other man would ever know the taste of her.

Julian used his grip on her hair to arch her throat back like an offering. Sank his teeth into the frantic pounding of her pulse until her breath fractured.

"Duchess," he growled. "After seeing him put his hands all over you, I find I'm not a civilised man tonight."

She bit his lip. "Good. I don't want you civilised. I want you feral."

Grasping her jaw, he forced her to meet his stare. "Then get on your knees."

Caroline sank to the carriage floor. Anticipation sank barbed hooks under his skin at the picture she presented – lush and willing.

"Be a good girl and open that pretty mouth." He made quick work of his trouser buttons.

Her eyes caught his as she parted her lips and took his cock in her mouth. A low groan rasped in Julian's throat as wet heat enveloped him. Clever tongue tracing maddening patterns, threatening to sever the last tethers of his formidable control. She sucked hard, gaze locked with his.

A tight breath hissed between Julian's teeth. "Just like that. Take me deeper, duchess."

She would ruin him, render him wreckage; Julian read the intent in her feverish eyes. Her hunger matched the beast writhing beneath his skin.

He thrust between her lips, his fingers still tangled through her hair. Guiding her as she worked him. So beautiful. So ruthless. Her self-control as arousing as her submission.

When her hand crept between her thighs, Julian caught her wrist.

"None of that," he chided. "I told you I'm not feeling civilised tonight. So you don't get to find your pleasure yet."

Fever-bright eyes lifted to clash with his. "Julian—"

"Beg me for it," he whispered.

She smiled. "No."

Julian felt himself grinning slowly in response. She was just as uncivilised tonight – revelling in her chaos, the power she had over him.

He yanked her back up into his lap. Their mouths crashed together, the kiss all teeth and grasping hands. Savage. Possessing. Marking. She would wear proof of his claim for days.

Then her lips were at his ear, her voice a temptation in the dark. "If you don't fuck me right now, I'll finish myself off in your lap and leave you unsatisfied."

Julian's tenuous control snapped.

He claimed her mouth again as he positioned her hips above his rigid cock. He swallowed her cry as he pulled her down hard, burying himself in one ruthless stroke. She was perfection – slick, tight heat.

Nothing civilised existed here in the shadows – nothing but wet heat and fevered skin and harsh breaths. The slick friction threatened Julian's reason as the beast inside roared in triumph. She was his, only his, to fuck and take and mark. Nothing existed but the push and retreat of their joined bodies – no past, no future. Only the relentless present.

*Mine*, Julian's hands said. *Mine*, his teeth echoed against her throat.

Caroline arched and shuddered in his arms, as desperate for him as he was for her.

He withdrew, then surged back inside. Pounded into her, forcing his cock deeper. He grasped at her hips, bruising pale skin beneath his fingertips as he guided her movements in time with each punishing plunge. The rhythmic drag and friction swelled exquisite pressure low and deep, threatening to shatter them both.

When her eyes drifted shut in bliss, Julian grasped her chin. "Look at me." He would not allow retreat or half measures. Not from her. "Eyes open, duchess."

Eyes locked with hers, Julian slipped his fingers between their joined bodies. Stroked her nub in relentless circles even as he thrust into her.

"I want to see you break." His voice was a ruined rasp against her ear. "Now."

Caroline's body went taut. Her sharp cry was ecstasy and agony as she found her peak, shuddering through each merciless wave. Watching her come undone around his cock splintered the last of Julian's control. His own release slammed into him with brutal force, and the world dissolved into fractured light as he spilled himself inside her.

Much later, after the long carriage ride ended, Julian sat beside Caroline in bed and peeled back the cotton bandage on her side, exposing the healing gash. He wet a cloth in warm water from the basin and dabbed away the dried blood, cleansing the aggravated laceration.

When the injury was cleansed to his satisfaction, Julian selected a tin of salve. He coated his fingers and leaned in again, keeping his touch featherlight. But Caroline still tensed, breath escaping in a pained hiss.

"I'm sorry for aggravating this," he murmured. "And for losing control earlier."

Caroline regarded him evenly. One pale brow arched. "Since when have I objected to you losing control? I believe I specifically requested you be more feral."

"Be that as it may, your health is paramount," Julian said. He brushed the softest kiss onto her wounded skin. A benediction. "I'll be more careful in the future."

"And I suppose making wild, animalistic love is off the table until I fully recover?"

A rough noise rumbled in Julian's chest. He lifted his gaze to hers, wry amusement flickering. "If you're angling for another round already..."

"I'm always angling for another round. I missed you." She gave him a wry smile. "Did you miss me back?"

Missed her? As if his searing, visceral need to reclaim her was anything less than the desperate thrashing of a drowning man. Yes, he'd fucking missed her.

Julian exhaled slowly. "Every damned day. Of every damned year."

Her palm found his jaw, turned his focus back to meet her searching look. Something tender moved behind those perceptive eyes. "I have a confession."

He brushed his lips to the delicate skin of her inner wrist, overcome. "A serious one, I take it. Very well, then. I'm listening."

She took a slow breath. Gathering courage, steeling herself. "I want to have children with you."

Everything slowed. His pulse. His measured breaths. The world beyond their solitary orbit ceased to matter. There was only her words – impossible, unbelievable words – shattering the oppressive silence between them.

Julian searched her expression, awaiting the usual signs of evasion. But Caroline returned his stare without pretence.

"You're sure, my duchess?" he managed at last.

She offered a tremulous smile. "Yes. I think I'd like that very much."

Julian smoothed his knuckles along her jawline. Then he gathered her close – and kissed her.

Made promises etched silently into her skin.

# 32

The windows were dark as Julian stood outside the tenement in Whitechapel, not a single candle lit in the entire building – and somewhere in that place lurked the bastard who'd put a bullet in his wife.

"I want you to stay out here while my men and I go in." Wentworth's low voice at his shoulder.

"No," Julian said. "I'm coming in with you."

Wentworth cut him a sharp glance. "I won't have London's most powerful duke charging into a potential deathtrap. Her Majesty will have my bollocks for earrings if I let you stub your toe."

"He shot my wife." Muscles coiled in Julian's shoulders, unease threading through him. "I've earned the right to see his neck snapped."

The spymaster inhaled slowly through his nose. "You'll follow my lead in there, or I'll eject you myself. Titles mean nothing right now."

Tension arced between them. After a long moment, Julian looked away, back to those lightless windows swathed in shadows. He gave Wentworth a terse nod.

The spymaster lifted his hand in a series of quick gestures, directing his men to surround the premises. They melted into the darkness, slipping through the tangled maze of alleys and rookeries. Unseen, unheard.

Wentworth grasped the worn iron latch and pushed. The door protested, screeching on its hinges as it swung inward to admit them into musty blackness. Upstairs, all remained still – not a creak or cough to betray any occupants. Wentworth eased over the threshold, pistol drawn. Julian's heart pounded as he followed.

Step by measured step, they crept up the narrow stairs. Julian's ears strained for any noise past their own hushed breaths and the treads groaning faintly beneath their cautious steps. On the top landing, Wentworth jerked his head left and took position by the farthest door. Julian mirrored him on the right, bracing his shoulder against the warped wood. Their stares locked across the dim passage.

*Go.*

Wentworth kicked open the door, splintering wood. A scuffle from one of the rooms broke the fraught silence, then a heavy thud. Pritchard lurched out from his bedchamber, looking half drunk, clearly unused to such rude awakenings. When his bleary eyes landed on Julian, the colour leeched from his scruffy face.

"You," he croaked.

"Check the rooms," Julian said to Wentworth.

As Wentworth swept through, Julian focused on Pritchard, pinning the man in place.

"All empty," Wentworth confirmed, returning to the hall.

Julian advanced on Pritchard, fury coiling beneath his skin. "Where is he?"

The veneer of the polished aristocrat had cracked, and violence seeped through the fissures.

Pritchard's eyes bounced from Julian to Wentworth's men, now stationed at the door. "Don't know who you mean."

Julian's fingers twitched with the urge to throttle the bastard. "Don't play the fool. Yesterday at the Brimstone, you mentioned another tenant. Edgar Kellerman, born Theodore Warrington."

He drew nearer, letting his imposing height carry the threat. "Where. Is. He?"

"He must have sneaked out while I slept." Pritchard's voice shook.

"How convenient," Julian said coldly, backing the man into the flaking wall. He shoved his forearm under Pritchard's chin, relishing his panicked wheeze as he cut off his air. "And where might our rat have scurried off to in search of new shelter?"

Pritchard's face purpled. "Anywhere. He has money from robbing you toffs."

Julian pressed forward, savouring the chokehold. "Because I have a deeply personal interest in finding the man who shot my wife. Think harder."

"I don't… know," he rasped.

Through the red haze edging his vision, Julian felt a firm hand grasp his shoulder. "Ease back, duke," Wentworth said. "Let's focus on locating our real target, shall we? We need him able to talk if we're getting answers."

With effort, Julian uncurled his fist and released Pritchard, who sagged back against the wall, wheezing.

Wentworth withdrew his pistol, thumbing back the hammer with an ominous click. "Details on Kellerman. Now."

But despite the panicked sweat coating his sallow face, Pritchard offered no answer.

Wentworth sighed. "No? Pity."

Without blinking, he aimed the pistol and fired.

The gunshot split the cramped space like thunder. Pritchard howled as the bullet punched through his kneecap and out the back of his leg. Before he could collapse, Wentworth slammed his hand into Pritchard's shoulder, shoving him against the wall.

The spymaster re-centred his pistol over Pritchard's good leg with casual menace. "Feeling chatty about your dear friend Kellerman's plans and whereabouts now, I trust? Useful words keep you limping out of here intact. Further waste of my time, and the next one goes through your other kneecap."

Pritchard just whimpered in reply.

"No? Not talkative yet? Last chance," Wentworth warned. He thumbed back the pistol hammer again. The dark eye of its barrel hovered inches from Pritchard's left kneecap. "What's Kellerman planning? I could shoot you, or I could let Hastings take you apart piece by piece, but somehow, I think the bullet might be a mercy."

Sweat slicked Pritchard's face. "He didn't tell me anything."

Wentworth's finger tightened on the trigger. "Hm. That's a shame. Going to be a bugger getting around with two ruined knees. Rather not make the lads drag you out of here. Maybe I'll shoot your hand instead?" His eyes slid to Julian in invitation. "Hastings?"

Rage seethed beneath Julian's skin. "I'll bloody remove it."

Pritchard broke. "I just helped with the con, I swear it! His motives were his own."

Julian's jaw clenched. As much as he might relish watching the blackguard squirm, it was clear Kellerman didn't trust anyone with his vendetta. "Did he keep papers here?"

Pritchard bobbed his head. "Aye. Rooms were always locked. Hid things."

"Where?"

"I don't know where," he said, licking his lips. "He didn't show me."

Wentworth narrowed his gaze. "Lads? Take him for me. We'll see if he conveniently remembers anything tonight."

At his word, the men dragged a whimpering Pritchard off, leaving a glistening crimson trail behind him. Julian watched him go, lip curled in disgust. Let him suffer. He'd earned far worse than a bullet to the leg.

Julian proceeded with Wentworth through the rooms, searching for hidden latches or secret caches concealed in the walls and floorboards. But their hunt turned up nothing. Until—

"Wait." Wentworth's sharp bark split the heavy silence. "You smell that?"

Julian focused his senses. Beneath the clinging stench of mould and decay, he detected it too. Faint yet unmistakable. Kerosene.

Their gazes locked. Wentworth pointed to the far wall shared with the next building, and they moved to the scarred wainscoting. Wentworth's fingers danced over the panels until pausing over one section.

A whisper of draft teased Julian's face – a hidden latch.

With grim purpose, Wentworth eased his blade beneath the warped edge. The concealed door popped open on protesting hinges, exposing the darkness within. The stench of lamp oil intensified. Moonlight slanted through the small window to limn the battered surface of a humble writing desk tucked against the far wall.

The papers scattered on the desk pulled Julian like gravity – but just as his boot touched down inside, Wentworth's grip locked on his shoulder, yanking him short.

"Careful. Remember what I said about Her Majesty wearing my bollocks for earrings?"

Bloody hell. Julian had nearly blundered straight into the windowless room. Into what was likely a deathtrap.

"Wait here," Wentworth said. The spymaster slipped into the dark room beyond the doorway – barely a whisper of clothing to mark his passage.

The next moments passed in taut silence as Julian waited, poised on the threshold. He tensed at each floorboard creak as Wentworth conducted his unseen investigation, nerves straining for any cue to action. Finally, the faint scrape of a match sounded, followed by Wentworth's muttered satisfaction.

"Clever bastard." His gruff voice echoed against the hidden room's walls. "Rigged the lamp to erupt if moved without disarming the mechanism first. Amateur work, but enough to kill us both if we didn't notice the tripwire. It's on the floor just there, Hastings. Ease over it."

Julian released a slow breath and stepped over the thin wire suspended above the floorboards. Inside the tiny study, the anaemic flame illuminated a jumble of books and papers strewn across the desk. He catalogued the materials – leather-bound ledgers full of numbers, rolled documents that looked to be maps or blueprints. And beneath it all, a smaller folded letter sealed in wax and addressed to him in bold, arrogant strokes.

His stomach twisted at the sight of the taunt – Kellerman had expected Julian to find this place. Reluctantly, he broke the seal.

*Be seeing you again, duke. I hope you enjoy yourself with your wife.*

Wentworth grunted. “A dark part of me wonders if he’s moved beyond his vendetta to tormenting you specifically.” He surveyed the letter, face grim. “If so, finding his old targets means nothing. He wants you as his new plaything.”

Julian shuffled through the documents, discarding anything nonsensical. “I’ll review these with Caroline and see if we can find anything of use.”

Wentworth nodded. “I’ll have my men patrol. See if they find him that way.”

They worked to gather the materials, alert for any more traps Kellerman might have set. But their search found nothing beyond an extra pistol and box of lucifer matches tucked in a floorboard cache, like an afterthought. Soon, they were leaving, satchels laden with coded papers.

# 33

Sunlight slanted through the windows of Caroline's art studio, spilling over polished wood floors and glinting off the easel splattered with paint. The earthy tang of oils mingled with the reek of turpentine, perfuming the air with the familiar scents of creation and destruction.

Caroline stood before her canvas. With small, controlled strokes, she brought the meadow scene to life in vivid hues, losing herself in a world far removed from the coded documents scattered across her worktable like fallen leaves. One page after another, filled with columns of numbers and threats penned in the heavy scrawl of a familiar hand.

The creak of floorboards made her look up. Julian paused on the threshold, sin given form even in his exhaustion. The way those pale blue eyes raked over her body made Caroline's belly flutter. She loved the way he looked at her.

"Don't let me interrupt," Julian said as he carried the fresh trove of papers inside. "Carry on. Would you like me to pose naked for you?"

Caroline bit back a smile. "Strictly landscapes today, you scoundrel. But I appreciate the offer." She set her brush down and turned to face him. "What progress have you made decoding that mess?"

He crossed the room and deposited the documents on her worktable. "I've organised it all as best I could. Columns of numbers, shipping schedules, unsent threats penned in Kellerman's sloppy fist..."

Caroline moved to his side, her skirts whispering over the floorboards. Her eyes skimmed over page after page of unintelligible figures and symbols, meandering lines of text. Kellerman's hand was as familiar to her now as Julian's.

"He seems rather besotted with you," she mused. "First, he tries to shoot you, and now he's writing you love notes. I hope you won't abandon me for this newer, angrier suitor."

Odd, to think she had become almost an afterthought in the game Kellerman was intent on playing with the Duke of Hastings – merely a means to provoke Julian into reacting.

Into making a mistake.

"Yes, nothing quite stirs the blood like written threats from a deranged killer," Julian said.

"Well, I can hardly fault the man for his infatuation," Caroline replied. "At present, half the ladies in the *ton* are ready to steal you. Why not include a murderous criminal in the mix?"

Julian's response was to grasp her about the waist and pull her against him for a hungry kiss. Caroline sank into him, lips parting beneath the onslaught.

"I hope that answers your question," he murmured.

She rested her hands on his chest. "Well. Maybe I should defend your honour, then, duke? Should I challenge him to pistols at dawn?"

"I'd prefer you avoid pistols, bullets, weapons or anything that explodes." He turned his focus back to the documents, spreading them on the table beside the divan. "Now come over here and have a look at these."

When he patted his knee in invitation, she settled onto his lap. His hands came up to knead the knots in her shoulders, working their way down her spine. She exhaled, the tension in her muscles unravelling under his ministrations. Julian always knew exactly how to disarm her.

"I've made some progress identifying patterns." He gestured to the columns of foreign symbols and figures. "But the variation is sophisticated."

Together, they pored over the nonsensical symbols filling page after yellowed page. He scribbled notes in the margins, elegant script flowing from his fountain pen. His fingers tapped out an irregular rhythm on the foolscap, matching the cadence of her heart.

When his fingertips slid beneath the thin muslin of her dress, tracing across her bare skin, it became impossible to focus. Caroline squirmed in Julian's lap as his hand inched higher.

"Behave," she murmured.

"You make it difficult," he said, nuzzling her cheek.

She forced herself to take a deep, steadying breath. "Here." She indicated a sequence of symbols repeated within the columns at set intervals. "A pattern. Shipping times?"

Julian frowned over the symbols, desire temporarily banked. "Can you work out where?"

She shook her head. "No, but this other page refers to renovations at a warehouse in Wapping. I'd wager that's where he's having supplies delivered. Incrementally, given the records."

"Supplies." Julian's eyes sharpened. "You mean explosives."

As Caroline reached for the page, Julian grasped her wrist. "I think you should go to Ravenhill," he said quietly. "Until this is over."

She bristled. "Absolutely not."

Julian's jaw tightened. "I ought to have sent you away after the incident at the ball."

"And miss all this intrigue?" Caroline brandished the foolscap. "Without me, you'd never have found this flat or decrypted these codes."

"And what if you're with child?" His voice was sharp. "We've hardly been restraining ourselves of late."

His words sliced through her like a blade to the gut. Caroline sucked in a breath as the papers slipped from her numb fingers. They drifted to the floorboards like falling leaves.

Pregnant. The notion was impossible to dislodge now it had been spoken aloud. When had she last bled? The days and weeks blurred together in her memory, lost in a haze of deciphering codes and evading villains. She hadn't paid her courses any mind.

Julian cursed. "Forgive me, that was poorly done. I shouldn't have—"

Caroline grasped his face in both hands and kissed him. He inhaled sharply in surprise, then his fingers tangled in her hair as he took control of the kiss, coaxing her lips apart.

In one smooth motion, Julian grasped her hips and eased her down onto the divan cushions. He settled over her, his fingertips tracing maddening patterns across her collarbone.

He kissed her until she was mindless with need, hands grasping his shirt to pull him closer. Coded missives were forgotten, and the outside world receded until nothing existed but his mouth scorching hers, his fingers sending sparks dancing over her body.

Julian rucked up her skirts and entered Caroline in a hard thrust, wringing a gasp from her. Caroline's back arched off the divan at the sweet invasion as he filled her, the blunt pressure exquisite. He claimed her with deep, relentless strokes, one hand clasping her hip.

Mine, each powerful drive seemed to say. Mine.

Later – much later – as the afternoon light gilded the rumpled papers spread out across her divan, Caroline turned her head where it rested on Julian's bare chest to study his profile. His eyes softened as they met hers, pouring warmth through her veins.

"I'll go to Ravenhill in the morning," she whispered.

When he finally responded, his voice was rough with emotion. "At first light."

Caroline nodded and pressed a kiss to his palm. "Don't take unnecessary risks in my absence."

His thumb stroked along her cheekbone in a tender caress. "Only the necessary ones. You have my word."

Then he kissed her until she saw stars behind her eyelids.

# 34

The grey light of dawn slanted through the carriage windows as Caroline left Stafford House. Julian stood on the steps, sharp lines etched deep with worry. This parting felt different from all the others. A note of grim finality hung in the air as the coachman shook the reins and cracked the whip.

She kept her gaze fixed on the familiar London streets rolling past. Looking back would destroy what fragile composure she still possessed.

Allowing her eyes to drift shut, Caroline focused on memories of nights curled in Julian's arms, his warm breath feathering across her hair as he whispered secrets. She clung to the fragile remnants of those faded moments – the small measure of comfort.

All too soon, the creak and rattle of the carriage wheels changed cadence as they rolled to an abrupt halt.

Caroline's eyes flew open. Unease skittered down her spine, raising the fine hairs at her nape. Her gaze darted to the window, taking in the cramped, shadowed side street. Why had they stopped here? This was not their intended route.

Heart pounding, she leaned towards the window, straining to spot the coachman. Before she could call out to him, the carriage door was wrenched open, and a hulking figure clambered inside.

Kellerman.

Caroline's voice froze in her throat, but before she could gather her wits, a damp rag was clamped over her mouth and nose, cutting off all sound.

Chloroform.

The sickly sweet scent overwhelmed her senses. Caroline thrashed, drawing in panicked breaths through the rag as she fought the pull of the drug. But the fumes dragged her down into darkness.

Her frantic breaths grew thinner and weaker, grey edging into her vision. Kellerman's grip on her wrists was an anchor weighting her into the void.

Then, nothing.

Cold. Twisted metal biting into her back and sides. The tang of rust flooded her nostrils. Caroline surfaced from the drugged void, senses returning in hazy increments. Frigid dampness kissed her cheeks, drops pattering faintly against her skin. Low thunder seemed to rumble in the distance.

Caroline's lashes fluttered open. Weak light filtered down from above, barely sufficient to make out her surroundings. She lay on her back, the rough metal cage on all sides pressing in close. Iron bars arched above her like the ribs of some ancient leviathan, chains suspending her prison from a high ceiling she could not glimpse.

Like a spider's victim, trussed and waiting.

Panic seized her then, visceral and choking. She tried to sit up, but her wrists were bound in front of her, rope biting into her tender flesh. She thrashed against the restraints until her cries dissolved into ragged pants, her chest heaving.

When the wild panic had reduced to a simmer in her veins, Caroline forced her mind to focus.

The box suspending her was perhaps ten feet long, the rusted iron reeking of the river. She craned her neck, eyes watering against the gloom. Just visible overhead, a hatch lay closed tight – the only means of escape.

Secured with a lock.

She studied it – an intricate mechanism, almost like a puzzle. With etchings like Kellerman's coded notes to release the bolt. Made to taunt.

Because Kellerman, like many men, thought she was just a useless duchess – a trinket to be displayed on Julian's arm. The gossip sheets, after all, had played their part in that. She was the wife who fainted in her husband's arms. Not the one snapping orders.

Not the one who helped solve his codes.

Caroline almost let out a dry laugh. "Idiot," she muttered.

Grunting with effort, she braced her feet flat against the metal floor. The new leverage allowed her to shift into almost a seated position.

The rope binding her strained with her movements. The bindings had inflamed her wrists, abrading the tender skin. But Caroline hardly noticed. All her focus was bent towards the crude mechanism overhead.

"Think," she urged herself through chattering teeth.

The temperature inside the iron coffin was frigid, sapping her warmth. Already, her fingertips had numbed. She curled them into her palms, trying to force blood back into the frozen digits. Her greatest asset in this moment was her intellect.

Caroline squinted upward once more at the lock. Five small, numbered dials protruded from the metal. Each dial possessed numeric symbols from zero to nine that could be rotated to form the proper sequence.

A distant rumble penetrated the walls. A sudden splash echoed very near her head. Icy water sloshed down through the opened hatch, splattering her upturned face. The frigid shock stole her breath even as understanding crashed over her.

The Thames was rising – submerging the hatch by increments.

And her time was running out.

# 35

The townhouse was too damned quiet without her.

Julian prowled from room to empty room like a spectre, his footfalls muted on the plush carpets underfoot. He lingered in the doorway of Caroline's art studio, gaze tracing over the half-finished canvases and abandoned brushes precisely as she had left them. As if she might reappear any moment to resume work.

Julian forced himself to turn away. Down the hall, his study beckoned, the chaotic mess of Kellerman's cryptic letters and ledgers still awaited deciphering – an endless pile of frustration. Setting his jaw, Julian settled himself in the leather chair and tried again to wrest some semblance of meaning from the seemingly random figures and symbols.

Outside, the sunlight swept over the trees as Julian worked. He transcribed letter frequencies, scribbled calculations, searched for the patterns that came so easily to Caroline's clever mind.

He tossed the pen down with a curse and pressed the heels of his hands against his eyes until bursts of light painted the insides of his lids. Bloody hell, he was exhausted. His mind was too wrung out for further progress deciphering Kellerman's infuriating codes. The numbers and letters were beginning to swim.

The mantelpiece clock's distant chime tore Julian from his spiralling thoughts. *Half past noon already?* He grimaced, rolling his stiff shoulders to work out the kinks.

"Your Grace?"

Julian glanced up. Percy hovered in the doorway, knuckles white around a silver tray. "A letter arrived, Your Grace. The lad ran off before I could ask who it was from."

Dread trailed icy fingertips down Julian's spine. Wordlessly, he accepted the folded foolscap. Percy slid back out and shut the study door with a hollow thud that echoed through the room like a gunshot.

Julian broke the plain wax seal and unfolded the letter crammed with rows of slanted script. No greeting, no signature, but he hardly needed either to identify the author.

> *When forced to decide between the woman you love and the country you serve, where would your loyalties lie? Two clocks now count down the hours. One life at the mercy of the rising tide, and the others at the clock attached to an infernal device. Choose, duke.*

The country you serve – dear God, Parliament was in session. And Caroline, at the mercy of the rising tide.

Julian's jaw clenched against the panic threatening his composure. He grasped a pen and dipped it in ink, hand shaking. Threatening to snap the instrument in half as he jotted a note.

"Percy!" The shout seemed to ricochet through the halls. Julian grabbed his coat off the stand and strode from the study, crumpling the letter in his fist. He thrust it at the wide-eyed butler. "Have this sent to Mattias Wentworth immediately. Bring my carriage round."

Outside, a chill rain misted the air. Julian descended the front steps swiftly and slipped into the waiting carriage.

"Where to, Your Grace?" the driver asked.

*A warehouse at Wapping*, Caroline had said.

"The docks at Wapping," he bit out. "And hurry, damn you."

The horses surged into motion as if sensing his urgency. Buildings blurred past the rain-streaked windows, ghostly shapes half glimpsed. Julian's hand curled around the door handle, prepared to leap out when they arrived. He'd search every building himself if need be.

When the carriage finally juddered to a halt, Julian tore himself from the cab without waiting for the footman. The groan of ships and slap of water greeted him, tar and brine mingling with the metallic tang of blood from nearby slaughterhouses.

Think.

*At the mercy of the rising tide.*

Somewhere with access to the Thames.

Julian raced towards the warehouses near the Execution Dock, where the Admiralty courts sentenced pirates and mutineers to death – leaving them hanging until they had been submerged three times by the tide.

There – a building a stone's throw from the dock, equipped with a private slip that flooded at high tide.

And the tide was nearly at its peak.

# 36

The hatch remained open just long enough for the small cascade to drench Caroline's head and shoulders before it slammed shut again.

A cat batting at a mouse, cruel and patient.

Caroline shoved down the stark panic clawing at her throat. She forced herself to think, shutting out the creak of rusted hinges and the hollow groan of currents. Five wheels coded with symbols from Kellerman's letters, each with thousands of potential combinations. Impossible to test each permutation before her air ran out.

The frigid water surged higher, sliding icy fingers down her neck and chest. Loud as cannon fire, new droplets bombarded the hatch above at regular intervals. The once-distant thunder of churning currents pressed against the metal tomb encasing her. Lapping at the rusting walls, eager for its prize.

Five wheels. What sequence? She ground her wrists raw against the rope until her skin bled.

Mathematics in a logical order, chosen by a mind viewing humanity as disposable odds and variables. Subtract the heart, and all that remained was...

The realisation stole Caroline's breath. Of course. She used the permutation she'd utilised to solve the coded notes about the warehouse in Wapping.

Cold salt water surged over her feet now, leaching away all warmth. The hatch would soon dip below the surface, sealing her fate. This was her only chance.

Caroline strained against her ropes. Her frozen fingers shook as she seized the first dial and wrenched it right to the seven. The second she twisted left to the three, the movements needle-sharp with desperation.

When she had set the last number on its seven, she collapsed back. Her heartbeat drowned out the roar of the incoming tide, chest heaving with prayers. Outside her tomb, the river rose. Icy seawater gushed through the opening overhead, soaking her to the skin. She gulped a breath just before the downpour sealed the hatch fully.

The world fell silent. There was no light, no sound save her thin breaths and the creak of chains. Somewhere below her feet, the inexorable tide swirled. Rising by the second. If she had gambled and lost, the choice was no longer hers.

When the icy water reached her lips, Caroline closed her burning eyes. She thought of Julian. Of the eight years without him. Of all the words she hadn't yet said.

The cold seared her lungs. Paralysis crept inward from her limbs, her thoughts growing sluggish and remote. Before the black water closed over her face, she gave one last push against the lock, clicking the final number in place, and it yielded.

She shoved upwards. But despite the hatch being open, she scrambled for purchase. She couldn't pull herself up, not with her wrists bound.

Above her, the square of pale light beckoned, impossibly far. Her bound wrists thrashed, the cuffs tearing her abraded flesh anew. She could glimpse the grey sky overhead, but the rising river pinned her down, just out of reach. Already, the frigid seawater reached up to her collarbone.

This was an elegant torture, engineered to torment the

prisoner with hope before the inevitable end. Even now, she strained upwards, desperate to prolong each agonising moment above the surface.

"Linnie!"

The hoarse shout fractured the stillness. She must be dreaming, her fevered brain conjuring ghosts in these last moments. And yet – there – a face eclipsed the light above.

"Julian." His name tore from her raw throat, ripped free by the savage riptide.

"Hold on, my duchess."

The reply echoed against the iron walls. Not a fantasy. He was real. Caroline wrenched her bound wrists upward with the last dregs of her strength.

"Julian," she choked again as the dark tide swallowed her. His blurred silhouette loomed against the square of light before everything vanished.

Hands plunged into the box. Strong arms encircled Caroline's body, heaving her towards sunlight and breath – through the open hatch into the chill air.

Then, she was held tight to a broad chest. Gasps sawed her lungs as the roaring in her ears slowly resolved into shouts somewhere nearby. She heard the strike of oars on the water. She sagged against Julian as the box receded below them.

"You're all right. I have you. Just breathe," he rasped against her temple.

She felt him fumbling at the rope binding her mangled wrists, freeing her.

Caroline's lips shaped his name, no sound escaping her burning throat. There was only this – Julian's heart hammering against hers, the warmth of his skin chasing away the chill.

# 37

Julian bent his head against the chill as he carried Caroline's limp body from the warehouse, her sodden gown wetting his coat. She remained still in his arms save for small puffs of breath that ghosted from her parted lips.

"I'll have you home," he urged, quickening his pace towards the waiting carriage. "I know you must be freezing."

The driver flinched at their bedraggled state but wisely held his tongue as Julian bundled Caroline inside. As soon as he had tucked his coat around her shivering frame, Julian rapped sharply on the roof overhead. The carriage jolted forward, wheels sloshing through abandoned puddles.

"Linnie?" When her dazed eyes found his, Julian risked a faint smile. "There's my ferocious wife. Back from the brink and itching for a fight, I've no doubt."

"After this…" she mumbled into his chest.

"Yes?"

"I'm not leaving bed for a month." She burrowed closer against him, soaking his shirt. "And I want chocolate. As much as you can get me."

He huffed a quiet laugh. "As you command, my duchess. A month in bed and all the chocolate you can drink."

The carriage rumbled through fog-smothered streets. Julian

cradled Caroline tighter, wrapping both arms around her trembling body.

He bowed his head, pressing his cheek to her tangled blonde curls. Salt and rust clung to the silken strands. His throat constricted at the memory of the iron tomb swaying in the current. The black water already lapping at her chin when he'd plunged his hand through the hatch. She'd managed to get it open. If he hadn't been there in time to pull her up—

*You survived this*, he silently told her. *So you can survive what comes next.*

What came next. The thought chilled Julian more than the icy rain pelting the carriage windows. He had left her once already. Left his wife broken because duty demanded it.

He stared down at her face, searching for answers in the smudged hollows beneath her eyes.

Her lashes fluttered open. "If you stay with me when others are in danger, I will throw all your belongings into the Thames myself. I know extracting me from a watery grave wasn't all Kellerman had planned for you."

Julian swallowed. "I won't leave you."

Not like before.

Not after Grace. Not after Tristan.

"We aren't the same as we were then," she said. "Understand me?"

Julian only brushed his lips over Caroline's brow. Through the fog's dark maw, Stafford House emerged. As the coach rolled to a jarring halt, Julian's grip tightened on her.

"Go." Her nails dug into his wrist. "Don't make me argue with you about this when I've only just escaped drowning, you insufferable oaf." She sounded utterly exhausted.

"I love you," he whispered into her hair.

"I know." She clutched a fistful of his shirt. "Now *go*."

With utmost care, Julian eased open the door and handed Caroline down to the waiting footman below.

"Take the duchess upstairs, put her in a warm bath." He

relinquished her limp body reluctantly to the man's steady grip. "I'll be back as soon as I can."

The man nodded, face grim. "Consider it done, Your Grace."

As the man bore Caroline up the front steps, some primal part of Julian snarled in protest. Wrong, wrong. She belonged with him.

But she'd asked him to go.

Somehow, he composed himself enough to give the coachman a terse order. "To Parliament."

Soon, the looming edifice of the Palace of Westminster came into view. Inside, Julian strode past empty benches and dark alcoves, following the growing sounds towards their source. There, in the oldest part of the labyrinthine building, he found Wentworth and his agents.

"Any sign of Kellerman?" Julian asked without preamble.

Wentworth's mouth flattened. "No. I received your letter and had already started evacuating when I got here, thanks to Pritchard conveniently recalling the plans after some persuasive questioning that may or may not have left him without some non-vital appendages. But finding a needle of a bomb in a haystack this size is near impossible."

Julian forced aside emotion and sifted his memory. Through the stacks of papers and scrawled missives littering his desk, inked visions of chaos and retribution. He sought one thread among the tangle. "He had times in his notes. Storage in Wapping for supplies."

*Renovations*, Caroline had mentioned when she noted the pattern. Timings Kellerman would have used to bring the parts for his explosives inside – using the construction as a front to smuggle in his supplies.

"The north wing repairs," Julian said. "Where they've torn up the original foundation."

Wentworth's eyes sharpened. He was already moving, falling into step behind Julian. "With me, lads," he shouted to his men, voice booming off the rafters. "And bring lanterns unless you fancy getting buried in the dark if this place blows."

They plunged through pools of lamplight and shadows, footsteps echoing off stone. Soon, they had descended a winding stair to an arched passageway lined with dusty crates and tools. Iron nails studded the low ceiling. The raw dirt floor had been churned to mud beneath countless workmen's boots.

At Wentworth's signal, the men fanned out. They advanced slowly, searching the cramped cavity's nooks and crevices. Seeking any wires or levers hinting at a deadly purpose. But the crowded space appeared mundane and harmless – just an abandoned worksite beneath London's skin like countless others.

Wentworth turned down a narrow side passage, crouching under crumbling timbers. Julian followed close behind, pulse thundering.

There. His boot scuffed something smooth and metal hidden in the mud.

Julian froze. Dread congealed in his chest as the lantern illuminated the object. A copper coil attached to a tidy line of explosives. The device Kellerman had smuggled inside brick by innocuous brick.

Wentworth went still, body coiled taut as a spring. His harsh exhalation was the only sound beyond their hushed breaths. Grim purpose hardened his features to granite. With his free hand, Wentworth gestured down the left fork. Towards a faint rim of light outlining a doorway just visible around a gentle curve.

Towards their prey. Waiting to spring his trap and bury them all.

They closed the distance. Pressed themselves to either side of the arched entrance. Inside came the scrape of a match, blooming to a dim glow. The shuffle of boots over dirt as a figure moved within the small chamber.

Wentworth's knuckles whitened on his pistol grip. Eyes meeting Julian's, he held up three fingers. Then two. One.

*Now.*

Wentworth tore inside, weapon levelled at the room's lone occupant. Behind him, Julian followed on the balls of his feet, coiled to strike.

At their sudden entrance, the man spun around. Recognition blazed in his eyes. Before Kellerman could lunge for his fallen lantern, Wentworth pulled the trigger. The report was deafening in the cramped space.

Kellerman crumpled to the ground, his forehead splashed with blood from the bullet that ripped through his head.

Julian glanced at Wentworth. "I suppose that's one way to deal with the problem," he said.

"Certainly the easiest way, given that he probably had a grand villain's speech all prepared about righting wrongs and toppling empires or God knows what nonsense." Wentworth wiped his sleeve across his face, leaving rusty smudges. "Go home, duke. Kiss your wife, have a rest. The lads and I will wrap up this mess."

By the time Julian arrived home, the light had faded from the sky. He took the stairs to the bedchamber, each footfall resonating through his weary bones. Inside, the lamps had been dimmed to a weak glow.

His breath stalled at the sight of Caroline tucked into mounds of blankets. Dark smudges of exhaustion still marred her face, but her skin had colour now. She looked impossibly small and fragile in the massive bed. Self-recrimination lashed Julian once more. He'd left her—

"What's that look for?"

Her hoarse voice fractured his grim thoughts. Julian glanced down to find one pale blue eye cracked open, fixing him with her familiar assessing stare.

"You're awake," he managed unevenly.

"Astute observation." The corner of her mouth twitched. "Now, come here and let me look at you. I want to ensure you're not concealing some grievous injury that will make me furious later."

Despite himself, Julian laughed.

He eased down to perch on the bed's edge. Her gentle hands came up, tracing his features as if needing the tactile confirmation he was whole and unharmed. Her touch loosed something inside Julian's chest.

"Kellerman?" she asked.

"Dead." He turned his face into her palm, breathing her in. Her wrists were bandaged from where the rope had rubbed her raw.

"Good."

"I'm sorry I left you." His voice fractured around the edges. "Christ, I'm so sorry."

Her blue eyes held his. "I told you we're not the same as we were eight years ago. Now come here."

Julian got into bed beside her. When Caroline's nails scratched the nape of his neck, he exhaled low and slow. Let her touch begin unravelling the cold dread still coiled inside him. With each tender pass of her fingers through his hair, the knots loosened their hold.

"You made me a promise," she whispered to him.

"Did I?"

"Yes." Her lips lingered along his temple. "No leaving bed for a month. And I want enough chocolate to drown an elephant."

# 38

Weak sunlight crept across the bedroom floors, gilding the edge of the rumpled sheets tangled around their bare limbs. Julian watched dust motes dance through the hazy morning light, content to lie still. To feel the gentle rise and fall of Caroline's ribs beneath his splayed fingers.

When she shifted, he gentled his grip at her waist, mindful of her still-healing injury. She slid her hand over his chest. He sucked in a sharp breath, desire coiling hot and tight inside him. Christ, he would never tire of this – of her. They had spent days exploring each other in this bed, learning all the ways to give and receive pleasure. And still, it wasn't enough.

Caroline offered him a sleepy, satisfied smile. "What are you thinking about?"

He traced a fingertip along her collarbone, following the delicate lines of her throat. "I was just contemplating all the wicked ways I plan to ravish you today. I believe I promised you countless deflowerings."

"Only countless?" She arched a brow. "Surely you can quantify your nefarious intentions towards my person a bit more precisely. I should hope you have at least…" She pursed her lips, pretending to consider. "Five depraved notions planned?"

His gaze heated. "I assure you, duchess, I'll surpass five with ease. I was thinking more along the lines of six or seven. Perhaps even ten if we never leave this bed at all today." He nipped at her bottom lip, relishing her breathy gasp. "Fifteen, if you're especially enthusiastic." His voice dropped to a rough whisper. "However many it takes until you're begging for mercy."

She laughed. "Fifteen? My, how ambitious we're feeling this morning."

"I'm always ambitious when it comes to you. But I suppose there's only one way to find out."

Julian growled low in his throat before crushing his mouth to hers in a searing kiss that stole the very breath from their lungs. When they finally eased apart, chests heaving, her bright gaze remained intent on his face. Assessing. Plotting.

Always scheming.

He arched a brow beneath that piercing regard. "Yes?"

Caroline traced the line of his jaw. "I was just reminiscing about our wedding vows. I should like to renew them."

"Here?" He couldn't help but laugh. "Now? In bed? While we're both still naked?"

"But of course. I'll keep it brief."

And then she was sinking down onto his cock, scattering all thought beyond pure sensation. He strained up into her slick heat, starved for more. But she would not be rushed. Caroline set a slow tempo, savouring the slick drag of their joining. Drawing out each devastating stroke, she leaned in to brush her lips along the shell of his ear.

"To have and to hold from this day forward." Her whisper sent sparks skating down his spine. Julian's fingers constricted at her hips, but she kept her measured pace. Taking them both to the brink with agonising restraint before easing back again.

"For better, for worse. For richer, for poorer." Another roll of her hips stole his breath. Julian panted into her open mouth, drowning in her. She consumed his thoughts, his senses, until nothing else existed beyond their shared skin.

Caroline finally increased her pace. Yet even then, she did

not relent, her soft litany whispered between kisses. "To obey only when you're a very, very good husband… and pleasure me thoroughly. Multiple times a day."

"That's not…" Julian's laugh hitched on a groan. "That's not from the Book of Common Prayer."

"Oh, it's in the special appendix for very naughty duchesses." Her palms swept his chest, his shoulders. "Till death us do part, my duke."

Those sweet, devastating lips branded tender oaths on his jaw, his parted lips, until Julian shook with the force of it. As the keen edge of bliss dulled to afterglow, Julian cradled her. He pressed his lips to the vulnerable nape of her neck. Breathed in the scent of them mingled on her skin.

"There now," she said. "You still have fourteen more ways left to make love to me today. If you're up for the challenge."

He nipped at her jaw. "Very well, duchess. I suppose I'd better rest up before I get started. Next time, I'll be the one to say the vows."

# Epilogue

## Ravenhill

*Five years later*

Sunlight dappled the blanket, wavering shades shifting with the breeze. Around them, the meadow rioted with colourful wildflowers.

Julian looked down at the small figure on the blanket beside him, fingers toying idly with a fallen petal. "I know you're meant to be napping," Julian said. "Your mother will have my head if she learns you tricked me into shirking your bedtime."

The boy flashed an impish grin. "Who says she'll find out?"

Henry was getting to be a handful.

Julian sighed, though inwardly he was delighted by his son's precocious wit. Much like his mother's. "I see you're already educated in deception. Don't let your mother discover what else you've learned from Mr Grey."

He looked up as two forms crested the hill. Julian's elder son sprinted on gangly legs, and at his heels raced Caroline, skirts scandalously hiked as she gave chase. Their youngest collapsed in squealing delight as she scooped him up and spun them both into the soft grass.

Julian propped up on one elbow to watch his wife.

Caroline shot him a look. "Don't think I've forgotten your role in this criminal enterprise, duke. Aiding and abetting delinquent napping habits. For shame."

Julian clasped his hands over his heart. "I would never interfere with my son's rest." At her pointed look, he amended, "At least, not more than once a week. Twice at most."

Laughing, Caroline collapsed onto her back and tugged their sleepy-eyed younger son beside her. Julian watched her stroke the cowlicks back from his forehead. Watched the boy nuzzle her.

While the boys drifted to sleep in the grass, Caroline joined Julian on the blanket. She sighed as she settled against his side. Julian curled an arm around her shoulders, drawing her close. She came willingly, fitting their bodies together with the ease of long practice. No space was left between them for ghosts to creep through.

"If they don't sleep after all that frolicking, I may have to procure one or two dogs to keep them entertained," she mused. "I'll resort to begging, borrowing, or stealing if I have to."

Julian made an agreeable noise, then dropped a kiss to her temple. "Just one or two? I suspect you'll need three at least. Then perhaps their poor, exhausted parents can manage a lie-in."

She nipped his jaw in reproach. "Is that what we're calling it these days?"

"We have to use euphemisms now that Henry has decided to mimic everything we say."

He drew her down for a kiss. As she melted into him, Julian softened his grip, mindful of their audience nearby. When they finally eased apart, her cheeks were flushed.

"Behave. Unless you want the boys telling everyone in the village how their parents kiss."

Julian winced. "God forbid. Can you imagine?"

"Hm. Seeing your stern façade crack might be worth it." Her eyes danced. "Remember when John blurted out that word he learned from the stable master?"

"I thought Percy might faint into the soup tureen."

In the lengthening afternoon shadows, their boys slumbered on. Grass stains marked the fine linen of their little lordling suits.

And Julian and Caroline would soak up every skinned knee and muddy coat while they could.

As if sensing his pensive mood, Caroline gave his fingers another squeeze. "What is it?"

Julian studied their clasped hands. Traced the elegant outline where her wedding ring encircled her fourth finger. That band of gold made his throat ache even now.

"Only reminiscing," he said. He crushed her close, burying his face in her neck. Just breathing her in. "I love you, duchess."

Words that came so easily. Spoken so often in the five years since they'd retaken their vows skin to skin in London.

Caroline eased back, smoothing her thumb over the furrow between his brows. "There, that's better. Now you almost resemble a man whose two young sons actually let him sleep."

"Get the three dogs, my duchess." He leaned in and whispered, "If they're outside playing, I can take you in every damn room I please."

Her wicked grin flashed. Before she could respond, their sons – who had just been sleeping only moments before – suddenly ploughed into them in a tangle of gangly boy limbs. Laughter and bold demands for dinner drowned out tender words.

"Four dogs," Caroline called over her shoulder as she chased Henry and John. "Perhaps a dozen other animals. A menagerie. We may need reinforcements."

He sighed, wanting to kiss her, but there would be time enough for that later.

For now, Julian didn't mind the interruption.

# Acknowledgements

As ALWAYS, I'm so grateful to my lovely editor, Rosie de Courcy. Her insightful notes and feedback are always such a joy to read, and I feel blessed to have her guidance throughout this series.

I also want to express my heartfelt appreciation to the fantastic team at Head of Zeus/Aria/Bloomsbury and Kaye Publicity, who have worked tirelessly on this series. I'm truly fortunate to have all of you.

To my agent, Danny Baror, thank you from the bottom of my heart for being such a strong advocate for me and my work, especially during this past year.

And last but certainly not least, to you, my wonderful readers: I know some of you have been patiently waiting for this book, and I hope it was worth the wait! Your messages, words of encouragement, and love have kept me going, and I can't thank you enough for your support.

# About the Author

Katrina Kendrick is the romance pen name for *Sunday Times* bestselling science fiction and fantasy author Elizabeth May. She is Californian by birth and Scottish by choice, and holds a Ph.D. from the University of St Andrews. She currently resides on an eighteenth-century farm in the Scottish countryside with her husband, three cats, and a lively hive of honey bees that live in the wall of her old farmhouse.

www.katrinakendrick.com